25.95

I0623785

THE UNDERGROUND RIVER

BENEATH THE BURNING GROUND

Book I

THE UNDERGROUND RIVER

JEANNE WILLIAMS

Five Star • Waterville, Maine

First Edition
First Printing: September 2004

Published in 2004 in conjunction with Golden West Literary
Agency.

Set in 11 pt. Plantin by Christina S. Huff.

Printed in the United States on permanent paper.

Library of Congress Cataloging-in-Publication Data

Williams, Jeanne, 1930–
    The underground river : a frontier story / by Jeanne Williams.
        p. cm.—(Beneath the burning ground ; bk. 1)
      ISBN 1-59414-003-0 (hc : alk. paper)
      1. Kansas—Fiction.   2. Farm life—Fiction.   3. Rural
    families—Fiction.   4. Fugitive slaves—Fiction.   5. Children
    of clergy—Fiction.   6. Antislavery movements—Fiction.
    7. Frontier and pioneer life—Fiction.   I. Title.
    PS3573.I44933U55 2004
    813'.54—dc22   2004049701

For Michael, brave soldier, beloved son

Chapter One

It was the day! The day the Wares' new home would be built.
Christy Ware's heart sang like the orioles flashing among the
limbs of the great walnut as she climbed it and clambered
from limb to limb, tying the ropes fastened to the corners of
the wooden quilting frame till Ellen Ware, her mother,
judged it to be at the right level. Neighbors were coming from
miles around to help, most of them strangers. The women
had sent word that, if Ellen had enough blocks pieced, they'd
help her make a quilt while the men raised the house.

The giant walnut sheltered the Ware family that spring
while they camped in the wagon after the long journey from
Illinois. Spreading branches, feathery with new leaves and
catkins, shielded them and nesting birds—the orioles, scarlet
tanagers, and yellow-throated vireos—from rain and sun and
caught the brunt of early April winds. If winter never came,
thirteen-year-old Christy would have been happy to live
under the tree forever—no floors to sweep or scrub, no windows to wash, and no furniture to polish except for her
mother's piano which stood under the thickest cover of the
tree and was protected by a piece of canvas except when her
mother played nearly every night before her father read to
them, more often from Marcus Aurelius or Plato than from
the Bible, even though he was a Universalist minister.

"Isn't it strange," Jonathan Ware said, looking up at their

leafy roof, "that black walnut's favored for cradles, but it's also the wood the Army, and everybody else, likes for gunstocks?"

Christy didn't much mind doing dishes after supper to the chorus of chuck-wills-widows, their smaller cousins the whip-poor-wills, and the whistling plaint of screech owls quavering amongst the hoots of great horned and barred owls. A fox watched the humans inquisitively now and then; Robbie barked raccoons away; a mother bear with her cub, small in the spring but growing fast with summer's bounty, often paused close enough to be seen outside the campfire's circle of light.

"That's a musical bear," Jonathan Ware teased his wife Ellen. "Or maybe she's exposing her cub to culture."

To avoid the jeers of her older brothers, Christy didn't say that the bear looked almost like a person when she stood erect on her back legs and reached for something. Christy believed the bear was the spirit of the forest and thrilled when it appeared, a moving shadow against the trees.

Sleeping under the sky was delightful, waking to the whole wide world, but winter would come, however hard it was to believe that in this heat of early August. The pigs, chickens, and sheep had pens and sheds where they could be shut at night to protect them from foxes, timber wolves, and panthers. Zigzagged rail fences, secured near the corners by upright posts, surrounded the cornfield and garden and discouraged wild hogs and the Wares' cattle and horses, if not the deer. Now it was time to build the humans' house.

Christy helped her father and brothers carry big flattish rocks for the foundations of what would be two cabins connected by a roofed breezeway or dogtrot. Piled in stacks perhaps eighteen inches high about six feet apart, foundations discouraged insects that could bore into the logs and destroy them. Jonathan and the boys had cut oak trees tall enough to make logs twenty and sixteen feet long. Piles of these ranged around the foundations, trimmed and hewn on two sides as smooth as broad-axe and foot adze could make them.

The Ware men folk rived out what Jonathan reckoned were close to 5,000 oak shingles to roof the cabins and the ten-foot space between. Everything was ready.

As Christy scrambled back and forth, adjusting the ropes, she thought of the neighbors she knew best, Ethan Hayes and Hester Ballard, and how she'd met them.

As soon as Ellen's pride, her Silver Laced Wyandottes, the most vulnerable of the Wares' creatures, had a log house, Christy's father and brothers, fourteen-year-old Thos and sixteen-year-old Charlie, cleared and plowed several acres of bottom land. Stumps of black walnut, hackberry, oak, and hickory jutted from the broken earth to be grubbed or burned out as time allowed. Logs that could be used for fences or buildings were snaked by the oxen or horses to wherever they'd be handiest.

Christy and Thos had planted that first field to corn, following rough furrows that were little more than big clumps of sod bound by interlaced roots, ancient, undisturbed by the fires that swept through prairie and woodland after the first frost when sere high grass would explode from lightning or a chance spark. The family had sold their harrow, so Jonathan had made one by attaching four stout-limbed branches to an oak bar the horses could drag across the plowed land to break up the clumps.

Brother and sister carried hatchets. Where they found no cleft in the earth, they chopped niches in clods and covered the seed corn. They also planted pumpkin seeds to be protected by the growing corn, and string beans to grow up along the stalk. In Illinois, Jonathan and the boys had done all the planting, but, here, Christy had to help and she was glad.

Planting was much more to her taste than carding, spinning, and weaving. The earth smelled rich and moist and, where it was crumbly, felt good to her bare feet. And it was magic that seeds would grow into green bladed corn taller than her head, leafy vines with plump orange globes, and other vines weighted with flavorful green beans.

Nor had it all been work. As summer came on and the creek warmed, Christy and her brothers had swum in a limestone-bottomed hole near the house, and often there'd be a free hour or two when they could explore up and down the creek and in the woods around their clearing. Their best discovery had been a cave in the bluffs to the south. A low entrance opened into a chamber large enough for a score of people, and fantastic shapes formed by drips from the ceiling glittered in the muted light. It must have been used by Indians because a limestone slab near the opening had been hollowed out for grinding. A stone pestle rested at the edge. Who had used it last and when?

These pleasures, though, had been surrounded by all that had to be done. The shorthorn oxen, Moses and Pharaoh, brass knobs gleaming from the tips of their curving horns, broke an acre for sorghum cane, and a small plot for a garden. The sleek white animals, each weighing about 2,700 pounds, worked best for Thos. He praised and rubbed them down after their labor and put dollops of sorghum molasses in their grain.

While the men folk had planted the cane that would produce the family's sweetening once the big barrel in the wagon was gone, Christy and her mother had attacked the clods of the garden with spade, pitchfork, and hoe, but the sod roots had to decay before the earth could nourish tame seeds. Still, they had planted chunks of potato, each with two eyes, and were planting peas when a plump woman with light brown hair escaping her sunbonnet had jogged up on a little white mule with a couple of big sacks tied behind the saddle.

"I'm Hester Ballard, and please don't 'Miz Ballard' me." She had slid off the mule and given it a soft word and a pat. She had an open kind of face, eager and waiting, like a flower turned toward what the heavens sent, rain or sun. "I'm your nearest neighbor. Live a mile up the creek with my boy Lafe. Reckoned you'd be putting in a garden. Thought maybe you could use some watermelon, cucumber, turnip, and cabbage seeds, some rhubarb that was getting so big I had to divide the roots, onion buttons, and some cabbages I've had buried all winter. Plant them now and they'll grow seeds for next year."

She was about the age of Ellen, likely in her middle thirties. They had smiled, seeming to take to one another on sight. Christy could read her mother's mind, that it wouldn't be as lonesome here as she'd feared.

"Thank you kindly," Christy's mother had said. "I'm Ellen Ware and this is Christy. We'd be grateful for whatever you can spare, especially the onion buttons."

"Guess you know to plant them in the same row with cabbage. The onions' stink keeps away those pesky moths that lay eggs on the leaves to hatch into worms that'll just gobble up your cabbage."

As she spoke, Hester had dug in her apron pocket and handed Ellen three small cotton bags before she untied the lumpy sack from the saddle, lowered it to the ground, and carefully lifted out a dozen big cabbages. You could tell they'd been buried from the dirt that stuck to the leaves.

"Now, of course, you know to plant onions and turnips and 'taters, all the things that grow underground, in the dark of the moon, like you plant peas and such plants as grow above ground on the new moon."

"I'm afraid I don't know much about that, or planting by signs, Hester." Ellen had sounded apologetic. "I was brought up in town and my husband . . . well, he thinks all you need to do is plant when the ground's warm enough."

Hester had chuckled, a deep mellowness rising from her full bosom. "Lige Morrow does that when he leaves off hunting long enough to scratch out a little corn plot. Sits on the ground, bare-bottomed. When it don't chill him, he reckons the ground's ready for seeds. 'Course, you need to plant 'taters and onions a lot earlier. Maybe in March." Her eyebrows had puckered together over a snub nose that gave her somewhat the aspect of an opulent cat. "Once you plant by signs, you'll never do it any other way."

That sounded like more magic. "How does it work?" Christy had ventured.

Hester had puffed out her cheeks. "As well as paying attention to the moon, you keep track of the twelve signs of the zodiac. I use Doctor Jaynes's almanac . . . be glad to lend it to you. Each sign comes around twice a month and rules for two or three days. Plant cabbage when the signs are in the head, potatoes when they're in the feet. Mostly, you plant from head to heart, then from the thighs on down." She had given her head a decided shake. "Never plant in the bowels. Even when seeds sprout, they'll rot."

It *was* magic. Ellen had made a polite murmur, but Christy had said: "I'd truly like to read your almanac, Missus Ballard." She loved to read anything, and, although they'd each brought some of their favorite books, many had been given to the academy where Jonathan Ware used to teach.

After the planting was done, Jonathan had wanted to start on their home, but Ellen had said: "What's the use of planting if wild hogs and deer get at the sprouts? And I saw a big wolf slinking up to the sheep yesterday. It was all Robbie could do to run him off. Build fences first, Jonathan, and shelters for the pigs and sheep. We can wait."

That was when big, yellow-haired Ethan Hayes, long legs and moccasined feet dangling from his white mule, first had come to help. "I run a tannery a couple of miles downstream." The fringes of his supple buckskin shirt had swayed as he slid off the mule and hobbled her. "Been too busy finishing hides for some Cherokees up from Indian Territory to be a good neighbor, but my woman and boys can look after things today while I help you split rails, since that's what you're doing." He handed Ellen a plump cotton sack and a small covered tin pail. "Butter my woman churned last night and some walnut meats."

"Please thank her for me, Mister Hayes," Ellen had said. "I hope to meet her soon."

"Maybe when we raise your house," the young giant had said. "Allie stays right busy with the three boys and our baby girl, not to mention the tannery, but she's glad to have close neighbors."

Without being bossy, Hayes had soon led the work as they chose the straightest and longest of the previously felled black walnuts. Jonathan and the boys had split rails before, but Hayes had used his axe with deft ease, trimming off boughs before measuring off lengths and chopping his log in two with such accuracy that one side of each cut looked as if it had been sawed. He had taken Thos for his partner while Jonathan and Charlie worked on another log.

Hayes had made four oak wedges, tossed two to Jonathan, and made two mauls from oak limbs about six inches thick and the length of an axe, trimming handles with his pocket knife. Hoisting his well-sharpened axe, he had brought it down in the middle of the larger end of the log. Thos had set the iron wedge in the cut. Three blows from Hayes's maul had driven it in and split the log halfway open. As directed, Thos had thrust the wood wedges in to hold the crack open while Hayes set the iron wedge farther down the log. A few more swings of the maul and the log had cracked in half. The halves and resulting quarters had been split in the same way.

By dinner, there were piles of rails ranged around the field and all the best felled walnut trees were used. Hayes had started to pile into the food, but stopped, blushing, and bowed his head as Jonathan asked a blessing. As he had heaped his plate with cornbread, ham with gravy and wild greens, Hayes had said: "Mister Ware. . . ."

"Jonathan, please." Jonathan grinned. "We're neighbors."

"Jonathan." Hayes's sun-bleached eyebrows met above his clear blue eyes. "Mind a straight question?"

"Not if you don't mind a straight answer."

"When you prayed just now you said something about all men being brothers. Did you mean Negroes?"

"Why, yes." Jonathan smiled at Ellen. "I mean women, too, though the language could be clearer. If what you want to know is whether we think slavery is right, the answer is no."

"Kind of figgered that. I don't favor it myself, though I'm sure no Abolitionist." He sighed, chewed a few bites, and put down his fork. "Something awful's happened, Jonathan, Missus Ware. I didn't want to tell you till I got a notion of what kind of folks you are. Andy McHugh, the blacksmith near Trading Post just a mile or so west of the Kansas line, Andy brought some hides for tanning yesterday. And some real bad news." He glanced at Christy.

14

"Our children live in the world and have to know about it," Ellen said, although she was pale.

Hayes took a deep breath. "You'll likely know that Missourians who want Kansas to enter the Union as a slave state crossed the border in droves at the territorial election last year, threatened Free Staters away from the polls with guns and Bowie knives, and voted in a proslavery territorial legislature that still runs things. So the Free Staters elected their own legislature and governor. Early this month, a grand jury indicted the Free State leaders on charges of treason, so last week, May Twenty-First, proslave bigwigs like used-to-be Senator Atchison and George Clarke, the Indian agent down at Fort Scott, led what was well nigh an army into Lawrence and helped proslave lawmen arrest the Free State leaders for treason."

Ellen's hand went to her throat. "Lawmen took part in this?"

Hayes gave a harsh laugh. "Bless you, ma'am, Sheriff Jones hollered it was the happiest day of his life when the Free State Hotel was blown up. Two newspaper offices were wrecked to smithereens, and the proslavers looted stores and houses before they rode home."

"But. . . ."

"There's worse." Hayes shook his bright head. "When word spread about Atchison bringing in his Platte County Rifles from Missouri, Free Staters from all around hurried to defend Lawrence, but it was sacked before they got there. Naturally they were mad enough to kill . . . and old John Brown and his boys did just that."

Into the silence, Jonathan asked: "Who's John Brown?"

"A devil or prophet right out of the Old Testament, accordin' to your lights." Ethan frowned. "For sure, he's a red-hot Abolitionist. Five of his sons settled over on

15

Pottawatomie Creek in the winter of Eighteen Fifty-Five. He joined them last fall. They got up a militia, the Pottawatomie Rifles, that went to help Lawrence."

"So when they knew the town was ravaged. . . ."

"Old Brown had his men kneel while he prayed. Andy McHugh says he called long and loud to Jehovah, Lord God of Moses and Gideon and Joshua, the Liberators. Then he told his men he was going to do something that had to be done, that they all knew how proslavers on the Pottawatomie had warned Free Staters to get out or be killed. Old Brown said he wanted only those men with him who would obey him without question."

Ethan paused, swallowed, and went on in a strained voice. "His son, John, Junior, must have had an idea of what was coming. He wouldn't go. But four of Brown's sons did, and several more of the militia. That night they camped a mile from Dutch Henry's Crossing, sharpened their short swords, and decided who to call on. Next morning they went to Patrick Doyle's place. The Doyles were dirt poor and had no slaves, but they were strong proslavers, and the sons, one of them only eighteen, had run Free Staters away from the polls at the last election.

"Brown's party took them outside. Patrick tried to run. Old Brown shot him." Hayes shuddered. "That was the only pistol fired. Brown's sons hacked the young men to death with swords. They did the same for Allen Wilkinson, who was elected to the proslave legislature . . . when Missourians were allowed to vote and Free State men run off. Dutch Henry Sherman, a loud proslaver, wasn't home, but the Browns took his brother to the river, killed him, and threw him in."

"God have mercy on them," Ellen whispered.

"All of them, the Browns, too." Jonathan's lips were pale. "What horrors in the name of God! They must be insane."

"It's said a streak of it runs in old Brown's family."

Little Beth was fussing. Ellen picked her up and cradled her closely. "What will happen now?"

"Why, ma'am, the proslavers will try to get Brown, but I have a notion we'll hear a lot more about him before he's done. Free Staters like Andy McHugh hate what happened, but they've got to defend themselves or be run out of the country."

Jonathan looked grave. "I'm afraid it won't be settled till Kansas, slave or free, enters the Union."

"Maybe not then. But there's not much we can do about it except be glad we live in Missouri." Hayes stowed away his last few bites of food and got to his feet. "Let's go chop trees and make rails."

That afternoon, two to a tree, the boys and men chopped from either side. Fist-size chips flew till the trees wavered, groaned as the heartwood wrenched apart, and fell.

"That Ethan's a master with the axe," Jonathan Ware said after the young man had vanished into twilight and the woods. Christy was sure her father was trying to make things seem normal and right after Ethan's terrible news. Jonathan gave his wife a hug. "Two hundred rails! We'll start building fences in the morning. When we get tired of that, we'll split more rails, and, when we're tired of that, we'll rive white oak to cure for our floors."

The boys looked glum. They hadn't had a chance yet to swim or fish or just explore. Jonathan caught their look and grinned, gripping them by their shoulders. "Cheer up, lads. There's so much work on a new place that you've always got a choice of it."

"I'm glad we have lots of the same birds we did at home . . . in Illinois, I mean." Ellen smiled at the bluebird braving the Wyandottes to pursue a bug near the chicken house. She poured cornbread batter into the Dutch oven setting among the embers of their cook fire. "It makes this place seem friendlier. Like Cavalier, the Silver-Laced Wyandotte rooster, crowing and showing off to his wives."

"No wonder he crows." Jonathan chuckled. "He has a house while we're still roosting under this tree."

Ellen sighed and pinned dark braids tighter on top of her head before she sat down in the rocking chair to nurse Beth who was not quite a year old. The chair and rosewood piano looked strange beneath the tree, but Christy understood that they gave her mother a lot of comfort. She'd need it after hearing about old John Brown. Christy shivered and pushed away the imagined glint of those whetted swords, escaped to memories of their journey.

The Wares' possessions had been winnowed down to what would fit in the big covered wagon pulled by Moses and Pharaoh, and the Dearborn wagon drawn by Queenie and Jed, bays of Morgan blood, who could plow all week and race on Sunday. Queenie's chestnut colt, Lass, in spite of her mother's anxious whickers, skittered ahead, around, and behind while she was fresh of a morning, but, after a few hours, the little filly trudged closely as she could to the mare.

Of humans and creatures, only the chickens, Ellen, and the baby Beth rode all the time in the Dearborn wagon, the cages roped securely on top of Ellen's piano. After the space between the piano's legs was packed tightly with dishes wrapped in bedding, panes of glass for windows in their new home, and other fragile things, it was swathed in featherbeds and quilts which in turn were protected by heavy canvas. Except for the carved maple rocking chair that had soothed four generations of Jonathan's family as they spread west from Rhode Island, the family brought no other furniture. The wardrobe, table, and chairs Ellen's mother had brought from Kentucky were needed less than the John Deere walking plow with its steel-share Jonathan bought from the nearby factory at Moline, Illinois, or scythes, hoes, spades, axes, and other tools.

"I helped my uncle in his carpenter's shop," Jonathan consoled Ellen when she wept to see their four-poster bed and his treasured desk hauled away by the neighbor who'd bought them. "I can make everything you want, love."

Their marriage bed? The cradle she and her children had slept in? The great oak chest her great-grandparents had brought over from England? She turned against him and sobbed. "Oh, Jonathan!"

He stroked her soft dark hair. "Remember why we're going, Ellen. This small farm can only support one family. The boys are growing up. With what we've got from selling this place . . . and, yes, our treasures . . . we can take up one hundred and sixty acres in western Missouri for a dollar twenty-five an acre, enough land for Thos and Charlie, if it came to that, but, when they're twenty-one, each can buy his own quarter section."

"Yes, but. . . ."

"Otherwise, in four or five years, my dear, they'll head West and we'd be lucky to ever see them again." He looked at her with that coaxing supplication in his blue eyes that his wife could never resist.

"But where will you find a school to teach at or Universalists to preach to?" she asked. "From all we hear, Missourians outside of Saint Louis are hardshell Baptists and Methodists with a sprinkle of Presbyterians."

He laughed fondly. "Folks will come to services just to hear you play your piano."

Her eyes were troubled. "Slavery's strong there."

"Only along the Missouri and Mississippi Rivers where big planters grow tobacco and hemp. We'll settle in the southwest where there's plenty of the kind of land not wanted for plantations, but where a family can make a living."

"I suppose I have to be grateful that you don't want to go to Kansas!" Remembering that conversation, Christy shivered again. All they'd known about Kansas Territory, then, was that it was a forlorn place where settlers fought tooth and nail over whether it would join the Union as a slave state or free one.

Ellen wiped her eyes and went back to packing.

They'd brought milk buckets, candle molds, a churn, spinning wheel, loom, tubs, sad irons, the big iron kettle for washing clothes and making soap, smaller ones and a Dutch oven and skillets for cooking, all with feet so they could stand in coals and ashes in the fireplace. The iron tea kettle had feet, too, but the griddle hung from a crane.

The new kitchen, at least, would soon seem familiar with the wooden spice box with six drawers, coffee grinder, crocks, and wooden bowls and spoons. Besides Ellen's cherished silver and china, for everyday there was glazed blue earthenware delft, and iron forks, spoons, and case knives.

Speeded by traveling by steamboat down the Mississippi to Hannibal, then overland to pick up the Boone's Lick Trail west, they'd jounced along the roads and taken ferries across the rivers. Cavalier, the arrogant Silver-Laced Wyandotte rooster, frequently squawked with indignation and glared at the people who dared coop him up, flaunting his rose comb above the demure ones of his two dozen wives. They had, with difficulty, been chosen by Ellen as the best of her more than a hundred hens. For them, Jonathan contrived three long cages with perforated false bottoms that let droppings fall below into a drawer that could be pulled out and dumped as necessary. In spite of this consideration and plenty of grain, Cavalier pecked if a hand came near, and crowed any time he felt like it, which was often in the night.

Jonathan, Thos, and Charlie took turns driving the oxen while walking at their side, driving the team, or herding along the fawn-colored Jerseys—Lady Jane, Guinevere, Bess, and Goldie—who were all heavy with calves, and Mildred, Cleo, and Nosey, the Suffolk ewes, who lambed on the journey. Most laggard and apt to stray after last fall's acorns or a succulent mushroom were the Poland China sows, Patches and Evalina, whose white-spotted black bodies were swollen with piglets. Robbie, the little border collie, kept them moving with firm patience till he got a thorn in his paw. For a day, he rode across Jed's withers. They were the best of friends. When Jed was grazing, Robbie often jumped to his back and had as much of a ride as good-natured Jed was inclined to give him.

They had traveled so long that it was still hard to believe that this was where they'd live always, on the knoll above Clear Creek that flowed into the Marais des Cygnes River. Very near the Kansas border they were, only two miles. So close that five of the ten women now working on all four sides of the quilt lived across the boundary and hadn't been known to the Wares, except by name, till they came with their men folk to help that morning.

As if by common consent, no one brought up old John Brown's slaughter on Pottawatomie Creek or the turbulent events that had followed, news Ethan Hayes had passed along from his customers. A company of Missouri sharpshooters had gone to take Brown, but been defeated. Federal troops kept the Free-State legislature from convening in Topeka. James Lane, a Free-State firebrand, brought 600 like-minded settlers in through Iowa and Nebraska to make up for those stopped by Border Ruffians at the Missouri border, and Free Staters were besieging four proslavery strongholds.

On this neighborly day, though, no one spoke of the fury raging in Kansas Territory. Tall, fine-boned Lydia Parks, eldest daughter of widower Simeon Parks, a Quaker, who had a grist mill just across in Kansas on the Marais des Cygnes, took tiny stitches to finish off a corner. She made such a neat job of that critical task that Lucinda Maddux decreed: "Best you finish all the corners, Lydia. You've a rare knack for it."

Lucinda, graying and ample, took authority as the oldest woman there. She lived with her husband Arly and their youngest son Tom across the creek from the Hayeses on the road to Butler, the Bates county seat. Their oldest son, she'd explained, was still hunting gold in California, the two middle ones and their families had settled in Oregon, and two married daughters remained in Tennessee.

Lydia Parks's pale skin warmed with a blush at Lucinda's compliment. That turned her almost pretty, although she made her thin face even more so by combing her black hair into a knot as tight as any of the older women's. She must have grown up mothering twelve-year-old David whose birth caused their mother's death. Their brother Owen was married to Harriet, the young woman with braids plump and golden-brown as ripe wheat, who kept leaving the quilt to nurse her fretful baby.

"The mite's teething." Harriet's mother, Mildred Morrison, was buxom where her daughter was pleasantly rounded, but they had the same bright blue eyes. "Don't hurt a baby to cry. Oh, well, that'll come with the next one."

Harriet flushed and tightened her lips, taking up her

22

needle with a jerk. Apparently Mrs. Morrison shared the young couple's cabin, but, from several overheard remarks, Christy surmised that the widow would be glad to relieve Lydia of keeping house for Simeon.

Smoothing the rumpled moment, Susie Parks, black hair escaping a French knot to wave softly about her face, smiled at her hostess. "Let's embroider our names on the back of the quilt so you'll never forget us."

"Not much chance of that." Ellen smiled around at her neighbors. "You've all been so kind. . . ."

"Lord, child, what are neighbors for?" Lucinda, to Christy's fascinated horror, took a pinch of snuff. "Wish we'd had help when we came here. We lived in the wagon, under and around it, till Arly and Tom got a round-log house built. That was just to do us till there was time to make a good hewn log cabin, but we're in it to this day." She looked admonishingly at the younger women. "Don't ever let your man entice you into a round-log hut, my dears, or there you may stay the rest of your days."

"Then there's them as thinks they're too good for logs, and freight in lumber from a sawmill." Nora Caxton was as withered as her husband Watt was sleek and dapper. They lived on the other side of the Hayeses. Watt raised mules and traded in them, cows, and horses. Nora's scraggly rust-hued hair was knotted on top of her skull. Wisps of it jounced as she gave her head a sharp nod and stared accusingly at Lottie Franz. "Both my grandads fought the British in Eighteen Twelve. I had a great-grandaddy at Valley Forge. Don't seem right that some come in from foreign lands and, right off, have things better than us who been born in this country four generations or more."

Lottie regarded the other woman with wide, calm eyes. "But, Missus Caxton, Emil fought in the War of Eighteen

Twelve. He had just come to this country, a boy of sixteen. He limps because a musket ball shattered his leg. His only son, my husband, was killed in the war with Mexico seven years ago."

"You're sure not foreigners," Hester said. "Anyway, except for Indians, everybody's family came from somewhere else. Not that long ago, either."

Christy wandered over to watch her father, Ethan Hayes, Simeon Parks, and Owen Parks split out two-inch-thick puncheons or floorboards. Sill beams the length of the cabin had been positioned on the foundation; floor beams hewed off at the ends rested snugly on the sills about four feet apart. Emil Franz, Andy McHugh, and Watt Caxton trimmed off the underside of the ends of the puncheons to fit tight over the sleepers.

The boys had the task of smoothing the boards with adzes and knives. Besides Thos and Charlie, the oldest Hayes boys, tow-headed Matthew and Mark, there was a flame-haired skinny Irish orphan who lived with the Parkses, David Parks, and Lafe Ballard. Christy liked Hester so much that she'd expected to like her son, but, on the occasions he'd stopped by, he'd watched her with his pale eyes till she felt handled, and once he'd trod hard on Robbie's tail and pretended it was an accident.

Barrel-chested Arly Maddux, shaggy gray hair and beard framing his red face, moved from group to group with suggestions. Ethan said weeds grew higher than corn in his fields. That didn't matter much since his fences were so poorly kept that hogs and cattle were in the field more than they were out. He was of vaguely Baptist persuasion and his favorite theme was infant damnation.

"A hair more this way, boys!" he called to Andy McHugh, the gaunt red-haired blacksmith from across the border, and Owen Parks, as they placed the first end log in the space left before the first sleeper and lap-jointed the edges to fit over the sill.

After the second end log was in place, Ethan, the acknowledged master at notching, hewed two sides of the end of a log and hewed the top at an angle. The end of a second log, hewn at the ends by Andy, was placed crosswise on top of the first. Using a straight board to measure the angle of the bottom log, Ethan notched the top one to fit perfectly across the first, then did the same to the other end.

The men and big boys settled into a rough rhythm, some laying the sills and sleepers of the second cabin, others splitting puncheons, and Jonathan and Andy hewing log ends and placing them for Ethan's notching, so accurately that he seldom had to lift up a log to trim it more. The resulting dovetails locked the logs so tightly that the cabin would stand solidly as long as the logs were sound, and they were oak, so that should be till long after Christy had grandchildren, hard as it was to believe she ever would.

Cabin-raising was much more absorbing than quilting. When Beth first roused and whimpered from her quilt beneath the tree, Christy hoped she'd quit fussing, at least till Ethan finished this notch. Alternating sides, the logs were now waist high.

Beth's fretting changed to a howl. Sighing, Christy turned from watching Ethan and started for the baby. She stopped with a gasp. That Irish boy of the Parkses—Dan O'Brien. He was cuddling Beth.

He'd trimmed puncheons so smoothly that Ethan had praised him, and the Parks sisters said he was a rare fiddler, but what could he know about babies, American ones, anyway? What if he dropped her?

Avoiding playing children and the sprawl of Watt

Caxton's hounds, Christy sped to the rail-thin lad and reached for Beth, who treacherously gurgled. The baby patted a broken nose that was brown enough to almost hide the freckles that spilled over high-angled cheek bones.

He grinned at Beth but ignored Christy, even turned a bit away. "Here, I'll take her," Christy said. She hoped their mother hadn't heard Beth wail or seen this Irisher get to her before Christy did.

"Indeed, you were in no hurry before."

Stung, Christy snapped: "I came as soon as I heard her."

"That you did not." A foreign lilt flavored his words, but he spoke with precision that must have come from living some years with well-educated Quakers. "You cocked your head this way when the little one fretted, but then you went back to watching Ethan Hayes."

"If you've nothing better to do than spy on a person. . . ."

"I do. This." He smiled at the baby and said something soft in his own tongue. That widened his narrow face, brought a shine to smoke-gray eyes, and made him almost nice to look at.

"She needs changing," Christy snapped. "Are you going to do that?"

It was a chore Thos and Charlie avoided like the plague although her father often did it. "Bring me a diaper," said this unbelievable boy.

"No!" she hissed. "Give her to me. Right now!"

He shrugged and handed her over, but, before he moved away, he pierced Christy with a cool smoke-gray stare that expressed his opinion of her care-giving.

Hateful thing! Christy lugged Beth to the wagon and changed her, cleaning Beth's petal-soft skin. Ellen Ware was particular about keeping the baby dry and fresh so she wouldn't get a rash. Thank goodness for the safety pins that made the task easier. A supply of them, regular pins, and needles were in her mother's sewing basket.

"Do you know you're almost a year old?" Christy asked. Beth laughed and made an assortment of sounds. "You won't remember Illinois at all, or camping under the tree, or how the house was built. But I'll tell you. . . ."

"Christina!" called Ellen. "Grind the coffee, fill the water buckets, and then bring butter and milk and cottage cheese . . . buttermilk, too . . . from the cold-box."

Ellen didn't like to get their drinking water from the creek, and it was a chore to fetch all they needed from a quarter mile away, so Jonathan and the boys had dug for water in a dozen places, but still hadn't struck water for a well. They'd try again when they weren't so busy, but, till then, they'd dug a hole to fit a deep trough made of oak. This was kept full of water in which to place crocks of the rich milk, butter, buttermilk, and cream that came from Lady Jane, Guinevere, Goldie, and Bess after their calves had all the milk they needed. Rived clapboards fastened together with pegs made a cover.

As she ground the roasted coffee beans, Christy reflected that the oldest girl in a family should be twins to help with all the woman work. Charlie and Thos put in long hard hours, but they got to sit and eat while she jumped up for more corndodgers or gravy, and they settled back in comfort while she did the dishes. They wore the knees and elbows out of the clothes she helped her mother sew, and that *after* carding, spinning, dyeing, and weaving the cloth.

After she filled the water buckets, Christy brought the butter she'd churned yesterday, the cream she'd skimmed that morning from last night's milk, the cottage cheese drained out last night from simmered curds, and crockery pitchers of fresh milk and buttermilk. She put these on the beautifully grained walnut table her father had made as soon as the wood had cured enough.

As the women on each side finished an arm-length of quilt, they rolled it up and hurried to put out their contributions to the feast. When there wasn't an uncovered inch on the walnut table, a long table improvised from floorboards for the loft laid across sawhorses was soon crowded to the edges. Christy used tongs to fill a basket with roasting ears pulled from the ashes, steam-cooked to juicy tenderness in their husks. From the Wares' garden came bowls of green beans, creamed peas, beets, and sweet potatoes mashed and sweetened with molasses, and, of course, Ellen had made lots of cornbread and pones.

Hester swung a kettle of hominy up beside her crock of corn pudding. Yellow-haired Allie Hayes was a robust match for her big husband, but it was all she could do to carry a wood platter holding two roasted wild ducks stuffed with nuts, herbs, and sweet potatoes. The Caxtons brought fried squirrel, and the Madduxes contributed stewed doves.

Boys carried up watermelons and musk melons put in the creek to chill. It was hard to say whether the greatest treat was light bread made from wheat ground at the Parks' mill, or the apple and blackberry pies Lottie Franz brought from their wagon while Emil set a basket of grapes on the table and stowed a tub of fragrant apples underneath.

"This old rooster pecked me one time too often," Catriona McHugh said, as she nudged a Dutch oven of chicken and dumplings a safe distance from the table edge. "Onery as he was, he ought to have plenty of flavor!"

Jonathan Ware was a Universalist minister, but, of course, he invited Arly Maddux, as a guest and Baptist parson, to ask the blessing. Arly was in high flight when Watt Caxton's slumbering hounds roused and set up clamorous barking.

"Call off your dogs, Watt!" boomed a voice from the creek.

"I'll bid mine stay here and we'll have no ruckus."

"Willin' to bet mine can't whup yours?" Watt bellowed.

"You want a fight, Watt, I'll give you one."

"Treat your dogs like they was human," Watt grumbled, but he yelled and swore at his hounds that cowered to their bellies and hushed.

The man ambling up from the creek was tall and lank. With summer, Ethan had quit wearing his leather shirt, but the stranger wore one and pants as well, with beads worked along the fringed seams. His sun-streaked sandy hair was tied back with a thong. He carried a rifle under one arm, and the other hand gripped the legs of a big turkey slung over his shoulder.

Beside him like a whisper moved a dark, slender girl in red calico, the only dress that hadn't been made from homespun material. Like the man, she wore beaded moccasins. Her black hair was braided with red ribbon into a single plait that hung below her waist. She carried a covered wooden bucket.

"Sorry I didn't get this turkey to you in time for dinner, but we were getting you some honey." The stranger dropped the handsomely feathered bird on the grass near the trunk of the walnut. He thrust out a hand to Jonathan. "I'm Lige Morrow. This is my wife Sarah. We live across the creek and up a ways."

Ellen came to greet the Morrows, accepting the bucket of honey with delight. "We can't take all of this," she demurred. "Let me pour some for us into a pail and. . . ."

"It's all for you." Sarah spoke better English than most of the gathering except for the Wares and Quakers. Her eyes tilted upward, golden green. Her skin was creamy rose and gold, so rich and smooth you wanted to touch her. "My bees send it willingly."

"Well, then," said Ellen with a smile, "thank them for us, very kindly."

Sarah nodded. "There are many flowers this year. They make much honey. So I ask six hives if they will spare honey for you."

"You didn't smoke them into the top of the hive?" Emil Franz's shrewd gray eyes studied the hunter's woman.

"No."

"You had to stun 'em some way," Nora Caxton argued.

Lige stepped closer to his wife. "The bees don't sting Sarah. She moves around the bee-gums with no trouble at all." He grimaced. "They'll sure take after me, though."

"Ain't natural." Nora squinted at Sarah and curled her lip. "Must be redskins have a kind of wild smell."

Lige's yellow eyes had the sheen of a great cat's, but his tone was genial. "Miz Caxton, I'll bet you venison for the winter that, if folks was to shut their eyes and sniff at you and Sarah, they'd say you're the one smells wild. Like a polecat that's been dead a week."

Chapter Two

Lige Morrow spoke with a smile, so gently that no one could believe their ears for a minute. Watt Caxton went red to the roots of his greasy black hair. "Why, you shiftless, woodsrunnin' squawman! I'll. . . ."

Morrow raised an eyebrow. "Take a pot shot at me from the brush?"

Arly Maddux puffed forward. "Now, neighbors! Put by your wrath. The Good Book says . . . 'Be kindly affectioned one to another with brotherly love.' "

Jonathan, too, had moved between them and looked from one man to the other. "I'll be grateful if you'll both forget the hard words and join in the feast. Indeed, we'd be grieved, my family and I, if our cabin-raising was marred with neighbors falling out."

Nora Caxton sniffled. "No need for you to jump on your high horse and gallop, Lige Morrow. All I said was. . . ."

"Sarah's half Osage and half French." Tautness flowed out of Morrow and he grinned at his wife. "Sweet as her honey most of the time but stings like her bees when she's mad."

"Otherwise, you wouldn't notice," Sarah Morrow retorted. She, a brilliant poppy beside a withered nettle, smiled at Nora. "I don't mind to be called a redskin, Missus Caxton. At the Osage mission, our priest used to say . . . 'An Indian scalps his enemies, but a white man skins his friends.' "

31

"Watt, she nailed your hide to the wall," chortled Arly, clapping the trader on the shoulder. "Gather 'round and let me finish the blessing before the food gets cold."

As the crowd drifted back to the tables, Christy heard Lafe Ballard whisper to Matthew, the eldest Hayes boy: "Wonder what color that squaw is . . . you know, in her woman parts?"

Matthew, tow-headed like Mark and Luke—their folks had just started with the books of the New Testament in naming their boys—reddened up to his big ears. "You hadn't ought to talk like that! If Lige hears you, *you'll* be colored black and blue!"

Lafe Ballard giggled. He had delicate features, girl-pretty, with a deep-cleft chin, eyes so pale a blue they had almost no tint, and waving silvery hair. "Bet you don't even know what women look like under their drawers. Sometime you ought to watch your mama. . . ."

Matthew knocked him flat. Lafe was up like a cat, but he didn't strike back although he and Matthew were fairly matched enough—Lafe taller by a few inches, Matthew heavier and broader. They were at the back of the gathering. Only Christy saw and heard them.

"I'll get you for this, Matt Hayes!" Lafe's snarl was muffled by the shirt tail he pressed to a bleeding lip.

"Hey," growled Matthew, clenching brown fists, "come down in the trees where no one'll stop us and I'll give you more'n you want!"

Lafe's eyes glittered like moonlit ice, but he turned and swaggered toward the feast Arly had finally blessed to his satisfaction. People here certainly seemed quick to fight, Christy thought. And Beth was fussing again. Christy sighed and picked her up, joining the older children who'd eat after the younger ones had been helped by their mothers. The men ate

first, of course, as they did on any occasion where everyone couldn't sit down at the same time.

After dinner, Harriet Parks and Christy did the stacks of dishes while Ellen Ware put together a stew from leftovers and more vegetables. Lige dug a pit and built a fire in it while he cleaned and dressed the turkey, stuffed it with peppergrass, wild onions, and nuts, molded clay around it, and put the fowl among the coals in the pit, raking some on around the sides and top. He covered the bird with earth and built another fire on top.

"Keep the fire going till the middle of the afternoon, will you, sis?" he asked Christy. "By supper that ole gobbler will taste plumb scrumptious!"

So she kept an eye on that fire, but, when she wasn't adding wood or minding Beth or running errands for the women, she watched the men lap joint ceiling beams to the lengthwise logs paralleling the sills, wall and floor the lofts, secure steeply slanted rafters to the ridgepoles, and split out lathing.

For the first time, nails forged by Andy McHugh were used—his gift along with hinges for the doors and shutters and a rod and kettle hooks for the fireplace. The ring of hammers reverberated as lathing was nailed to the rafters and shingling began with the bottom row. Two shingles were nailed side-by-side to the lathing, and a third nailed across the crack. The next row overlapped the first by about three inches, and, at the peak, the top shingle on one side overlapped the other by three or four inches so rain wouldn't find its way into the joining.

Meanwhile, Emil Franz and Ethan Hayes, the best craftsmen with wood, used axes and Emil's saw to cut out a door, fireplace, and two windows in each cabin. They then used cured walnut to make doors, shutters, and frames, peg-

ging them into the cut logs. Christy held the panes in place inside the frames of one window in each cabin while Emil pressed gray clay found near the spring around the edges on both sides. The other windows would be open in fine weather and, in foul, closed with shutters.

Much as she liked watching the men, Christy hurried to tend to Beth when she whimpered, not wishing that aggravating Irish boy to have another chance to fault her. As arm-length after arm-length of the quilt was rolled up, Sarah took tiny stitches that rivaled those of Lydia Parks.

"The nuns taught us," she explained. "We had lessons in reading, arithmetic, penmanship, history, and geography at the mission, but we learned cooking, spinning, weaving, and housekeeping, too."

Lucinda Maddux primmed her lips and yanked a recalcitrant thread. "You had to worship statues, I'll be bound . . . idolaters, that's what Catholics are!"

"We don't worship idols." Sarah Morrow gazed calmly at the minister's wife. "We ask the Holy Mother and the saints to intercede for us, but that's because they were human once. God is beyond our finite minds."

"Fi . . . what?" demanded Lucinda. "They taught you to sew, I'll have to admit, but what's the use of a . . . woman . . ."—she amended hastily—"learning all that stuff? I only got to go to school a few winter terms. I was needed to help at home, but I can read my Bible, write my mother back in Tennessee, and cipher a little. That's all a body needs. Arly can't read at all, but God called him to preach."

"If you can read your Bible, ma'am, you read very well, indeed." Sarah's tone was all respect, but Christy thought she detected a hint of a smile.

"Your dress is beautiful." Susie Parks, whose homespun linsey-woolsey, probably dyed brown with walnut bark, cast

34

wistful eyes at the crimson that would so become her fair skin and black hair. "The skirt's so full you could wear a crinoline under it."

Lydia frowned at her younger sister. "It's vanity to puff out one's skirts with a connivance of horsehair, and costly to boot."

"But it takes the place of at least three petticoats," Susie argued.

"I used to wear ten in Ohio," put in Mildred Morrison, "except in winter when some were quilted. It's so inconvenient to wash here, though, that I make do with five. I think I'll ask my son Barney to fetch me a crinoline from Saint Louis next time he's there. He freights on the Santa Fé Trail, you know." The buxom widow, whose taffy hair frizzed oddly at the temples, preened a moment before she sent a disparaging glance at her daughter Harriet, young Owen Parks's wife. "Barney's a fine son. Nothing's too much trouble for that lad if he reckons it'll please his mother."

"Maybe he thinks that can be done." Harriet, yellow-brown head bowed, stabbed her needle through the quilt.

Mildred sucked in her breath. Before she could blast her daughter, Lydia Parks said: "Father said only yesterday that he hopes ladies here won't feel obliged to keep up with the frivolities of fashion."

Mrs. Morrison looked annoyed. She had made quite a fuss of forcing seconds of her blackberry cobbler on widower Simeon. Appearing not to notice, Lydia finished the last corner and got to her feet, flexing her fingers and sighing with pleasure in a task well done.

"There you are, Missus Ware. It's a beautiful quilt."

Lottie Franz nodded and her blue eyes glowed. "Always you'll remember, when you look at it, this happy day your home was built."

"It will be a happy house." Sarah Morrow's laughter trilled with the tanager's hoarser song, flashing above them, his scarlet brilliant as her gown. "I will ask the Holy Mother to ask her Son that this quilt warm and comfort all who rest beneath it." She said it as matter-of-factly as Mildred Morrison had announced her intention of asking her son for a crinoline.

Before Lucinda Maddux could say something to match her scowl, Ellen said: "Thank you, Sarah dear. It will pleasure me every time I see the quilt to remember all of you. Christy, you can't climb the tree with the men folk around, so go ask Luke Hayes if he'll shinny up and untie the frame on the near end. We'll leave the curtain hanging on the frame to show the men we've accomplished something, too."

Thousands and thousands of tiny stitches must have gone to make the quilt. It was the Tree of Paradise pattern Ellen had copied from one of her grandmother's before moving to Illinois. Every good piece of cloth was carefully saved from any worn-out garment and cut and pieced into the patterned blocks, but Ellen had dyed newly woven linsey-woolsey a lovely heaven blue for the border and spaces between the blocks.

It hung, bright and beautiful, from the great tree. Christy decided sewing wasn't completely dreadful if something that wonderful could be made, something that would last a lot longer than Thos and Charlie's trouser knees and shirt sleeves.

"Look!" Sarah pointed. "Your doors are on their hinges, Missus Ware!"

"Real glass in the windows!" Lucinda Maddux shook her gray head. "Ten years we've lived here, and all I've got is oiled hides to let in a little light." She turned accusingly to

Sarah. "Thought I saw sun sparkin' off window panes at your place as we passed by."

"Lige brought back panes when he went to Independence last fall. My bees gave me enough honey to trade for them."

Jonathan came, smiling, to Ellen, chestnut hair tousled, blue eyes shining. He took her hand and said to the others: "Won't you come, ladies, while I ask a blessing on our home and all our neighbors?"

He had deferred to Arly at dinner, but Christy knew he wouldn't want anyone else to preside at this moment. Bowing his head, he prayed: "Oh, Lord, we thank Thee for the bounty of Thy forests that have yielded the means to build our home. We thank Thee for these friends and neighbors who have been kind and strong and skilled to help us. May we live here in a manner pleasing to You. Ever mindful of Thy gifts, may we share them with others. May this roof shelter those who have none. May these walls protect any caught in a storm. May there ever be food and warmth and welcome for the hungry or the weary, for this is not our house only, dearest Lord, it is Thine." He opened the heavy door with the long wrought-iron hinges. "Lord, we pray Thou wilt bless the coming in and the going out of all who pass this door and let Thy peace reign within."

There was a chorus of "Amens". Lines formed at the tables, Arly gave thanks at considerable length as if to compensate for not being asked to say grace over the house.

Lige had broken the clay off his turkey and carved it on a wooden platter. Christy got a few scraps and bent to fill her plate with stew from the iron kettle sitting on coals at the edge of the fire.

Someone bumped her arm, knocking her wrist against the kettle. She cried out, dropping the ladle, and turned to meet Lafe's gaze. Only a pale rim of iris glowed around the enlarged pupils of his eyes. His lips were parted, as if to taste. She saw his teeth were small and white.

" 'Scuse me," he said, as his mother hurried up. "Didn't go to bump you."

She knew he had. Knew he enjoyed her pain. But she was one of the host family and, anyway, she couldn't accuse him with Hester looking so sorry and so worried. "Come, hold that wrist in cold water, honey. That'll ease it more than anything. Lafe, Son, watch what you're doing, 'specially around a fire."

"I will, Ma." He spoke meekly, but his eyes glittered. "I'm sorry."

Liar! Christy wanted to shout. But Hester, poor Hester, to have her only child like to hurt people and think dirty about women! The cool water did relieve the sting. "Just keep it under water for a while," Hester bade. "I'll bring your stew and you can eat."

"We'll put sweet butter and a bandage on it later," Ellen said, touching Christy's cheek. "Where the veins are so close to the skin, we don't want it to make a bad sore."

Sarah brought her a chunk of cornbread covered with amber honey. "Honey's good for burns," she said. "Trouble is, it's sticky and draws flies."

"*Mmm.* It tastes so good!"

"Yes, and there's still plenty from my bees through the winter."

"How do you get them to stay at your place?"

"They can sip from the log Lige hollowed out for the birds to bathe and drink. Whenever I see a pretty flower or vine, I wait till it goes to seed and try to grow it, so there are blooms from early spring till frost. Bees love the wild plum tree by the cabin, and there's a blackberry thicket big enough to get lost in. I did once." Sarah laughed. It was charming to hear, she was enchanting to watch, and Christy tumbled worshipfully in love.

"Oh, may I come see you?"

"Of course. You'll meet the bees. In a few years, if they like you and are willing to stay with you, I'll give you some bee-gums."

"Gum trees?" Christy puzzled.

"No, pieces of hollowed log with roofs. You'll see." She went off with a swirl of crimson skirts, her kindness sweet as the honey in Christy's mouth.

By the time she had eaten, Christy could hold her wrist out of water without much pain. Her mother gently applied unsalted fresh butter to the red weal that ran almost the width of Christy's wrist, and secured the bandage by running the strip torn from old pantaloons between thumb and index finger before looping it again around the burn.

"No dishes for you till it heals," Ellen said. "What a shame, dear."

"It doesn't hurt much now." Christy wanted to tell her mother that Lafe had jostled her on purpose but, with great effort, held her tongue. That would worry and upset her mother, and supposing she decided she should tell Hester? Whatever it was with Lafe, Christy sensed deeply in her bones that it wasn't anything to be cured by whipping, shaming, or grieved entreaties. What she had seen in his eyes was evil, what her father called the lack of the presence of God; only Christy thought the devil had rooted himself where God was not. She would tell her brothers, though. They needed to be on the watch for him. Besides, she wouldn't care a bit if they waylaid him sometime and thrashed him till he'd never try his tricks at the Wares' again.

The women cleared the tables in the last glow of sunset. The Franzes had cows to milk and took their leave, Emil promising to bring them some Catawba grapevines and Maiden Blush saplings once they went dormant and could be safely transplanted. Matthew and Mark Hayes raced off home to do chores and return. The rest of the assemblage either had no animals requiring care or had arranged with neighbors to take over that evening. Charlie and Thos slipped off to milk, and pen the hogs and sheep. Christy held the egg basket in her bandaged right hand and collected them with her left. Located where it was, this burn was going to be an aggravation, but worse, even after it healed, it would remind her of Lafe's meanness, the devil twisted deeply inside his comely flesh and bone.

"Now we'll get to hear your piano, Missus Ware," bubbled Susie Parks as the men carried it inside the cabin that would serve for everything but sleeping.

It was placed to get light from the glass window, but although the moon was almost full, it was dark enough inside now for candles. Ellen extravagantly placed six in the silver candelabra that had been her grandmother's. The mellow light reflected from the polished rosewood, but the sheen in Ellen's eyes was that of tears.

Was she happy that her piano and candelabra made at least that spot like her old home? Or was she thinking how strange they looked in that cabin, log walls still unchinked, fireplace opening agape?

Whatever she felt, when Jonathan brought the walnut bench he'd made to replace the brocaded one she'd had to give to a friend in Illinois, Ellen seated herself with a graceful sway of skirts and played "Praise God from Whom All Blessings Flow" with such spirit that those who didn't know the doxology hummed it. Next was Jonathan's favorite "To be a Pilgrim".

Then Ellen smiled at Dan O'Brien whose hair caught the

light even from his far corner. "Won't you play your fiddle, Dan? The ladies say you can bring the birds down from the trees."

"Maybe a screech owl, ma'am."

"Come, lad!" called Andy McHugh. "Give us the dance I taught you from the Isle of Skye, the one called 'America'."

"Aye, laddie," old Catriona urged. "Even I'll prance my best to that one! It was the last dance I ever stepped on that dear soil before we took ship and came so far, so far." Her voice caught. "This land's been good to us. No landlord to drive us from our croft, no laird raising regiments for the wars of the English queen. But, och! Never to see the shining lochs or the mists on the mountains. . . ."

"Or the laird's deer destroying our fields," her son reminded her. "His sheep devouring the grass, his agent and the constables tearing down our houses, firing our roofs. . . ."

He turned to the Irish boy who must have seen things as bad or worse, for he was old enough to remember the famine years. "Play the song, Dan." The broad-chested, red-haired blacksmith held out his hands to Susie Parks who reached about to his heart. "Will you dance, lass, and show our friends the steps?"

Whatever the McHughs had lost or left in Skye, that Western Isle of Scotland with its magic name, it was clear Andy had found his love here on this frontier border, old to the Indians, new to the whites. And whatever the powers in Ireland had done to the flame-haired orphan boy, it left him music.

Thin face bent to the satiny instrument, he played joy and hope out of sorrow and longing. Christy's heart softened, although she assured herself he'd had no right to accuse her of neglecting Beth. Ethan drew Sarah into the dance, and Lige made a surprisingly courtly bow to Allie Hayes. Their baby girl slept in the other cabin so Owen and Harriet Parks joined in, as did the Caxtons. Jonathan claimed Ellen. Hester, in spite of Mildred Morrison's scowl, smiled invitingly at Simeon Parks who grinned back and met her at the edge of the reel.

"We don't hold with dancing," Arly Maddux said, pushing Lucinda toward the door. "And I'm purely astonished, Mister Parks, that Quakers do."

Simeon chuckled. "We heed our inner light. Mine tells me it is not wrong to move nimbly with one's neighbors so long as there be no drunkenness or wanton behavior."

"How about wantin' behavior, Sim?" hollered Watt Caxton in a way that hinted that he, at least, might have imbibed something stronger than buttermilk.

"We'll be on our way," snapped Arly.

Jonathan and Ellen thanked the Madduxes, and Jonathan went out to help Arly hitch up his team. Ellen sat down by Lydia Parks, the only young woman who hadn't been asked to dance. Catriona clapped and called encouragement. Mildred Morrison glowered at Hester.

When Jonathan came back in, one of their silent messages passed between him and Ellen. Approaching the ladies' bench, he drew Lydia up with laughing gallantry.

After a few numbers, Watt Caxton and Nora were panting. "Time we went home," Watt said loudly, pushing back his greased hair. "I've tricked me a big old sow bear into my pen along with her cub. Goin' to have a bear-baiting tomorrow. Men with good bear dogs are comin' from all over. Usually you just turn six, seven dogs at a time in on the bear, but this 'un's so big and mean, 'specially with her cub to protect, that I'm bound she can handle a dozen at a time . . . till she's hurt bad. That should take a while. Quite a while, if the cub shows fight."

"Mother!" Christy gasped. "That must be *our* bears!"

Sarah's hand went to her throat. Lige said: "What'll you take for that bear, Caxton?"

"More'n any buckskin hunter's got. Bring your dogs over, though, and prove they're some account."

"I don't hold with bear-baitin'."

"No," sneered Watt, "and you don't like the way I train my dogs, do you?"

"I kill wolves, but I'd never hamstring one's back legs so's all he can do is sit there while a pack tears into him."

Ellen made a muffled sound. Again a look passed between her and Jonathan, who said: "If you'll let the bears go, Mister Caxton, we'll keep you in milk, butter, and eggs all winter."

"You will?" screeched Nora. She caught her husband's arm. "Watt, think how nice that'd be!"

He shoved her hand away. "I've sent word around. The best dogs in the county'll be there. Unless God or the devil turns them bears loose, they'll be there tomorrow, and there they'll die when we've had our fun!"

With a defiant smirk, he swaggered out, trailed by his wife. Jonathan didn't go help harness their gaunt team. The neighbors looked at each other, most of them distressed and shamed that one of their kind could be so wicked.

Simeon Parks shook his white head. "Shall we seek God in silence, trusting him to change the heart of our brother?"

"He's not my brother!" vowed Lige.

"I don't know why you're all carrying on so," sniffed Mildred Morrison. "Goodness' sakes! They're only wild beasts. You'd think they had Christian souls!"

"They have spirits," Sarah declared. "All living creatures do."

"If those nuns taught you that. . . ."

"They didn't. My grandmother did, before she died." Sarah's tawny eyes smoldered. "No one will ever unteach the things she told me."

"Missus Ware," Dan O'Brien said, "will you play? I . . . I hurt my fingers this afternoon. It's hard to fiddle."

"Why don't we settle down and just listen to the music?" suggested Lige.

Susie Parks nodded gratefully. "I don't think any of us feel like dancing now. That dreadful man!"

"Pray for him," her father urged.

Christy saw white light spill through the square cut for the fireplace. The trapped bear and cub must see the moon they had known for all their lives, but did they sense this was their last time to watch it? To die torn apart by hounds after hours of fear and torment?

No! It wasn't going to happen! Not if God, Sarah's wise old god of the spirits, if not the Christian one, would help. Christy had never been to the Caxtons, but she knew their place lay across the creek a little beyond the Hayeses. The Caxtons' shambling old team wouldn't travel faster than she could if she ran a lot.

But that pack of dogs.

She'd just have to get there ahead of them. All eyes were on Ellen, who was playing one of Jonathan's favorites—a sonata by the young German composer, Johannes Brahms. Would the bears ever again hear the strange human music that had seemed to enthrall them so?

Christy slipped out the dogtrot and ran.

Chapter Three

A burning stitch in her side made Christy press her fist against it. She panted when she came level with the whining creak of the wagon and rumble of wheels. She could make out the Caxtons in the pale light, although she couldn't see their faces. The hounds had scented something and bayed along the creek till Watt profanely called them off. He had no time to hunt that night with the bear-baiting next day.

The hounds must smell Christy but had doubtless grown accustomed to her scent during the day and recognized it as one they needn't herald. If only that tolerance would remain on Caxtons' territory! Better yet if she could find the pen and free the bears before the Caxtons arrived.

They must be heading for the ford Ethan maintained upstream from the tannery. That would make their way home easier but longer. Hoofs and wheels of settlers had worn this rough track that was still far from a road but less difficult than driving across this brushy, rocky, wooded region. For closeness to water, the Caxtons' house would be as near the creek as flooding would allow. If Christy crossed now, she was bound to find the cabin as long as she stayed near the creek, and she should get there before the wagon did.

Where pebbles and sand were scoured away from the limestone bottom, the creek was over a tall man's head, but at other stretches it flowed no more than a foot or so deep. She and her brothers hadn't explored this far, so Christy, not wishing to get her clothes wet or swim, hurried along watching for a likely place.

A sandbar with willows reached far into the creek. The current had carved a sharp angle around it and gnawed earth away from the roots of a huge tree on the other bank. From the sound of the water, it ran deeply here, but Christy thought she could leap to the gnarled roots that resembled a contorted giant serpent.

Although she and her brothers ordinarily went barefoot, they had put on shoes for the evening's festivities. Christy took hers off, as well as stockings and pantaloons that reached below her knee, made a bundle, and threw it across. Kilting skirts and petticoat to free her legs, she took a deep breath and jumped, struck the lowest root, caught a grape-vine, and sprang upward, scrambling up the bank.

There! She wasn't wet at all. Resuming her pantaloons, she decided her shoes' protection was worth their pinch and the time it would take to put them on. She mustn't lame herself on a stob or rock or briar.

The groaning wagon rattled a little ahead of her now, but she ran in the spangled moonlight, holding her skirts to keep them from catching. A whippoorwill's lament sent a chill through her. She was grateful when several barred owls called to each other: *"Who cooks for you? Who cooks for you all?"* She soon outdistanced the ill-cared-for team. You'd think a man who traded in animals would know the importance of looking after them, but, from the sound of it, Caxton depended on cursing and the whip.

Slowing now and then to catch her breath and ease the pain in her side, Christy hoped she wouldn't be missed at home. She and the boys had permission to go on sleeping beneath the tree till the weather chilled, and, if her mother noticed her absence, she'd probably think Christy had gone to rest outside, too.

A clearing, jagged with rotting stumps, was strewn with logs that hadn't been used or burned. Winded, Christy paused at the edge. Weeds grew high as the tallest stalks of corn in a small patch given little protection by a half-hearted rail fence. A single cabin of round logs squatted near what was probably a smokehouse.

Despair gripped Christy. Where was the bear pen? She had expected it to be near the house. Above the pounding blood in her ears, she heard the distant clatter of the wagon.

Oh, bears! she wailed silently. *Where are you?*

What was that peculiar noise, a sort of muffled, gentle grunting? Scanning the edge of the clearing on the far side of the cabin, Christy could now make out a square log structure with a pole roof.

Let it be the pen, and not a crude barn. Let the gate be one she could open quickly. With silent entreaties, she ran toward the building. The screech of wheels groaned nearer at every second.

No gate on this side . . . or this. . . . Turning the corner, she smothered a scream as she almost ran into someone. Someone who started and whirled on her.

"You!" She and Dan O'Brien spoke in the same breath. And then, again in chorus: "What are *you* doing here?"

"Never mind," growled Dan. "Push in on this spavined gate so I can work the rawhides off the posts. Quick!"

She shoved with all her might, smothering a cry when she bumped her burned wrist. The shift gave Dan the bit of an inch he needed to work off the wide, tough leather loops that held the heavy gate to the upright pole forming the end of one wall.

A strong smell came from inside, but there was utter stillness. "Now," panted the strange Irish boy, "run around the pen to the far end! I'll open the gate. If the bears won't come out, you make some racket down there to send them this direction. Get along with you now!"

No time for speeches of independence, or asking why he'd come. She couldn't have opened that gate alone—and neither could he, unless he had a knife to cut the leathers.

The gate scraped back. No sound from the captives, but their smell was strong through the unchinked logs. The wagon was close enough that Christy could faintly hear Watt's complaining voice. Locating a chunk of wood, she struck the wall.

No response. Good grief! What if they wouldn't come out, what if they stayed frozen till the wagon came? Christy banged harder on the wall, trembled with relief as there was a scuffling. She looked around the corner in time to see the bear and cub lunge into the trees.

Dan forced the gate shut, grabbed her hand. "Hurry!"

The wagon was almost upon them. No time to dash across the clearing toward the creek. Dan and Christy plunged after the bears. Thank goodness, instead of climbing trees where the hounds might trap them, the crunch of twigs testified that they were running.

Since the mother had to find places she could get through, the boy and girl could follow through the trees, now and then catching a glimpse of the cub.

"Can't . . . can't we double back to the creek now?" Christy puffed.

The dogs began to yip, and then to bay. Caxton's distant swearing exploded into a howl of outrage. The hounds' behavior must have caused him to check the pen. Dan hadn't had time to replace the leathers. Caxton probably couldn't recapture the bears, but killing them would be some satisfaction, and with great luck, if he baited the pen again, he might still have a quarry dangerous enough to content the men who were bringing their dogs, maybe a wolf or panther, if not a bear.

Would the excited hounds attack people? Christy didn't want to find out. *Oh, Lordy, Lord!* A bluff loomed before them, pale gray rock bleached by the moon, seventy or eighty feet high, stretching out of sight on either hand.

For an instant, the bears showed dark against the cliff. Then they were gone. "Must be a cave!" Dan gripped her tighter. "Come on!"

Lungs burning, sobbing for breath, Christy dragged Dan up when he tripped on a vine. He steadied her when she stepped into an old root hole. But there was no cavity, no hiding place in the side of the cliff.

"Go on!" Releasing Christy, Dan gave her a push and picked up a limb. "I'll keep the dogs busy as long as I can."

"No!" In turning back to him, Christy saw a hole in the rocky ground. "Look! Down there! That must be where the bears went!"

"We've got to try it." Dan gripped the rock edge of the opening. "I'll go first."

He dropped the limb through the opening and let himself down. There was a thud. Christy prayed hard. In a few seconds, his voice echoed upward. "Hang onto the edge and drop! I'll catch you!"

As she let herself down, she saw the dogs racing toward her, bellies low to the ground, caught a glimpse of Watt swearing his way through the trees. She closed her eyes, let loose of the rim, and plunged.

Not far. Dan's arms closed around her. They went down in a heap in the moonlight spilling through the hole. "Let's go," Dan ordered in a whisper. "I don't know if those dogs'll jump into a sinkhole, but we don't want to find out."

"But we can't see. We might run into the bears."

Indeed, beyond the halo circling the bold splash of full moonlight, it was pitch black.

"I'll test the way with this limb," Dan promised. "Hang onto the back of my shirt."

The dogs bayed at the hole, but none, so far, had ventured to leap. In a few minutes, Watt's curses streamed downward. He was telling the bears what he'd do to them if he ever caught them, but he must not have been eager to jump down and meet the bears by himself. Apparently he hadn't seen Christy and Dan. He knew, of course, that human hands had worked off the rawhide loops, but wouldn't know who to blame it on.

"Shall we wait till Mister Caxton takes the dogs away?" Christy asked beneath her breath.

"He may stay up there a good long time, hoping the bears'll come out." Dan sounded worried. "Sinkholes like this can be where the top caved in over an underground river. There's one not far from Whistling Point, close to where we live on the Marais des Cygnes. Sometimes the hidden river's dried up and leaves long tunnels like this. Sometimes the river's still running. You can toss a log in a sinkhole and it may tumble out miles and miles away where the river breaks out from underground."

"So you're saying this cave or old river, or whatever it is, may reach a long way off? But what if there's no way out?"

"I'd like to find out . . . when I have some candles."

Christy shivered. "*I* wouldn't!"

"Caxton won't want to give up on the bears and lose all that money and fun he was counting on. He may stay up there quite a spell."

"The bears are somewhere ahead."

"Or behind. The cavern runs both ways." His hand on her shoulder made the dark less scary. She'd always been afraid of the dark. When they were younger, Thos and Charlie had gotten most of their rare whippings for jumping out of dark corners and sending her into shrieking fits. She found she was getting to like the lilt of the Irish boy's voice.

What would she have done if he hadn't been at the pen? She couldn't have loosed the bears. If she had somehow managed to hack or break the loops, would she have dared follow the bears down the sinkhole? Thankfulness melted away the last bit of her aggravation at him for chiding her care of Beth.

"What do you want to do?" she asked.

"Go ahead as far as we can without passing any side caves that could mix us up if we have to come back. If we come to another sinkhole, we can climb out and try to figure about where we are."

"What if this cavern just goes on and on and on?"

"*We* won't," he said positively. "If we don't find a way out in an hour or so, we'll come back here and hope Caxton's gone."

"Won't your folks miss you?"

"I told Susie I was walking home and asked her to bring my fiddle." There was a smile in his tone. "They know I like wandering in the moonlight, like a cat or an owl, they say."

She clutched his shirt again—the Parks sisters wove excellent homespun—and followed gingerly. The limb he held scratched on rock.

"Down there, be ye, you mangy devils?" Caxton's bellow resounded distantly, but the explosion echoed along the rocky walls. A flying chip hit Christy in the back as shattered rock crashed from where the shot had struck.

At Christy's flinch, Dan turned. "Are you all right?"

"Just a little sting from a rock piece," she whispered. "Let's hurry. He might lean down and shoot our direction."

This was the deepest night she had ever known. A density to the blackness made it stifling and almost palpable. "I don't smell even a whiff of bear," murmured Dan. "I think they went the other way."

"I hope so . . . and I hope they get out."

"Why do you care? Why did you come?"

Christy hesitated, then decided he deserved to know the truth even if he made fun of her. "The bears used to listen to my mother play the piano. At least they seemed to. They stayed at the edge of our firelight for the longest times."

"Probably smelled your food."

"*I* think they liked the music."

He laughed with soft but not unkind derision. "Oh, aye. For sure, it was the music."

Vexed, but not enough to let go of him, Christy demanded: "Why did you come?"

He was silent.

She tugged at his shirt. "Why? It's not fair not to tell when I told and you . . . you laughed."

After a moment, he said: "You have the right of it, Christy Ware. But . . . you'll not be telling this to a soul?"

"Cross my heart and hope to die. . . ."

"Don't say that!" He kept his tone muted, but it was fierce. "Don't ever hope to die, my girl. 'Tis a sin against life and God."

"It's just a verse."

"A brainless yammering."

52

"Never mind. Why did you want to set the bears free?"

Each word came as if pulled by force from a hidden, hurting place inside. "Killing a beast is one thing. But tormenting it, making sport of any creature's fear and pain, laughing at it . . . that I cannot bide."

"I'm glad you can't . . . Danny."

He stopped moving.

Christy faltered: "Is something wrong?"

Starting out again, he spoke so softly she could scarcely hear. "The gentry, they drove by in their carriages while I rocked Bridget in my arms, trying to get her to sleep. When she'd starved to her wee bones, she didn't cry any more. . . ."

"Oh, Danny, Danny!"

"You would have it."

"Bridget . . . what . . . ?"

"She died a week before her second birthday."

Christy burst into tears. Through her sobbing, matter-of-fact rather than bitter, Dan said: "I know now the gentry didn't laugh at us. They didn't even see us."

"Your parents . . . ?"

"They died of chills and fever in Eighteen Forty-Seven, but it was starving killed them, and being turned out of the farm where Da had worked. I was six. Old enough to try to steal a bite for Bridget when I couldn't beg it."

No wonder he'd gone savage when Christy ignored Beth's crying. What wouldn't he have given to have his sister back—and there was no way he could, not on this earth, ever.

"That's how my nose was broken." Once he remembered the past, he seemed to want to talk. "A woman fetched me a clout with a great iron spoon when I made off with a few of her 'taties." He chuckled at the memory with a certain amount of pride. "Blood poured like I was butchered, but I pelted on. Bridget and I ate that night, though I doubt raw potatoes were the best food for a baby. But she laughed and reached for the pieces. Aye. She laughed."

"Why didn't someone help you?" Such misery, with people all around, was beyond anything she could imagine.

"The schoolmaster did. Shared his hut and the little food he had. Till he died." Dan's voice quickened. "Do you know any Choctaws?"

"Choctaws? Aren't they Indians?"

"I should say so. And they're the reason I'm alive . . . them and the Quakers."

"How . . . ?" Christy broke off in puzzlement.

"The Quakers gave out food and clothing and tried to find shelter for those without a roof. The government of England didn't care if we starved, but good people there and around the world sent help." His voice hardened. "Did you know there was plenty of food in Ireland, Christy? It was only 'taties failed those famine years, the crop that kept life in poor folk. Beef cattle, sheep, wagons loaded with grain . . . all that was shipped to England."

There was nothing to say. But how, with his parents dead and he and his sister starving, he must have hated the gentry and the owners of the food he saw driven past while he and his sister starved.

"I got a fever after Bridgie died," he went on. "Woke up in a kind of hospital the Quakers ran. One of the ladies is a second cousin to Simeon Parks who had written her he'd undertake to raise some Irish orphans. Three of us traveled to America on Choctaw relief money."

"I think they're one of the Five Civilized Tribes that have reservations in Indian Territory. That's south of Kansas Territory and west of Arkansas."

"Don't you think I found out where they live? When I'm older, I'll go to see them and find a way to thank them. They pitied the Irish, I believe, because they could well remember being hungry and sick when they were driven out of their lands in the East."

Christy was too young to remember that although her father had preached sermons on the wickedness of exiling Indians to make room for whites. "At least, let white settlement cease at the Missouri border," he had urged. "True, California and Oregon are settling up, there are old Spanish towns in New Mexico and Arizona, and the Mormons are established in Utah, but the vast region between should be reserved to Indians already living there and tribes forced out of the East."

That had been government policy for a time, as much as there was a policy. For one thing, the plains and deserts and mountains were considered poor farm land. But the Colorado gold rush sprouted towns, and there was growing clamor for a transcontinental railroad. Jonathan Ware was increasingly gloomy about the Indians' hope of keeping the spacious interior.

"What happened to the other orphans?" Christy asked

"Peggy O'Donnell was twelve when we came to the Parkses in Ohio nine years ago. She married a young farmer, Harry Shepherd, before the Parkses moved here, two years since. Her brother Tim . . . he must be almost twenty now . . . stayed to work on his brother-in-law's farm." Dan halted. "Is that fresh air?"

Christy sniffed, drew in a longer breath, and gripped his arm. "It must be. Dan, doesn't that sound like water running?"

"That it is," he said after a hushed moment. "Now wouldn't it be a fine kettle of stinking fish if there's a way out but we can't get to it?"

"Maybe the water won't be very deep." Christy spoke

hopefully although her heart sank at the prospect of retracing their steps to the sinkhole and risking Caxton and his hounds being there when they tried to climb out.

"We'll just be careful and go as far as we can," Dan said.

The muffled flow grew louder. Then it gushed free. "Must still be a river beneath where we've been walking," Dan guessed. "Here's where it's worn through rock." He tapped with the limb. "A ledge runs along this way. Let's see how far."

Christy took care not to crowd him, although she tightened her hold on his shirt. How strange it was down here in this hidden world with no one knowing where they were. Dan had told her things he might not have in an ordinary time and place. She didn't think she could ever get really angry with him again. Not after hearing about small Bridget.

"Light ahead," exulted Dan. "Did you ever smell such sweet good air? If this ledge just holds out. . . ."

Christy hoped the river would break out of some hillside as a fine spring so that they could easily get through the opening, but, as they neared the glow, it came from the top like the one near the Caxtons'. At least, if the ledge continued that far, they might be able to scramble to the top. Wherever that might be.

Almost anywhere was better than the Caxtons'. How good it was to reach light again. It seemed brilliant after the total dark. As Dan turned to her, she scanned the thin face with its broken nose and cleft chin, memorized his features.

He'd told her things in the tortuous cavern that she was sure he hadn't talked about in a long time. He was like no one she'd ever known, and she knew him in a deep and special way. Beside him, her brothers were children—and so was she.

He smiled. What a marvel people could heal, could be happy again after the grief he'd lived through. "Now then,

Christy girl, let's see if there's a way up. The river runs on, but we'd better get out now if we can at all."

Moonlight splashed rock and rippling silvered water, but the aperture was discouragingly far above them. Dan appraised her and shook his head. "Even if I boosted you up on my shoulders, you couldn't get a good hold on the rim."

"Maybe we can find some rocks."

He shrugged. "It's worth a look, though we sure haven't been tripping over any."

"The top had to cave in," she pointed out.

"For sure it did." He struck his forehead in mock shame. "Some chunks should be here, if the water hasn't swept them all away. I'll look here and you feel around over there. Don't fall in the water, mind! It could carry you out some place in God's good time likely, but in a state you might not fancy."

Christy groped along the wall, explored cautiously with her feet, keeping one planted firmly while stretching the other out as far as she could. "Here's a rock!" she cried. Bending to trace it with her hands, she said in disappointment: "It's all jaggedy and doesn't reach to my knee."

"Here's a whole jumble right at the edge of the river. Must be where the roof fell in. If we can heap them up. . . ."

Christy scurried to help. Some rocks were too heavy to shift, but the largest of these was close enough to the hole to serve as a firm base for smaller stones. Together, they dragged over the one Christy had found and banked other rocks around it till the crude platform reached Christy's waist. Dan cocked his head to study the rim. "Reckon I can scramble on top, then lean over and haul you up."

The rocks shifted beneath his weight, but his head and shoulders were above the edge. "Here's luck. There's a ridge I can get a hold on."

"Be careful, Danny!"

He pushed from tiptoe, hefted himself up. "Now for you, Christy!"

"What if I'm too heavy and drag you in?"

"There's a kind of dip where I can anchor myself. Don't fret about me. Just hold up your hands and hang on to my wrists while I grab yours."

She yelped at the very thought. "Don't you dare touch my burned wrist!"

"I'll take your hands, then," he said patiently.

It seemed a long way yet to the top when she stood on the rocks, but she sighed with relief when she saw that she could indeed reach Dan's hands. They closed, warm and strong, around hers, locking with her fingers.

"Up, up, up and away-y-y!"

He was laughing. That gave her heart to trust his hands. In no time, he had her on the rim. As soon as he released her arms, she threw them around him, buried her face against his chest. "Oh, Danny, I'm so glad we're out of that hole!"

"Me, too, but we were mighty lucky the bears showed us how to get into it."

He patted her on the shoulder—as if she were a baby. Attempting to regain some dignity, she pulled away and scrubbed her eyes with her sleeve. "I hope the bears found a way out."

"I expect that smart old mama will. Shucks, she may even have known where she was going. She must have been in every cave and hidey-hole in this neck of the woods."

Cheered, Christy looked around. The sound of water came through the ragged hole but, otherwise, there was no hint of that dark world beneath. "I do hope Mother thinks I went to bed and doesn't look. Do you know where we are?"

He, too, glanced around and gave a soft whistle. "I

think. . . . Just a minute!" Springing up, he ran to the crest of the ridge above them. "Whistling Point's just down from here. I can see the mill and our cabin."

"But. . . ."

Chuckling, he trotted back, helped her to her feet. "Remember, I told you there was a sinkhole not far from Whistling Point? This is it!"

"But it must be four miles to the Caxtons from Trading Post!"

"The underground way's a short cut." He looked at the moon that had traveled considerably since she had slipped away from home. "It seems a lot longer, Christy, but I reckon we were in the cavern less than an hour."

"It seemed like forever!" It had changed her life. Their journey through the dark, what he had told her, and the way she had trusted him, made her in a curious way closer to Dan O'Brien than to anyone in the world.

"Well"—he grinned—"now forever's over, we've got to get you home."

"Just show me the way to go." She tried to sound brave.

"Don't be a goose! Come along. There's a foot log across the river and a fairly good track wagons have made coming to the mill or going to the tannery."

"A . . . a *foot* log?"

"Haven't you ever used one?"

She shook her head. Her new sense of having suddenly grown up dissolved in a need to justify herself. "Back home we have proper bridges."

"To be sure." He spoke politely although that frequent smile lurked in his voice that was deepening to a man's. "But you'll find this quite a proper foot log. It's smoothed flat on top, and Uncle Simeon and Owen and I strung a cable from trees on either side." He tweaked the end of her braid. "You can hang onto the rope and prance along with no fear of slipping even when the water's high."

"Is it high?"

"No. There's places we could wade it, but why get wet?" He tossed over his shoulder: "You can hang onto my shirt with one hand and the cable with the other."

"Thanks very much. I'll hold onto the cable."

He only laughed.

Yes, they were back in the real world, on solid earth—but would either ever seem as real or solid now she knew what flowed beneath?

Chapter Four

Davie Parks stirred sleepily as Dan O'Brien settled beside him on the shuck mattress. Rubbing his eyes, he mumbled: "You sure must have come a long way 'round in the moonlight."

"Uncle Simeon's not worried?" Dan asked, recalling that as they'd driven home from the steamboat landing that fine autumn day nine years ago, Dan and Peggy and Tim O'Donnell, their new guardian, Simeon Parks, had said: "You can hardly dwell with us and call me Mister Parks, youngsters. I know you remember your fathers and you should give that name to no other man. Would Uncle Simeon be agreeable to you?"

The schoolmaster Dan and Bridget had lived with for a blessed space had taught Dan some English, and he'd picked up more on his journey, but he was glad this graying, keen-eyed man spoke slowly enough for him to get the gist of it.

Peggy and Tim understood more English than they spoke. They implored Dan with their eyes to answer for them. "Entirely agreeable, sir, and we are thanking you."

He had slept with Davie that night, too, while Tim had piled in with Owen, and, although at first Dan kept well to his side of the four-poster, by morning they were snuggled together for warmth, warmth that had melted some of the ice that formed inside Dan since he'd watched his parents die.

Lots of that ice was still there. He thought it always would be. But he had been lucky, oh, so lucky, to come to America and live with the Parkses.

He looked up to Owen, would have instantly died for Lydia or Susie, and Davie—well, in spite of their occasional huffs, the younger boy was the one person in the world Dan might have admitted he loved.

Slanting moonlight from the loft's one window now showed Davie's indignant face. "Well, you don't think I went down and told Pa you weren't here, do you?"

Dan tousled his hair. "Thank you kindly, young 'un." He was tempted to tell about freeing the bears and his escape with Christy Ware, but decided the fewer people who knew about that, the better. Davie wouldn't give him away on purpose, but something might slip.

He did tell Davie about the sinkholes and the underground river, though. "Slithering snakes!" Davie breathed. "Let's see how far it goes. Can't we, Danny? Can't we?"

"When the fall work's over. We'll take rope and candles and be real careful." Dan gave his foster brother a playful cuff. "Go to sleep. It's worn out I am, if you are not."

"I'm too excited about that cavern," Davie protested. But he rolled over and was asleep before Dan finished peeling off his clothes.

A few days later, Dan and Davie pulled fodder, stripping green blades from the stalks of hardening corn. After the blades cured a few days, they'd be bound and carried to the end of the rows to be hauled to the barn. Dan wasn't fond of hoeing weeds out of the corn, a constant battle till the stalks got shoulder high, but he never minded working by the harvest moon to tie blades together after dew had softened them enough for one to be twisted around the others and tucked under. The stalks gave out a sweet, clean smell that put him in mind of Christy. He grinned to imagine how indignantly her gray eyes would flash if he told her she smelled like fresh-dried fodder.

"What's the joke?" demanded Davie.

"I was thinking how sweet new fodder smells."

"In a pig's eye! You've been acting peculiar ever since that cabin raising." Davie's green eyes were both worried and re-proachful. "A bat with hydrophobia must've bit you in that cave."

"I'll tell you when you're old enough," Dan teased. He dodged a fist.

The sound of hoofs made them whirl. "What's Andy McHugh in such a rush about? And why's his mother hanging on behind him?" Davie wondered. "I didn't know that old sorrel mare of his could go faster than a trot."

"Let's go find out. It's time for a drink, anyway." Simeon never grouched at them to stay on the job. He simply ex-pected them to get it done in reasonable time, so they did, in-stead of finding ways to thwart him.

Simeon and Owen Parks came out of the mill house to greet their neighbors. Andy McHugh dismounted and swung old Catriona down. "Will you look after Mother while I go help James Montgomery run off Clarke's raiders?" The young blacksmith's glance swept the Parkses. "I know Quakers don't hold with fighting, Simeon, but George Clarke, the Land Office man at Fort Scott, crossed from Westpoint, Missouri, northeast of here, with hundreds of ras-cally proslavers."

Simeon and Owen exchanged dismayed looks. "Are you sure, Andy?" pressed Simeon.

"You bet I'm sure. They're burning out Free Staters, trampling crops, stealing . . . telling us to leave or be killed!"

Simeon drew himself together. " 'Tis against my belief to

fight," he said quietly. "However, I'll protect your mother and my womenfolk with my life."

"Let me go, Father," Owen urged. His Harriet was chalk-faced, and, from her hip, small Letty whimpered.

Lydia, Susie, and Mildred Morrison were trying to help Catriona, but she waved them off, red hair spiking out from beneath her ill-tied bonnet.

"All I need's a cup of tea, if you have it, and to get off that knife-spined old nag. Told Andy I could handle any Border Ruffian that's ever been born . . . what be they compared to constables and scoundrel lairds? But he would have me up behind him, rattling my few poor teeth from my jaws."

The white-haired miller seemed to pray silently before he turned to his tall young son. "Owen, you must decide according to your inner light."

"I'll take Zephyr?"

Simeon Parks nodded. Zephyr and Breeze were fine bay geldings, strong enough to plow, clean-footed enough to pull a carriage or ride.

Harriet's full lips trembled, but she said: "I'll put food in a sack for you." Then she froze. "You don't have a pistol or rifle, Owen."

"He can use one of my Colts." Andy McHugh had a Sharps in a saddle scabbard and carried two bone-handled revolvers in leather cases attached to his belt.

Dan said: "Might I have the use of the other, Andy?"

"You, laddie?"

"I'm fifteen."

Simeon's white brows knitted. "If harm befell you, Daniel, I'd feel to blame."

"Please, Uncle Simeon! I have to help chase that gang away from here. They might burn the mill and cabins, scare the womenfolk and little Letty."

After a pained moment, Simeon met Dan's eyes. "I won't forbid you, son, but take all the care you may. Ride Breeze."

Dan and Owen hurried to fetch the horses from the near pasture. Davie had the saddles, bridles, and saddle blankets ready when they led their mounts to the log stable by the barn. Harriet tied her husband's food sack and a blanket behind his saddle. Lydia did the same for Dan, and Susie added apples, gingerbread, and smoked dried beef to the corn pones that were all the provisioning McHugh had bothered with.

He caught her hand to thank her. She looked up at him, hazel eyes wide with fear and admiration. "Oh, Andy, do be careful. And watch out for my brothers."

It warmed Dan to hear her call him that so naturally. He'd be chopped to pieces before that bunch of cut-throats could come near his . . . family. Yes, they were that. He could claim them wholly now that he had a chance to protect them, pay back a little of all they'd done for him.

Andy allowed himself to smooth back a tendril that had escaped Susie's braided crown of black hair. "I have you to come back to, Miss Susie. You know I'll be careful. And be sure I'll watch out for Owen and Dan."

He turned to them, taking off his belt and slipping off the holsters. "Each of you put a holster on your belt. Best show you how to use these revolvers."

The six-inch barrel of the weapon in his hand sent a chill down Dan's spine. This was real. He would carry this revolver and shoot it at men, kill or wound them if he could—he, Dan O'Brien, who'd seen so much misery he couldn't stand to let a bear be tortured.

Christy's eyes watched him in her imagination. *I have to do this,* Dan told her. *Have to or the devils might hurt my family, burn them out or worse.*

"These Navy Colts hold six rounds," Andy explained.

"Susie, could we have a couple of little bags so I can divide up the cartridges?" She hurried off. "Now, then," he demonstrated, "press the hammer back with your thumb, aim along the sights, pull the trigger . . . and don't expect to hit anything that's more than fifty yards away. When the cylinder's empty, you knock out this wedge just in front of it and the cylinder comes out to reload."

Six shots without reloading! Such power! Fascinated and repelled, Dan stared at the revolver in his hands, the naval battle engraved on the cylinder, the seven-and-half-inch octagonal barrel, the polished walnut stock. "Where'd you get such choice revolvers, Andy?"

"A man heading for Oregon with his family traded them for a plow and my shoeing his oxen. After all the trouble in early summer, I laid in a supply of cartridges when I went to Independence for supplies, but I've got powder, bullets, paper and percussion caps if we need them."

Owen looked as blank as Dan felt. Andy raised a rusty eyebrow at them. "You lads have never rammed a charge home, never fired anything? Don't you hunt?"

Owen crimsoned. "Pa won't have firearms on the place."

Andy shook his head. "Then maybe he shouldn't have come out here. I'm mightily afraid it'll be many cruel years before anyone along this border can be safe without weapons."

Simeon approached in time to hear the last statement. "Is anyone safe with them?"

"I'd rather die making a fight. . . ." At the pained look in his prospective father-in-law's eyes, Andy broke off. He swallowed and turned to mount.

"Kiss your old mother good bye, lad!" shrilled Catriona.

He did, but the way he looked at Susie made it plain he longed to kiss her, too. Blushing, she hugged Owen and Dan.

Lydia's cool lips brushed Dan's forehead, then her brother's. "We'll pray for your safe return . . . and that you do no murders."

"Fine with me so long as we run them out of Kansas," Andy retorted.

Davie looked up wistfully as Dan climbed into the saddle. "I wish I could go."

Susie put a protective arm around him. "You're much too young."

"I'm only three years younger than Dan."

"Three years is a lot at your age," Lydia chided.

He caught Dan's knee. "Mind now, don't get yourself hurt."

Dan leaned over to squeeze Davie's shoulder. "Scared you'll have to pull all the fodder yourself?"

"God be with you!" Simeon called.

Dan wished he hadn't. How could God be with you when you meant to kill somebody?

A long, high, forested hill with a ledge of stone around its crest rose north of the little hamlet of Trading Post. The Marais des Cygnes flowed against the west end of the great hill and ran south for a quarter mile before sparkling eastward. The rapids at the turn formed a good crossing for the Military Road that ran south from Fort Leavenworth, staying near the Missouri border down to Fort Scott from whence it wound all the way to Fort Gibson in Indian Territory and Fort Smith over in Arkansas.

Here by the crossing was the trading post started by a French trapper twenty years or so ago. In the early 1840s, General Winfield Scott had started a log fort there but moved his dragoons south to establish the outpost named after him—to his considerable disgust. After his victories in the

Mexican War, he thought he deserved a better namesake than such an isolated, unimportant place.

Apart from the abandoned fort at Trading Post, there were only a few cabins—or had been. Blackened ruins were all that remained. Not a person or animal was in sight. Dan's backbone went cold and his scalp prickled. In Ireland, his family and countless others had been driven from their homes, but he'd never before seen homes destroyed on purpose.

Were these the first of many? Would there be a real war? One of grief and terror that would wreck the Parkses' cabins and mill, ruin what he thought of as the Wares' happy house, and all their lives? If Christy couldn't stand the thought of bear-baiting, how would she endure war?

Why did he feel as much worry for her as he did for Susie and Lydia? He'd only known her a little while. But they had worked together, freeing the bears, and then they'd made their blind journey underground. Even if they never met again, Christy would always be special to him.

He patted Breeze's gleaming neck as they followed the road over the pass between the rock-crested hill and a large smooth hill on the east. From the top of the pass, prairie stretched north and east with mounds of every shape rising against the sky. Some were cones, others flat-topped oblongs, but they were all grassy and treeless.

Dan's gaze was drawn from this wide expanse by Andy's cry. "They've burned out Sam Nickel!" Tall, husky Sam Nickel brought his grain to the mill, of course. He was memorable for his golden hair and one blinded eye, but Dan didn't know his family.

Smoke still curled from the heavy sill logs of a cabin east of the road at the bottom of the pass. Four fair-haired stair-step boys, the oldest maybe Dan's age, and a slender woman poked among the ashes. At one side was a straggle of black-ened rescued items. A gold-haired baby lay on its back, kicking for pleasure, cooing to a feather it gripped in one chubby fist.

Beyond the cabin were charred outbuildings. A heap of headless white chickens was piled beside what must have been a chicken coop. When the horsemen came in sight, the woman snatched up the baby and a butcher knife. The biggest boy gripped a broken hoe. The others poised the sticks they'd been dragging through burned rubble.

"It's me, Missus Nickel!" called the smith. "Andy McHugh, and Owen Parks and Dan O'Brien from the mill. Where's Sam?"

"He left some hides at the tannery while he went on to Osceola to trade butter and cheese for salt and gunpowder." The sunbonnet hid all but a few wisps of light brown hair. Mrs. Nickel was a pretty woman in spite of dark circles beneath her eyes. "I'm glad he was gone . . . and the team was, too. Clarke was looking for him. Sam doesn't care who knows he's a Free-State man."

"Speaks his mind." Andy frowned, looking at her closely. "Are you all right, ma'am?" He jerked his head toward the charred wreckage. "They didn't . . . do anything but this?"

"Isn't it enough? Thank goodness, the cows were resting under the trees when we heard the gang coming." She nodded toward the taller boys. "I sent William to take the cows deeper into the woods, and told John to run warn the folks at Trading Post and then find his brother and hide out till the rascals left." A wry smile twitched her lips. "Figured men who brag on being Southern gentlemen wouldn't hurt little boys and a woman."

"Looks like they didn't." Andy's voice was deep with re-lief.

The woman shrugged, nuzzling her baby's curls. He squealed and patted her face. "They held a pistol to my head to make me tell where Sam was hiding, and they cuffed the boys for sassing them." She gave the smaller lads a prideful glance. They puffed out their scrawny chests. "Those varmints ate the mush and side meat we were having for supper and ransacked everything, but, of course, we didn't have any cash money or fancy stuff. When Sam hadn't come by sundown, they reckoned I was telling the truth about him being gone to Osceola, and they went over the pass."

"But your place is burned. . . ."

"They came back after dark, maybe fifty of them." Mrs. Nickel held her baby closer. "They still hoped they could catch Sam. Made them mad as fire when he wasn't here. They tossed the oldest quilts at us and told us to get out while we could."

She broke off, tears filling her eyes. Her biggest son, taller than she was, put his arm around her and went on with the story. "They had a wagon and team they stole at Trading Post half full of things they thieved before they burned the cabins. They snatched the brass candlesticks our great-granny brought from England, and her little inlaid sewing box. One wanted the maple rocking chair Pa made, when I was born, so Mama could rock me to sleep." He clenched his fists and his blue eyes smoldered. "William and me wanted to try to stop them, but Mama hung onto us and cried."

"Things are things, Billy," she soothed, touching his cheek.

"They carried out the cedar chest Grandpa made Mama for her wedding," he growled.

She sighed. "I purely loved that chest. It smelled so good I kept my best quilts in it." Sadness gave way to outrage as she glanced toward the dead chickens. "The worst thing, what I can't understand at all, is they went in the chicken house and cut the feet off my poor hens! There'd be some sense to stealing them, but to do that. We killed the poor things out of pity."

"We'll give you some hens and a young cockerel who was headed for the frying pan," promised Owen.

"Maybe they won't raid you," she said hopefully. "They were likkered up last night, but, from what I could hear, they meant to burn out Free Staters at Sugar Mound, southwest of Trading Post, and then march . . . or carouse . . . north to Osawatomie to get old John Brown." A shudder went through her in spite of the sultry day. "They said two hundred and fifty militia with a cannon were headed for Osawatomie. Dave Atchison's leading a bigger mob . . . over two thousand men . . . toward Lawrence to finish what he started in May. One of his officers said he was bound to kill an Abolitionist. If he couldn't shoot a man, he'd kill a woman. If he couldn't find a woman, he'd get a child."

Dan gasped. Apparently shocked speechless, Andy recovered after a moment and said confidently: "Jim Lane'll stop them, or the U.S. Army will. James Montgomery and fifty men with Sharps rifles are after Clarke and his hooligans. We're trying to catch up with Montgomery."

"That little Campbellite preacher who lives northwest of Sugar Mound?" Mrs. Nickel shook her head. "They've been burned out once. Friends helped him build a hewn-log cabin with walls eight inches thick and portholes in the loft to shoot from. Sam says, when Montgomery doesn't sleep out in the fields, he and the family have pallets on the floor to be under the line of fire."

"Maybe they won't have to do that much longer,"

McHugh said, and lifted his reins, but hesitated. It was hard to leave the family sifting the ashes of their home.

"You're welcome to go stay at the mill with my family," Owen said.

"It'd scare Sam into fits to find this mess and us gone. Thank you kindly, but we'll stay here. Might as well start cutting trees for a new cabin. I hid the axe under the cabin. The handle burned some, but we can use it."

"You don't have any food," Dan protested, wincing at the trampled stalks in the cornfield, the garden where horses had been galloped up and down till not a plant or vine stood. He began untying the sack from his saddle. "This isn't a lot, but. . . ."

"Keep it," she ordered. "Are you forgetting that pile of chickens . . . nineteen good hens and a rooster? The boys will help me pluck and clean them. We'll have our fill of stewed, fried, and roast chicken. What we can't eat before it spoils, we'll smoke." She gave a bitter chuckle. "There'll be plenty of feathers to make new pillows and comforters. And we've got cows to milk. The rapscallions didn't ruin all the potatoes, and there's wild plums. We'll do fine." She looked up fiercely. "You just hurry after Preacher Montgomery and teach that bunch a lesson."

Andy nodded at a spider in the sooty array of salvaged things, a three-legged skillet to set over the coals. One leg was broken off. "I can fix that for you, Missus Nickel. Just have Sam bring it to my place."

"You'll have a sight of worse-broken stuff to mend," she said. "Don't fret about us. Get after Clarke!"

They rode.

It wouldn't do to exhaust their horses. As the day burned hotter, they never urged them faster than a trot. Osawatomie was northwest where Pottawatomie Creek joined the Marais des Cygnes, so they left the Military Road and struck across country.

Dan couldn't get the Nickles family out of his mind. His gorge rose at thought of the chickens, their senseless mutilation. It was the kind of trick bullying schoolboys might pull if they dared.

"When you've helped build a cabin and know how much work it takes . . . how every log's cut and hewn and notched, puncheons smoothed, shingles split out, that makes it seem more wicked than ever to burn one down."

Owen nodded, wiping sweat from his forehead and eyebrows. "Yes. And when you've plowed and harrowed and sowed corn, hoed weeds all summer, it fair looks like murder to see the crop ruined."

"If anyone maimed my mother's hens like that, she'd scream like a banshee." Andy grimaced. He drew up, adding the shield of his hand to that of his hat brim. "There's Middle Creek ahead. Can you make out that swarmin' of horses and cattle and men?"

"It has to be Clarke!" Owen's voice rose. "Looks like they stole every wagon they came across!"

"And everything worth carrying off, you may be sure." Andy frowned as his eyes swept the horizon. "Where's Montgomery? This is the time to hit Clarke, while he's having his noon rest."

"Horsemen southward!" Dan pointed.

Andy veered his horse. "Let's make for them and hope they're not stragglers from Clarke's gang. The timber along the creek should hide us till we're almost into camp." He threw back his head and laughed exultantly. "Och, the whelps of Satan! Won't they be surprised?"

Chapter Five

Fifty Sharps carbines greeted the newcomers. They lowered only when the smallest man of the avengers laughed and raised his hand. "Welcome, Andy McHugh! You're just in time!"

"Glad of it." Andy swept his arm toward his companions. "Captain Montgomery, here's Owen Parks and Dan O'Brien from the mill. Reckon you don't know them since you use the mill on Mine Creek."

Dan felt as if Montgomery's gray eyes penetrated his inmost self. "You're young, lad, for this kind of outing." The leader's voice was deep and pleasant.

"Not too young," Dan said.

Montgomery looked at Owen. "Are you not a Quaker?"

Owen colored. "I am, but Pa let me follow my conscience."

"I'm no man to go against conscience." James Montgomery had a smile of amazing sweetness. His neatly trimmed beard and moustache were a few shades lighter than his black hair that waved softly back from a long face ruled by a straight, thin nose. He turned in his saddle and called to his men.

"Friends, neighbors, you have your Beecher's Bibles and testaments. Let's preach these scalawags a sermon they'll never forget. Spread out as we near the camp but keep to this side so we won't shoot each other. When I wave my hat, fire."

74

"Testaments are what they call cartridge boxes," Andy said with a grim laugh.

Dan's heart seemed to rise to his throat and pound there as the horsemen advanced across the prairie toward the trees. From the roistering jollity carried on the wind along with the smell of cooking meat, the raiders had found whiskey along the way.

Apparently they had no suspicion of pursuit. A sentry would have warned them a good while ago. Dan fumbled as he took a dozen cartridges from the bag and stuffed them in the holster after he worked the Colt out of it.

Montgomery's force was almost into the timber, Sharps glinting, fanning out to cover the sprawl of the camp Dan could glimpse through the trees—loaded wagons, cattle, horses, men lounging around several fires. Dan took a deep breath, thumb ready on the hammer, and watched Montgomery.

Slowly, deliberately, the gray hat lifted, then swung down as Montgomery sighted and fired. In the same instant, fifty other Sharps spewed cartridges. The carbines had to be reloaded, but most of the Free-State men had pistols or revolvers and fired these as they rode into the shouting, howling chaos.

Taken unawares, a few of Clarke's men returned fire, but most made for their horses and spurred away, some bootless, some hatless, some without coats or vests.

They hadn't the slightest notion that they'd been routed by a third of their number—they doubtless thought Jim Lane was upon them—but, if Montgomery pursued them, they'd discover their mistake, rally, and attack.

"They're headed for Missouri, boys!" called Montgomery. "Let them run. We'll take their plunder back to where it belongs . . . and share out their belongings with folks they burned out." He scanned his men. "Praise God, none of you was hurt, but look, here's two of them."

One dark young man held his hands to his thigh. Blood seeped through his fingers. An older whiskery raider bled from shoulder and leg as he tried to crawl to a rifle that had been left behind.

A slim, short man, who could have been taken for a boy except for his scruffy dark beard and moustache, sprang down from his horse and kicked the wounded man away from the weapon, aiming a revolver.

"No, Doctor Jennison!" Montgomery reined between the Missourian and the small man who seemed to be all high boots and hat, a peculiar brimless tall hat that reared from his narrow forehead like a grotesquely elongated furry skull.

"Best kill these two, Captain." Jennison didn't lower his revolver. "That'll make a pair who'll burn no more Free-State cabins!"

There was a chorus of approval. Montgomery quelled it with a glance. "I will exact an eye for an eye, according to God's law, but no one was killed in this marauding."

"They beat an old man at Linnville senseless when he tried to defend his ailing son," grated Jennison.

"He'll recover before these two do."

Jennison spat near the man he had kicked.

Montgomery spoke softly: "Will you honor the ideals of your profession, Doctor? Will you attend these men?"

"I'd attend *to* them if you weren't so. . . ."

A warning growl came from the other Free Staters. Jennison shrugged and swaggered to a pile of abandoned gear. "Who needs some Forty-Four Dragoon Colts?" He held them up with a flourish. "Who needs cartridge boxes? Who'd fancy a spotted calfskin vest? And look at these fancy boots with fancier spurs? I'll have the spurs, but someone else can take the boots."

While Jennison doled out booty and others joined in appropriating the raiders' effects, a spry gray-haired man came to kneel by the dark young Missourian. Glancing up at Montgomery, the older man spoke in an Irish accent that gladdened Dan's heart: "Now, didn't I help surgeons patch up many a poor lad in the Mexican War, Captain? Sure, if someone'll rustle me up some clean cloth and water, I'll do what I can."

" 'Blessed are the merciful, for they shall obtain mercy,' " said Montgomery. "You're a good man, Hughie Huston. I'll take these men home, and my wife will nurse them." He turned to the others. "Now, friends, distributing arms is sensible, since we're the protectors of the region, but whatever else was left behind must go to the raiders' victims, including these kettles that have already cooked our dinner."

"What about Osawatomie and old John Brown?" demanded Jennison.

Montgomery shook his head regretfully. "Whatever was fated to happen is over by now, but who'll ride there and find out how the Free Staters fared?"

Andy McHugh had never dismounted. Now he volunteered to make for Osawatomie, and rode northwest. There was only subdued muttering as the other men dismounted and gathered variously around plunder and cook fires.

Dan and Owen hunted through the raiders' baggage and found some clean socks and a clean shirt. There was no water in the camp, although there were emptied jugs testifying to a drink stronger than water.

Dan took a pail and dipped it in the swiftest flow of the creek, hoping that would be the purest. Admiration and gratitude for Montgomery welled up in him. He'd fired the Navy

Colt, and, if he'd killed someone, he thought he could live with it after what he'd seen at the Nickles' place, but he couldn't have watched Jennison murder wounded men—and that probably meant Jennison would have shot him, too.

Old Hughie Huston had cut away the white-faced invader's bloodied trousers and said to Dan: "Will ye pour the water over his hurt easy-like?"

Dan obeyed. His stomach roiled at the dark blood that oozed across the pale skin as fast as he rinsed it away. "You're in grand luck, boy." Hughie's tone was brisk and not unkindly. "Yon bullet didn't nick your artery or you'd have bled out by now. It passed clean through, so I won't be digging around for it." He reached toward Owen. "A pair of those socks, if you please, and tear or cut me the longest piece you may of the shirt."

Hughie deftly packed the heavy socks over the wounds front and back, bade Dan hold the dressings in place, wrapped the strip of shirt around the thigh, and knotted it securely.

The young man's eyes opened. "I'm obliged," he gasped.

"Enough to keep on your side of the border, I hope." Placing a lost hat over the sweating pallid face to shield it from the sun, the old man rose somewhat creakily and surveyed the older, ginger-whiskered marauder who glared at him from bloodshot eyes.

"Mind how you handle me, you damned Irisher!"

Hughie grinned at his helpers. "Now isn't it the fine, courteous tongue he has hid by that filthy beard?"

"I'm an Irisher, too," said Dan, but he went to fetch more water.

The bewhiskered one-eyed Owen shrugged and said: "I'm a Quaker."

"Oh, my God!"

"Ye may well pray, spalpeen," said Hughie severely. "Thank your Creator for sending ye help, instead of Jennison's bullet. Now shut your gob so we won't swoon away from that skull-varnish on your breath."

Hughie hunkered down. None too gently, he used his pocket knife to cut blood-soaked clothing from the shoulder and leg. The man howled and cursed as Dan tipped the bucket on the wounds. "Had I good lye soap, wouldn't I scrub out your mouth for ye!" scolded Hughie. "Stop your blaspheming or I'll let Doc Jennison at ye."

The profane one glowered but held his peace except for an occasional yelp as Hughie probed out the bullets and, with Owen's aid, dressed and bandaged the hurts.

Neither injured man wanted food, but both drank thirstily from the cup Dan held to their lips. Then, for it had been a long time since breakfast, Dan filled a stolen crockery plate with hominy and ham looted from someone's smokehouse.

When Montgomery's men had eaten and loaded the invaders' belongings into the wagons, Dan helped the captain, Hughie, and Owen hoist the wounded on top of purloined Free-State featherbeds and quilts. Tersely Montgomery detailed men from around Trading Post to return livestock and goods plundered from there, some of which was their own, and take a share of things left by the fleeing pillagers.

Dan and Owen exchanged elated glances when they saw a cedar chest, some brass candlesticks, and a rocking chair. "Those are Missus Nickle's," Owen said. "Let's follow along to see her face."

Dan nodded. Montgomery shook hands with them and thanked them as did Hughie, who asked where Dan was from, and than explained that he himself left County Cork in the starving years and joined the U.S. Army straightaway since work was far scarcer than penniless Irish folk.

"It's better here, lad," said the older man, nodding. "Or will be once slavery's gone from the land. I be a preacher of the United Brethren, but I'll soldier again, if need be, and call it God's work." He glanced at the party breaking up to head for their respective homes. "There'll be quite some jollification at Sugar Mound when we turn up with these critters and all this plunder. Looks like we got back just about everything they robbed from Ebenezer Barnes's store before they burned it."

"We'll raise him a new one," said Montgomery. He glanced pridefully at his men. "We'll build back for everybody who lost a cabin. And in a few days I want some of you to ride along with me to call on proslavery men . . . not quiet ones who mind their own business, but the sort who spy for Border Ruffians and help them against us."

Jennison's eyes flamed. "I'll help you hang or shoot them all!"

Montgomery frowned. "There'll be no killing yet. We'll tell them plain that the shoe's on the other foot. They must leave Kansas or be driven out. . . ."

Lusty cheering interrupted him and shouts of: "We're with you, Captain!"

"We'll dose the devil spawn with their own physic!" cried Hughie. He shielded his eyes. "Yonder comes that young Scotsman, isn't it, Captain? Looks like his sorrel nag."

It was indeed Andy McHugh who'd encountered Free Staters returning home after being scattered by invaders who outnumbered them more than five to one and had a cannon as well.

"When old John Brown heard the Missourians were coming, he got together forty men," Andy said, slumping wearily in the saddle. "They posted themselves behind a stone fence near the river and held off the mob till the cannon blasted too many holes in the wall. Brown . . . and everyone else lit out."

"Was anyone killed?"

"Not in the fight. But Frederick Brown, old John's son, was going down the road alone when he met the raiders. They shot him down."

Montgomery bowed his head. "God rest his soul, and pardon him. He was one of the Brown sons who hacked to death the Doyle boys and other proslavery men at Dutch Henry's Crossing in May." He threw up his head. "Where are the marauders?"

Andy shrugged. "They burned four or five Free-State houses at Osawatomie, broke out their whiskey, and headed back to Missouri."

Plainly torn, Montgomery considered a moment. "We can't catch up to them, and, if we did, we can't tackle five times our number and a cannon." His jaw set. "But I'm not through with these malefactors. I'm a teacher and I'm going to teach them to stay on their side of the border."

A young, red-headed Irishman raised a carroty eyebrow. "Now, how will you be doing that, Captain? Preach them a sermon?"

"Why, Pat Devlin"—Montgomery smiled—"I think I'll find a teaching position around West Point and find out who Clarke's main supporters are."

"And then?" pressed Devlin.

"Then we'll raid *them*. Relieve them of enough to make up for what they destroyed over here."

"I'm your man," vowed Devlin, and was echoed by the others.

"I won't need all of you," Montgomery said. "But those who can take the time from your crops meet at Sugar Mound tomorrow morning."

Devlin's green eyes shone. "Will we be calling on the proslavers?"

"We will."

"And maybe lessening the loads and livestock they'll have to take across the line?"

"No robbing." Montgomery's eyes and voice were stern. "I say it now for all to hear . . . if we are raided, we'll raid back. From those who despoil us . . . those only . . . we'll exact compensation. If a Missourian kills one of us in less than a fair fight, we will take him, if we can, try him, and hang him." He paused, giving weight to each word. "We must be our own law since this territory is in the power of proslavers elected by Border Ruffians. But we *must* have law lest we sink to their level."

Jennison shrugged. "You're too much the parson, Captain Montgomery." He squinted a challenge. "What will you say if a proslaver captures a slave in Kansas . . . as federal law declares that he can . . . and then sells him or collects a reward for returning him. What then?"

"If we catch the man stealer, he shall be tried by a jury of twelve."

"And?"

Montgomery sighed, but his words rang clear. "If he is guilty, we will deal with him according to Exodus Twenty-One, Sixteen. 'And he that stealeth a man, and selleth him, or if he be found in his hand, he shall surely be put to death.' "

"Amen," said Hughie.

"Amen," echoed the others.

Dan's scalp prickled. This wasn't the end of border trouble. It would get worse before it got better. What if someone like Jennison burned the happy house just because it was in Missouri? Or if proslavers burned it because the

Wares were from Illinois and almost certain to oppose slavery?

"I'll ride with you tomorrow, Captain," promised Andy.

Owen looked sheepish. "I'll fight if we're invaded, but I don't feel right about forcing neighbors out of the country even if they are proslavery."

Jennison hooted. Montgomery checked him with a glance. "Abide by your conscience, young man. I would not for the world have you go against it. God speaks to us in different ways." Dismounting, he hitched his horse to the back of the wagon with the wounded men, and drove away with the main cavalcade and most of the rescued cattle and horses.

Dan and his friends soon outdistanced the Trading Post wagon that carried Mrs. Nickel's treasures. As the three came in sight of the farm below Prairie Mound, Andy whistled. "It looks like an Indian camp when they're smoking meat."

"Except Indian camps don't have burned cabins," said Owen. "Or cows being milked. Look, that woman and the youngsters have already made a shelter with branches trimmed off trees they've cut for logs."

The family swarmed out to meet the horsemen. When Mrs. Nickel heard the Missourians had been sent scuttling for the border and that her valued belongings would shortly be returned, a joyful smile turned her weary face young and pretty.

"Thank the Lord . . . and James Montgomery! That riff-raff won't be so eager to try driving us away when they know we're going to fight back. Light down, young men, and have some roast chicken. You can see there's plenty."

"We helped ourselves to the raiders' dinner, ma'am," said Andy, chuckling. "Anyway, we need to get home so our folks won't be worrying about us any longer than they have to."

"My sisters will come over tomorrow and bring you some

hens and a rooster," Owen promised. "You're sure you'll be all right here tonight?"

"We'll be fine now that thieving gang's run across the border. Besides, Sam might drop dead of apoplexy if he found this mess and none of us." Her smile broadened. "Anyway, won't I soon have my rocking chair to rest in?"

"That's a brave woman," Andy said after he'd collected the spider to repair and they waved and rode on. "She needs to be for what's coming."

Dan thought with a pang of his foster sisters and Christy Ware, of her gentle mother and baby sister. Christy was brave, he knew that, but would they, could they, endure what everyone seemed to believe lay ahead?

Chapter Six

The livid burn scar above the pulse of Christy's wrist throbbed as if probed with red-hot wire. She glanced catty-corner across the table. Lafe Ballard stared fixedly at the scar, then met her look with eyes so pale they were like ice under a winter sky. He smiled, lips parting over narrow teeth.

Christy forced herself to meet his gaze, but broke out in cold sweat when he went back to his ciphering. Her father hadn't seen—he was listening to Matthew Hayes and Tressie Barclay read from *McGuffey's Second Reader*.

Anyway, what had happened? Lafe had only looked at her. She had never told anyone that he'd burned her on purpose because she liked Hester so much. Sometimes Christy even wondered if she'd been mistaken, but the look she'd caught just now made her know it was no accident.

If he got the chance, he'd hurt her again. She'd do her best to see he didn't have that chance. It was a good thing the Hayes boys' way home ran a mile beyond the Ballard place so they saw the Barclay girls safe that far.

Christy tried to concentrate on Henry Thoreau's *Walden* that her father much admired and had assigned as her reading since she and Thos had already finished *McGuffey's Readers*. Her spelling and composition lesson was to look up words she didn't know, learn them, and use them in an essay. Her eyes caught the swirl of golden leaves drifting from the great walnut, and she thought back to that cold wind from the north that brought the first frost shortly after Christy's thirteenth birthday on the 10th of October, two weeks ago.

Overnight, the freeze shriveled sweet potato and pumpkin vines flat and black. Trees began to glow flame, russet, gold, and yellow and skies filled with the high-pitched call of snow geese flying south in long, wavering lines, honking wedges of Canada geese, and the bugling of sandhill cranes. Great blue herons winged silently, usually alone, necks drawn back in elegant S curves, and all manner of ducks landed to feed in the corn stubble where quail, chickens, and wild turkeys devoured both insects and fallen grain.

The great marvel was sky-darkening flocks of passenger pigeons settling like heavy clouds in the forest to gorge on the acorns so relished by Patches, Evalina, and their seventeen lusty white-spotted black offspring. The pigs were shut up in the evening but five of the younglings had fallen prey to wolves, foxes, bobcats, or panthers.

"The pigeons will stay till it freezes," Hester Ballard said as she stopped to visit, and they all looked up at a vast flight of birds. "In spring, they'll be back to gobble fallen acorns. The flock splits up then into pairs that go off to nest deep in the woods. The squabs are mighty tasty."

Jonathan Ware studied the teeming mass of feathers. Unlike ducks, geese, and cranes, the pigeons had no leader or formation. They simply swarmed forward. "From beak to tail, a pigeon's about sixteen inches long and its wingspread would be close to that," he mused. "So let's take a mile-wide, two hundred yard long cross-section of the flock and figure it twenty-five yards in depth, one pigeon above another. Allowing a cubic yard for each, that would make eight million eight hundred thousand birds per minute passing the cross-section." When Hester looked perplexed, he added: "Men who've watched flights for hours on end reckon there may be over two billion in some of them. Those who study such things think the pigeons make up a quarter to nearly half of all the birds in this country."

"There's aplenty." Hester gazed in awe at Jonathan. "Can you teach Lafe to calculate like that in his head?"

"If he has the knack."

"I hope he'll have a knack for something besides shooting. He brought home a deer the other day that'll help feed us this winter, but I wish he hadn't got it the way he did."

"How was that?" asked Jonathan.

"That no-account Watt Caxton hit on the notion of salting the ground and building a platform to shoot from. Deer watch for trouble at their own level, you know, not upwards. He invited some of his cock-fighting, bear-baiting friends." Her lips tightened. "They killed fifty deer in a few hours. That's not hunting. It's pure slaughter."

"Lafe's young," Jonathan said at last.

Hester shook her head. "There's a streak in him that worries me. I sure don't want him hanging out with the likes of Watt. I'm glad you'll have him in school soon, Jonathan. That should straighten him out."

Christy glanced at the scar on her wrist, the burn Lafe had caused. *Nothing will straighten Lafe out till he's laid in his coffin.* Startled and chilled by the certainty, she wished he weren't coming to school.

"You've got your walls all chinked against bitter weather," Hester approved. With a glint in her hazel eyes, she added: "Looks like your new chimney's not going to topple over like the first one."

Christy had thought they'd never finish chinking the walls inside and out, but at least the pure clay they found in the side of a gully didn't have to be mixed with lime. Thinned with a little water, it dried hard and almost white. After the chimney her father and the boys had made had crashed to the ground, Ethan Hayes had supervised the building of the next one, setting the rock foundation, deep and firm, in the ground, making sure the space above and behind the chimney throat was bigger than it was, and that the chimney narrowed down at the top to the size of the throat so that it would draw properly.

Once corn was in the cribs and fall wheat was sowed and harrowed, Charlie Ware had left to drive a wagon on the Santa Fé Trail for a well-to-do planter named Jardine, who he'd met at Simeon Parks's mill when he took their corn to be ground. Jardine had a controlling interest in the freight company and was one of the few landowners in the region who owned more than one or two slaves. Jonathan and Ellen couldn't have liked Charlie's working for a slave owner, especially one with a pretty daughter that Charlie blushed about, but they left the decision to him. The family all missed Charlie. It didn't seem right that he wasn't there for meals or when Ellen played the piano of an evening.

With farm work pretty much done till spring plowing and planting, school could begin. The study space was chosen to get the best light from one window and warmth from the fire once winter came. Ellen's loom was set up by the other window, close to Beth's crib. Jonathan and Thos made an oblong table of beautifully grained walnut long enough to fit over two benches that each seated four students.

Classes began at nine the first Monday in October. Maps of the world and the United States brightened the wall. Jonathan had a good supply of chalk and enough slates to supply the Hayes boys, whose only book to bring from home was a tattered hymnal.

Lafe brought his mother's old slate and Dr. Jaynes's almanac. The serious little brown-haired twins, ten-year-old Tressie and Phyllis Barclay, who lived beyond the Franzes, had slates, tablets, and *Webster's Blue Back Speller.* Jonathan had several copies of the speller, *McGuffey's Readers,* and texts of history, geography, and arithmetic. Allie Hayes had taught her boys the alphabet and to read a little, so Matthew and Mark went into the second reader with Tressie. Lafe simmered at being in primer with Luke Hayes and Phyllis Barclay, especially when he saw that Christy and Thos were through the readers and studied from their father's library, working mostly at composition and advanced mathematics.

Which, a few weeks later, brought Christy back to Thoreau. Taking care not to glance toward Lafe, she dipped the goose quill pen in the ink well and prayed not to blot her work with a disastrous drop. **Mr. Thoreau says he has lived thirty years without hearing a syllable of valuable advice from his seniors. It may be as well that he prefers to live alone.**

Jonathan rang the hand bell to signal morning recess. These respites were just long enough for the pupils to get drinks, visit the log privy, and race around a few minutes to work off the effects of sitting on a hard bench. At noon though, after lunches were consumed, they spilled out to play crack-the-whip, red rover, hide-and-seek, fox-and-geese, and drop-the-handkerchief. On rainy days, inside, they played old mother gobble wobble, do-as-I-do, forfeits, and London Bridge.

The older children took turns bringing pails of drinking water from the creek. This morning was Christy's time. In spite of digging in various places, Jonathan, much to his and Ellen's vexation, always struck solid rock that kept him from reaching water near the house.

Watching for cottonmouths, although it was time for any

sensible snake to den up for the winter, Christy filled the bucket. Leaning to one side from its weight, she toiled up the bank as Robbie barkingly announced a stranger on horseback.

Tall and gaunt, he wore a dark military coat with a red-lined cape. A slouch hat was pulled down to shaggy eyebrows jutting above dark gray eyes. He was clean-shaven and his face was deeply lined.

Jonathan and Ellen came out to greet him. If he gave his name, Christy was too far away to hear it, but she reached the house as Ellen was saying: "Won't you rest a bit, sir, and have some corndodgers and buttermilk?"

"Why, lady," he said in a voice that had the wild wind in it, "I'd welcome a bite, but I'll have it out here because, unless I'm much mistaken, you have a school and will be calling your scholars in."

He dismounted, towering over Jonathan, who was close to six feet tall, and with a soft word, tied his chestnut gelding to one of the stumps left for that purpose. He frowned at Christy's bucket as Ellen brought his refreshment.

"Wouldn't you like to have a well, lady?"

"My husband's started half a dozen wells, sir. We seem to have solid rock under us."

The stranger's smile used some of the wrinkles in his face and made him less forbidding. "Well, lady, when I've finished this excellent buttermilk, with your leave, I'll cut a willow branch and find a place for your good husband to dig."

"You can witch water?" Jonathan asked.

The cadaverous man's smile vanished. "No witch about it, sir. Does not God command that thou shalt not suffer a witch to live? It's enough that a forked willow branch points down for me where water flows beneath."

"There must be some law of physics operating," Jonathan mused.

"Rather," said the stranger, "call it the grace of God in aiding his children." He looked piercingly at Jonathan. "Before I find your well, I have one question."

"What?"

"If a fugitive slave stopped here for help, would you give it or turn him in for the reward?"

Ellen and Jonathan exchanged glances. Ellen put her hand on her husband's arm as he answered: "With God's help, we will aid anyone who comes to our door."

"If you're going to help a runaway, you'd better devise a good hiding place in case his master's hot on his heels." The stranger peered even more intently at the Wares. "Supposing that master . . . or a proslavery man . . . craved shelter and food?"

Ellen said firmly: "We'd give it, sir. Just as we did to you."

"I fear, lady, that helping all will get you the help of none when the shooting starts. Even the Son of God said he came not to bring peace, but a sword."

The Wares stood close together. They were not touching but it was clear they were joined, soul and mind. After a moment, the tall man shrugged. "I'll find your well."

Jonathan nodded. "We're much obliged for your efforts, sir. It's time I called my students in, but let me know if I can assist you."

Christy carried the bucket inside and set it on the small table that held the wash basin. As Jonathan rang his hand bell and Christy's schoolmates came in, rushing or loitering according to their interest in lessons, she saw the visitor cutting a forked willow branch. Coming up the slope, he gripped one fork in each hand, bending over, with the base of the limb

91

pointing down. She wanted to watch but another ring of the bell called her to her seat.

To settle his pupils down after their racing about, Jonathan usually read to them, or talked a while in a way that interested even the youngest.

"You all know Missouri mules are famous," he began, smiling at shy little Phyllis while keeping a quizzical eye on squirming Luke. "But did you know most of them descend from jacks and jennets brought from New Mexico in Eighteen Twenty-Three? Trading with Mexico and steamboating that began a few years earlier made Missouri prosper. She's still the gateway to the West and that makes her very important."

"Did Missouri belong to Mexico once?" puzzled Matthew Hayes. "Or was it Spain? Or maybe France?"

"France gave Spain New Orleans and all her lands west of the Mississippi in Seventeen Sixty-Two, but when Napoléon came to power after the French Revolution, he made Spain give back Louisiana. He needed money for wars against England, so he sold what was known as Louisiana to the United States in Eighteen Oh-Three. There had been French and Spanish settlers around Saint Louis, but, after the War of Eighteen Twelve, Americans like Daniel Boone swarmed into the eastern part of the territory."

"Weren't there lots of Indians?" breathed Mark Hayes.

"Yes. Some, like the Osages, Kansas, and Missouris, had been here a long time. Others, like the Sac and Fox, had been forced down from the north by the powerful Iroquois. Others, like the Shawnees and Delawares, moved into Missouri toward the end of the last century because American settlers were crowding them. All these Indians have villages and farms. They hunt a lot, but they also grow corn, beans, melons, and pumpkins, and many keep livestock."

"Did they fight each other?" asked Lafe.

"Of course, just like the English, French, and American colonists battled. As white folk poured into this region . . . they'd heard the ground was so rich that if you planted a ninepenny nail at night, by morning it would've sprouted crowbars . . . the government kept making treaties with the tribes to trade their Missouri lands for holdings in Kansas and what's now Indian Territory. By Eighteen Thirty-Six, there were no tribal lands left in Missouri."

"Our grampa fought in the Black Hawk War on the upper Mississippi in the summer of Eighteen Thirty-Two," said Matthew. "He saw Chief Black Hawk when he was a prisoner at Jefferson Barracks. Said he was a fine-looking man, proud as a king."

Jonathan nodded. "Black Hawk claimed the treaty ceding Sac and Fox land in Wisconsin and Illinois was signed by chiefs who had no authority. That's also what the Cherokees maintained twenty years ago when they were driven from the East on the Trail of Tears that led to Indian Territory. At any rate, the Indians who once lived in Missouri are now our neighbors across the line in Kansas and down in Indian Territory."

"Where, more shame to them, Cherokees and others of the Five Civilized Tribes hold slaves." Everyone whirled at the harsh voice from the door. "I've found your water, sir. Let me show you where to dig and I'll be on my way."

"Study your spelling while I'm outside," Jonathan told his pupils.

"I bet that's old John Brown," Lafe whispered. "I've heard he wears a caped coat like that and has eyes like a cold storm."

Matthew's blue eyes widened. "Wonder what he's doing over here?"

"Stealing slaves, of course," Lafe sneered.

"No one around here has any."

"It's not far to some who do, like Doctor Hamelton and Bishop Jardine." This last was the planter Charlie worked for. Apparently it wasn't against his religion to own slaves. Lafe chuckled in sudden inspiration. "I'll tell Watt Caxton on my way home. He says Brown ought to be tarred and feathered. Maybe Watt can attend to that."

"Watt's great for baiting bears, fighting cocks, and shooting treed panthers," Matthew said. "I don't see him getting in range of that Sharps."

Jonathan came in, the boys hushed, and Christy craned her neck to watch through the window as the stranger rode away. She thought about him all day. He, with his sons and a few other men, had murdered five men, two of them not much older than Charlie. That he had prayed first to the stern Old Testament God of Moses, Gideon, and Joshua only made the slaughter more terrible.

Still, if he rescued slaves. . . . Christy shuddered to remember how she'd overheard her father telling her mother about two slaves who had just lately been burned alive in Carthage for killing their master.

How tangled it all was, right and wrong. Yet Christy knew one thing. She'd help hide any slave who came this way, trying not to get her parents mixed up in it. That meant she needed to find a hiding place better than the corncrib or barn or loft.

What of the underground river?

Her heart raced as she remembered her escape with Dan O'Brien. The cavern, as best she could judge, ran under the ridge that reared gray palisades on the other side of the creek. There must not be any open sinkholes or she and Dan would have noticed the glow of moonlight as they groped their way, but there might be the beginnings of one, a crack that could be pried or hammered at to make an opening.

It was time to gather hickory and hazel nuts. If her mother let her do that Saturday, she'd look hard for a way into the hidden passage.

Saturday, as it turned out, she helped her mother wash in the morning while her father and Thos started the well with a pick and shovels. By afternoon, they had dug too deep to toss out the earth with shovels and handed up buckets of earth that Christy dumped for them. As the hole deepened, Jonathan rigged a log windlass to raise and lower the buckets. Christy stayed busy till time for evening chores.

Sunday morning was given over to simple church services. When neighbors learned that Jonathan Ware was a minister, although a Universalist one, they asked if he wouldn't preach for them. Arly Maddux's fire-and-brimstone Baptist sermons were too much for any of them, except the Caxtons.

"I'll speak of God's goodness and human duty," Jonathan had said, smiling. "It won't be what you're used to, but you'll get a blessing from the way my wife plays the piano."

So Hester, the Hayeses, Lige and Sarah Morrow, and Emil and Lottie Franz filled the cabin they'd helped to build and sang fervently, if not in tune. They listened attentively as Jonathan spoke on some parable, saying, or act of Jesus. After more hymns and a closing prayer, the women set out the food they'd brought to share, and it was mid-afternoon when they took their leave. The Caxtons had come once, the Sunday Jonathan had talked about Jesus's calling the children to him and saying that of such was the kingdom of heaven.

"Are you sayin' babies that aren't baptized still go to heaven, Ware?" Caxton demanded after the service.

"You can't believe God is wicked enough to send babies to hell, neighbor."

"God's ways ain't for us to question."

"He gave us reason. He must intend for us to use it. More, he gave us hearts. Who of us would throw a baby into an everlasting lake of fire? Does God have less compassion than his creatures?"

Caxton choked, muttered something about blaspheming, and hustled his wife outside.

Whatever the other neighbors thought of Jonathan Ware's trust that God was too good to send anyone to hell, most of them gathered at the Ware home Sunday mornings. It being the Sabbath, helping with the well after dinner was prohibited, but Ethan Hayes and Lige Morrow said they'd come next day and dig.

"Better get it done before the ground freezes or the weather turns nasty," Hayes pointed out. "It'll take you and Thos a mighty long time, Jonathan, if you just dig Saturdays and an hour or so after school."

"But you've already helped us so much!"

"What are neighbors for?" Morrow grinned. Clad in buckskins even for church, he shifted his tobacco to the other cheek. "Fact is, the meetin's and the good food, shared after, sure make us feel lots more like neighbors, don't they, Sarah?"

Her dark eyes shone. The store-bought yellow calico, exquisitely sewed with a pointed basque, was bright amongst the muted grays and browns of homespun. Lottie Franz's dark gray serge also came from a store, but the color and style were so somber that Hester whispered to Allie Hayes that it put her in mind of what a nun might wear.

"I love singing again," Sarah Morrow confided. "Anyway, since you hold school here and the children need water, it's only fair for the rest of us to help with the well."

"But you don't have any children . . . ," Ellen began, and broke off.

If that was a sensitive spot, Sarah didn't show it. "Children are everybody's, aren't they?" She laughed. "We'll certainly be better off if neighborhood youngsters grow up to be good people."

She passed her big wood bowl of honey-nut cakes. When they were gone and the dishes washed, the guests went home. Eager to start her search for a way into the cavern, Christy changed Beth's diaper without being asked.

When she looked up, her mother was smiling at her, which made it easy to say: "Could I go look for nuts if I watch the sun and get home in time to feed the chickens and gather the eggs?"

Ellen and Jonathan exchanged glances. Apparently they decided nut gathering was too uncertain an effort to be ranked as work that would violate the Sabbath. "Yes, but take Robbie with you," Ellen said, "and mind you're home well before sundown. Thos, do you want to go with your sister?"

He looked up from *Moby Dick*, a thick novel that Christy hadn't attempted to read. "Not if I don't have to," he said pleadingly.

"I'd liefer have Robbie," Christy retorted. She got an oak-split basket Lige had given them and ran out into the rich autumnal air.

The blaze of reds of golds along the creek made her catch her breath in wonder that was almost pain. The air filling her lungs was so rich that it seemed full of the glorious colors and afternoon sun.

Robbie alongside, Christy ran past the grapevines and maiden blush apple trees Emil Franz had given them, but had to slow down for the rough clods of the cornfield. Jonathan and the boys had plowed and harrowed about an acre early in September and planted it to wheat, but the broken sod of the rest would rot during the winter and, by spring, be much easier to plow. Stumps would be grubbed out or burned as time permitted.

Passing the thicket of papaw trees where she had gathered delicious fruit when its green-yellow turned brown, Christy slipped through the towering brilliance of sycamores, oaks, and walnuts and picked her way through the willows on the sandbar that reached so close to the other bank that she could leap it.

That plunge and her scramble up the snaky roots of a white-trunked sycamore caused an explosion of luminous green parakeets that winged off in a shimmering cloud. Christy watched them out of sight. Then, trying to keep her basket clear of luxuriant tangles of spicebush, sassafras, and young hickory, she found a dense thicket of hazelnuts and picked busily while Robbie lunged about after exciting smells.

Leaving plenty of nuts for the squirrels, she moved toward the ridge she believed must run above the secret passage. Hester had shown Christy several kinds of hickory and told her all had good nuts, except for the bitternut that had tighter, smoother bark than its relatives. "Squirrels like them," Hester explained, "but if you bite into one by mistake, you'll spit it out in a hurry."

As Christy picked from shagbark, kingnut, and mockernut hickories, the four-sectioned husks sometimes finished splitting from the shells. By shaking boughs she could reach, Christy soon filled the basket. Feeling virtuous at fulfilling her alleged purpose for the outing, she hung the basket over a snag on a dead tree and began to explore the ridge.

Falling leaves hid much of the lichen-crusted rock spine rearing above the forested creek bottom. Christy walked along, scuffing leaves and débris away from depressions and crevices.

If Dan O'Brien were searching with her, it would be more fun. Surely he could find a way into what had been their refuge. She frowned to remember the news her father had brought back from the mill, that Dan and Owen Parks had ridden with Andy McHugh to drive out the proslave invaders.

Dan was too young for that, only a year older than Thos! She shivered at the idea of her brother firing a gun or being shot at. Dan could have been killed. Somehow she knew his answer to that. He'd laugh and say he was lucky not to have died in Ireland.

A distant sound roused her from these thoughts. Dogs? Their baying, far off as it was, sent a chill through her. Even if they were Lige's hounds instead of Watt Caxton's, she didn't want to meet them in full cry, especially not with Robbie who was brash enough to take on a pack.

She called the dog, but he set up a furious barking at something under a ledge. Whatever lured him, fox, bobcat, wolf, or bear, she only wanted to get the little collie safely home.

"Robbie!" She hurried toward the ledge and grasped the ruff of his neck. "Robbie, come on! Don't you hear those hounds?"

"I hear 'em, missy," came a husky voice.

A man rose from his crouch beneath the overhang. His skin was dark as the shadows. He was tall. Big. Black. Christy smothered a cry and shrank away.

"For the love of Jesus Savior, little girl," whispered the man, "you know where I can hide?"

Chapter Seven

Should she take the runaway to her parents? She couldn't think of anything else to do. Frightened as she was, she knew his scent had to be lost in the water or the hounds would trail him.

"We'll hide you," she breathed, whirling, hushing Robbie. "But, first, you've got to follow along in the creek, then run to the cabin. I'll go tell my parents. Hurry!"

He plunged down the slope. Christy pelted after him, grabbing her basket as she passed the snag. It wouldn't do for the pursuers to find the abandoned harvest near the fugitive's spoor.

Heedless of scratches, she reached the creek in time to see the hunted man vanish around the curve that bounded the cornfield and thanked heaven for the uncleared woods that stretched on that side within fifty yards of the house. The hounds might pick up his trail again, but no one should glimpse him making for refuge.

Robbie barked toward the increasing racket of the hounds, but Christy called him and he came reluctantly, growling when he looked backward.

Bursting into the cabin, Christy gasped: "A man . . . a slave! Hounds are after him! I sent him down the creek and told him to come here."

Ellen's hand flew to her throat. She glanced around the room and toward the loft.

"The first place they'd look," Jonathan said. "Think of somewhere else. Thos, let's get some burning sticks in a pail. We're going to burn off the weeds and leaves to cover the man's trail on this side."

"Won't the men after him think that's strange?" worried Ellen.

"Most farmers do burn off dry grass and weeds in the fall," Jonathan assured her. "It helps new grass come up and keeps wildfires from being so dangerous. Ethan's been telling me I should do it."

The Ware men folk rushed out with their small torches. Christy stared at her mother. "The barn? Smokehouse?"

Ellen shook her head before a little smile eased the alarm on her face. "The well! We'll give him a quilt to wrap up in and then toss in enough dirt to cover him. If we have time!"

"Maybe the hounds will run up and down the creek a while," Christy hoped. "Oh, I wish he'd get here!"

"Maybe you'd better feed the chickens and gather the eggs. I'll start the milking. Whoever's after the poor man won't know that's Thos's chore."

The hounds! From across the creek, a good half mile away, their clamor froze her blood. What if her attempt to rescue the man got her father killed or their home burned, the happy house their neighbors had helped raise on that day that now seemed so long ago?

Outside, smoke rose from the cornfield and adjoining forest. Although her knees quivered, Christy took a pan and went to where cracked corn was stored in a covered barrel in the granary built onto the smokehouse. As she stepped out with grain for the chickens, she saw the colored man break from the trees. She set the pan on a stump and gestured him toward the well. The hole was perhaps ten feet deep. If the manhunters came this way, Christy hoped they wouldn't wonder why the diggers hadn't cleaned all the loose dirt from the bottom.

Christy got the shovels from the dogtrot as Ellen ran out with a quilt. She explained the plan as she wound the quilt around the panting, exhausted fugitive. "I'm sorry we'll have to cover you with earth," she said, "but it's the best thing we can think of."

The man actually chuckled. Christy saw he was young. A prime hand, a planter would say, with many years of hard work left in him. "Just so I'm not covered up permanent, ma'am." He leaped down without hesitation, tenting the quilt over his head so he could breathe. "Maybe," came his muffled voice, "your men folk will plumb burn up my trail and the hounds won't come here."

Even if they didn't, the pursuers would almost certainly stop to question the Wares. Heart pounding as the baying sounded just across the creek, Christy helped her mother shovel dirt from the pile beside the hole, trying to spread it evenly over man and quilt rather than dump it in a mass. When none of the quilt showed through, they put up their shovels and went about their chores with the din of the hounds approaching.

Christy's hands shook so much that she dropped an egg, which was too bad since the hens' laying declined with the shortening days. As she barred the door to keep them and haughty Cavalier safe from wild creatures that would fancy a chicken dinner, four horsemen at the edge of the cornfield were silhouetted in the dusk against the burning leaves and brush. They were talking to Jonathan and Thos, but it was too far away to hear what they said.

Hounds milled around the riders or lay as if exhausted. Robbie whined from inside where he'd been left to keep him out of trouble. Nape prickling at sight of the pack, Christy hoped they stayed where scorched soil and weeds should hide the scent of the fleeing slave. She liked dogs but she was deathly afraid of these.

Cold sweat formed beads and trickled between her small breasts as she went inside and put the eggs on the shelf. Beth was still asleep, thank goodness. It would take Ellen a while to finish milking, so, with dry mouth and blood drumming in her ears, Christy built up the fire, lit a candle, washed her hands, and poured cornmeal into a kettle of water. After a hearty dinner such as they'd had at noon, mush and milk was usually their supper.

Outside, voices neared. One was her father's. Thos called that he was going to help Ellen with the milking. Jonathan came in, followed by a well-dressed stout man with thick graying reddish hair, Watt Caxton, and Lafe Ballard, who, from behind the men, and with no warmth in his pale eyes, showed his teeth to Christy in a smile more frightening than a scowl.

"Christy, will you pour buttermilk for our guests?" Jonathan requested. "Bishop Jardine, this is my oldest daughter, Christina."

Charlie's employer. The one with the pretty daughter. Christy mumbled something and started dipping buttermilk from a crock into delft mugs. Jardine continued to appraise her from cider-colored eyes.

"You favor your brother, young lady," he said in a genial tone as she handed him his drink. "You must come visit my daughter for a month or so when your parents can spare you. Melissa gets lonesome, especially with her brother gone with yours to be a teamster."

This wasn't the time to say her parents would never let her visit a household supported by slaves. Christy thanked him and handed a mug to Watt Caxton. His acknowledgement was a jerk of the head that made his pointed black beard seem to stab his chest. Did he have any notion, Christy wondered, who had turned the bears loose?

It was certain that under the guise of needing refreshment Jardine was scrutinizing every niche of the cabin. Short of an outright confrontation, he couldn't let hounds search the property.

As he accepted his milk, Lafe grinned. Perhaps only to her did his—"Much obliged."—sound mocking, but there was no doubt that, as he sometimes did in school, he now stared at the scar on her wrist as if it gave him pleasure.

"Are you sure you won't have supper?" Jonathan asked.

"Obliged, but nothing's going to set well on my stomach till I catch that rascally Justus," growled Jardine. His glance fleered to Christy. "You didn't see my slave, Christina, while your father and brother were burning off the field?"

She hoped she answered swiftly enough and that her face didn't flush as hotly as she felt it was. "I didn't see your slave, Bishop Jardine." *I saw a man in trouble. I don't believe in slaves.*

Watt Caxton said in his braying voice: "Could be the nigger hid in the loft or outbuildings and no one saw him. You won't mind, will you, Mister Ware, if we have a look around?"

Jonathan said with perfect courtesy, meeting Jardine's gaze: "I'm sure you'll understand, gentlemen, that as an American citizen I must oppose the searching of my home by anyone but an officer of the law with a proper warrant." He didn't, of course, know where Justus was hidden.

Jardine sighed. From beneath his well-cut coat, he drew an ivory-handled pistol. At the same instant, Watt Caxton pulled a revolver. Lafe had nothing but his smile.

"I'm sorry for this necessity, Mister Ware." Jardine did sound regretful. "However, views you've been heard to express prove you no friend of owner's rights and you're known to be unorthodox, even denying the existence of hell."

"Brother, I affirm rather the goodness of God."

Jardine shook his head. "I paid a Cherokee planter twelve hundred dollars for Justus only a month ago, sir. I mean to have him back, even if it costs me more than that. I'll make him an example my other slaves will think about if they're tempted to head north."

Jonathan must have remembered what happened at Carthage, the awful thing he'd whispered to Ellen. "Bishop, you wouldn't burn him?"

"No, but my overseer, Blake, down there, who's watching the hounds, will open his back with a lash and fill the wounds with salt before he cuts off Justus's toes. Justus will be able to work, but, I assure you, sir, he won't run again."

Jonathan caught in his breath. "You should beg my daughter's pardon, Bishop, for speaking such wickedness in front of her. Even more, you should be ashamed before the God we both aspire to serve."

Jardine's ruddy face crimsoned darkly. For a moment, he almost raised the pistol before he controlled himself. "There were slaves in Jesus's day, Mister Ware. In Colossians Three, Twenty-Three does not Paul command them to obey their masters in all things?"

"Paul, not Jesus."

It was Jardine's time to gasp. "Will you dispute with the apostle, sir?"

"That I dispute often with Paul is one reason I'm a Universalist."

"God will judge you though man may do so first." Jardine turned to his companions. "I'll keep the Wares company while you check the loft and rest of the cabin and outbuildings." As Lafe got the ladder to the loft and cast a taunting grin at Christy, the bishop warned: "Don't damage anything, mind you, and keep an eye out for Missus Ware and the boy. I don't want anyone hurt."

Caxton took the candle and went out through the dogtrot to the other room. The ceiling creaked under Lafe's tread. He wouldn't find anything up there but Thos's pallet and clothes.

"The mush needs stirring," Christy said. She moved toward the fireplace with a half-formed thought to throw the steaming mixture on the bishop.

"I'll stir it for you." He did so, rather awkwardly, without lowering the pistol.

"Nothing up here, Bishop." Lafe dropped disgustedly down the ladder. "Shall I look in the barn?"

"Yes, but wait for Mister Caxton. He can hold the candle while you search."

"Does your mother know what you're doing, Lafe?" asked Jonathan.

"I was at Watt's when the bishop came along and asked Watt to use his hounds. But what Ma thinks don't matter, Mister Ware." Lafe's eyes glittered and he laughed. "I'm not coming back to your stupid little school."

"Lafe seems a lad of promise and I can use him," Jardine said. "Our freighting company has a contract to haul supplies to Fort Riley . . . that's located between the Oregon and Santa Fé Trails . . . to protect travelers on both routes. And there's more hauling than we can handle from Independence to serve merchants in towns not reached by steamboats."

"I'll wish you luck then, Lafe," said Jonathan.

"Thanks kindly, Mister Ware." Lafe's tone was civil but there was a curl to his lip. Christy longed to slap it off.

"I hope, Mister Ware," said Jardine, "that this necessity won't cause your Charlie to turn against me. I've taken quite a liking to him and he's a steadying influence on my son Travis, who sadly needs it."

"Charlie's doing a man's work. He must make a man's decisions."

"If you didn't tell him. . . ."

"Look, Bishop! You can hardly expect us not to tell our son about this outrage when he comes home. But you'll probably see him before we do. You can make your case first."

With the help of the prettiest girl Charlie's ever seen, Christy thought with a rush of anger and desolation. Could Charlie, *would* he, overlook this trespass? How could he go on working for a man who'd drawn a pistol on his father? An even more wretched question arose in Christy's mind. *Had Charlie been at the Jardines' when the slave escaped, would he have joined the hunt? No! He couldn't! It would break Mother's and Father's hearts . . . mine, too!* Yet to her horror and sense of guilt in doubting her brother, Christy wasn't absolutely sure. He fancied Melissa Jardine, was friends with Travis Jardine, and had been made much of by the wealthy planter. Swept along in the heat of excitement, yes, alas, she could imagine Charlie taking part.

But she *wouldn't* believe he'd approve of lashing Justus, packing the wounds with salt. Charlie had a kind heart, whatever else. Would that be enough?

She thought of Dan O'Brien. He'd never chase a slave. On that she'd wager her life. That certainty for the first time made her think beyond hiding Justus for the moment.

If only she'd found a way into the underground river! She could take Justus to that other sinkhole above the Marais des Cygnes and ask help from Dan or the Parkses, maybe even John Brown. He'd know how to get a runaway safely to Canada.

All these things churned through her head before Watt thrust his head in.

"Nobody there or along the wood stacked in the dogtrot, Bishop."

"Kindly go to the barn and outbuildings with Lafe," said Jardine. "Mind that you don't set a fire with the candle."

"Oh, these folks seem fond of fire, burning off their fields so late of an evening."

"I'm paying you well, Caxton. No fire. And don't discharge that revolver unless you find Justus and can't stop him short of a bullet in the leg. He's my property, remember. I don't want him damaged."

Caxton gave a disgusted shrug as Lafe joined him. Jonathan said to Jardine: "Would you care to have Watt Caxton approach your wife out of the night with a gun in his hand?"

"He'll obey or lose the money I've promised."

Jonathan's eyes smoldered. "What good is that if he hurts or insults my wife? Keep your pistol in my back if you wish, but let's make sure Caxton behaves."

After a moment, Jardine nodded. "I have no desire to alarm women. But my pistol's ready, sir. Christina, take your mush off the fire and come with us. Don't do anything foolish or, reluctantly, I will have to shoot your father."

Hating the unctuous planter with all her being, Christy set the bubbling kettle off the coals and followed her father outside. The moon had not risen.

Down at the barn, the candle wavered. Her mother and Thos must have had to finish milking in the dark, but they should be through by now. Well, let Watt and Lafe snoop around the barn.

Christy's heart stopped when her father warned: "Take

care not to fall into the well we're digging." He didn't know where Justus was. In fact, he wouldn't know that Justus wasn't in the barn. Beneath his calm, he must be agonized.

"Bring the candle here, Caxton!" Jardine called. "Let's have a look down this well."

What if Justus had moved so the quilt shifted from beneath the dirt? What if they tossed rocks down or stabbed with a pitchfork? Sick with fear, Christy squeezed her eyes shut as Caxton bent over with a grunt and held the candle as low as his potbelly would allow.

"Only the bottom of the hole," said Jardine. "Hurry with the barn, man. If that stiff-necked devil isn't here, he'll be almost to Kansas. Not that we'll turn back at the border if we're on his track."

"Can't search if you keep callin' me back," Caxton grumbled, but he hurried ahead of them to the barn where Lafe's silvery hair caught the light of the candle as they passed inside.

There was a yelp, no light, and a string of oaths.

"Who are you?" Ellen shrieked. "Why are you sneaking around our barn?" Her voice rose. "Jonathan! Jonathan! Help!"

"What's got into you, woman?" bellowed Caxton. "Why'd you throw milk over us? Bishop. . . ."

"Missus Ware?" called Jardine.

"Who else would it be, in my own barn?" Ellen had never sounded so—so shrewish. "Who, pray, are you?"

"Mordecai Jardine, your son's employer, madam. I regret the annoyance, but it's possible a runaway slave has hidden here without your knowledge."

"Well, he hasn't, sir! He's certainly not in the barn! I must tell you that I don't appreciate finding a man with a gun nosing into our barn!"

"I humbly apologize, ma'am, but your husband's views on slavery cannot but rouse suspicion. . . ."

"Suspicion's one thing," Ellen cut in. "Searching our buildings with guns is another!" For the first time, fear sounded in her voice. "My husband? Where . . . ?"

"I'm here and fine, Ellen," Jonathan reassured her. "Too bad you wasted our milk."

"I don't grudge it." Was that a hint of laughter in her tone?

Jardine cleared his throat. "Do I understand you to assert, Missus Ware, that my slave is not concealed in your barn or outbuildings?"

"I would swear it before a judge, sir. Indeed, I do swear it before the one who will judge us all."

"Then we'll take our leave."

"Bishop!" protested Caxton.

"We'll take our leave," Jardine repeated sternly. "Again, madam, my apologies."

Some demon prompted Christy to suggest sweetly: "Perhaps you'd like to take your overseer a drink of buttermilk, Bishop Jardine."

After a moment's astonishment, Jardine laughed. "He'll drink from the creek, young lady. Remember, you're invited to visit my daughter."

"Or," interposed Ellen, "your daughter may visit us."

Once more taken aback, Jardine stammered: "Though deeply obliged at the invitation, Missus Ware, I fear our opinions are too different for an impressionable girl to . . . to. . . ."

"Exactly," said Ellen serenely. "Good night, Bishop Jardine. Mister Caxton, I must say I'm astonished! And Lafe. . . ."

"Thos!" called Jonathan. "Is your bucket of milk safe? I hope so, for I'm hungry. Good night, sirs."

"Isn't it dangerous for them to go crashing around in the

dark?" Christy asked as the Wares went inside and Ellen lit another candle.

"I expect they're all used to hunting at night," said Jonathan dryly. "Now where in the world did you hide the man?" He nodded approval at Ellen's explanation. "Whew! And to think I called their attention to the well. We'd better leave our guest down there till we can be sure Jardine's crew is gone, but, Thos, go out and tell him we'll have him up soon and think of what must be done. If we can help him into Kansas. . . ."

Christy looked up from dishing out the mush, including a bowl for Justus. "There may be a way." While her family stared at her in amazement, she told them about how she and Dan had freed the bears and found the passage.

"Christina!" Ellen choked. "How will I ever rest easy now I know you may be wandering around in some awful cavern? If Caxton didn't kill you, the bear might have!"

"But aren't you glad the bears turned up again to listen to the piano?" Christy asked. It was only during the last week or so that the pair hadn't been glimpsed among the trees at dusk.

"I'm glad they weren't killed in that frightful way," Ellen admitted. "But Christy. . . ."

"You must try hard not to worry your mother." Jonathan's stern voice was betrayed a little by the pride in his eyes. "So, while you gathered nuts, you looked for but didn't find an opening to the underground?"

Christy nodded. Thos's eyes sparkled. "Wouldn't it be handy to find a way in? 'Specially if more slaves run our direction."

Jonathan pondered. "To be prepared, I suppose we'd better look for an entry, but I'm responsible for protecting this family. We're not going to become a regular station on the Underground Railroad, though, of course, we'll help fugitives who come to us."

Thos finished his second mug of milk. "Shall I get Justus now?"

"We'll take him some food," decided Jonathan, "but let's wait a little longer to bring him up."

Before Jonathan and Thos brought the young man in, Christy blew out the candle as an extra precaution so the room was lit by the fire only. Ellen, rocking Beth, spoke a soft greeting and asked him to sit down. He seemed to be favoring one foot.

"Lady," he said in a husky voice, "you look to me just like Mary holdin' Lord Jesus. And the rest of you shine bright as angels. I thank Jesus and all of you for helpin' me and I pray God to put it in my life to pay you back some happy day."

"We'll be paid if you get to freedom," Ellen said. "Have you hurt your foot?"

"Ran a stob into it. Paid it no mind with them hounds behind me."

Jonathan pressed him to a bench. "Thos, fill the wash basin with warm water. Put some of Hester's soft soap in it. We'll soak your foot while you eat, Justus, and then have a look."

Hungrily, but taking care not to cram his mouth or make a mess, Justus finished the mush, four eggs Christy fried for him in butter in the three-legged spider, and a chunk of leftover cornbread.

Smiling from his third mug of buttermilk, Justus said: "Nothin's ever tasted so good. First bite I've had since I run off night before last outside of some papaws and nuts."

"Looks like you'd have brought some food," said Thos, and got a reproving glance from Jonathan.

"Young master, I've been watchin' a chance to run ever

since Master Richard Frazer sold me away from my folks and the girl I married in the big house, with a preacher and all. Master Mordecai put me in a cabin with five other hands. Seemed like, nights, at least one of them was forever gettin' up or sneakin' in after sparkin' his sweetheart . . . or I'd fall asleep. So when they was finally all snorin' at once, I high-tailed it out of there."

"Bishop Jardine didn't beat you?" Thos asked.

"Thomas!" It was seldom Thos got his full name.

" 'Scuse me," he muttered. "None of my beeswax."

Justus shrugged. "Master Mordecai fed us good and kept us in decent clothes the slave women spun and wove the cloth for. His wife's crippled and don't care for nothin' but her childs and roses, but the woman cookin' for us slaves knew a powerful lot of herbs and cures. Everybody gets new clothes Christmas, and the hands hired or bought from other masters have a week off to go visit at home." His jaw set. "Master Richard and Master Jardine thought that ought to make me real grateful . . . that I could go see my folks and Hildy for a couple days a year with the trip takin' most of my week."

"But you can't go back to your old place," said Jonathan.

"No, but I can get up north or plumb to Canada, work and save money. Maybe enough to buy Hildy and my ma and pa, usin' a go-between." Justus considered. "My folks'd be cheap 'cause they can't work enough to earn their living."

Even at that, Christy wondered if the old slave parents might not die before their son claimed them. "After Hildy's mama died, she was raised up alongside Miss Lou, Master Richard's wife, so her white folks might not sell her for anything. If they won't, I'm goin' to steal her away."

Jonathan sighed. "Some day, Justus, no human being will be able to own another. I hope that day comes soon. Now let me see that foot."

After picking out splinters of rotting cornstalk, Jonathan swabbed the puncture with soft soap and packed it with a salve of marsh mallow, chamomile, and yarrow Hester had given them.

Ellen gave Beth to Christy, located a bit of homespun so threadbare it couldn't be salvaged, and bandaged the soft pad in place with a strip cut from an old hucking towel.

"Shamed to put you to all this fuss. No way to thank you." Justus looked at Christy. "You got a hold on me, missy, that no master could. If you hadn't brought me here, I'd be chewed by the hounds most likely 'cause I wasn't goin' back tame to Mister Blake's blacksnake. He don't whip often, but, when he do, it ain't forgot."

"Bishop Jardine doesn't have hounds?" asked Thos.

"Mistress can't abide 'em. They dug up some of her fancy roses a few years ago. She carried on till Master Mordecai gave the hounds to his brother who's got a plantation up by Independence."

Jonathan shook his head. "So if Watt Caxton hadn't joined in with his pack, you'd have had a good chance of getting across the border."

"Reckon I still do . . . a pretty fair chance." Justus stood, head almost brushing the ceiling. "They'll likely keep the hounds along the creek to pick up my scent when I leave the water. If I head west on the high ground. . . ."

"You're not going anywhere tonight," Ellen decreed. "You'll sleep in the loft, rest, and let your foot start healing."

"I've already taken our corn to the mill over in Kansas or I could do that and hide you in the wagon," Jonathan pondered.

"I don't have enough wool to cover you up or we could send it and you to the carding mill," Ellen regretted.

Christy made a rueful sound. "If I'd just been able to find

a way into the cavern! But I heard the hounds, and then Justus. . . ."

He looked up in sudden hope. "There's a cave somewheres around where I was hidin'?"

Again, Christy explained the secret river. "It's likely as dangerous to go back to Caxton's sinkhole as it'd be to go through the woods," she said. "But if there was some way into the underground just across the creek. . . ."

Justus laughed for the first time, looking too young to want to marry, much too young to die by hounds or a beating. "Maybe there is, missy."

"You saw one?"

"That rock I was hiding under . . . well, there was a fox ducked in ahead of me and it sure disappeared! When I heard you, though, somethin' told me to take my chance."

"A fox can squeeze through a little hole," Thos said. "They're mostly fur and tail."

Justus nodded. "Yeah, and any hole I could crawl in easy, so could the hounds."

"If there *is* a cave that leads into the main passage, maybe we could make the opening big enough for a human." Jonathan looked hopeful. "We'll see about it tomorrow. But while the bishop's hunting around, the best place for you, young man, is in the loft."

"If Master Mordecai came back here . . . ," Justus groaned. "No way I could forgive myself if I brought you good folks grief."

"I think the bishop believed my wife." Jonathan laughed softly and gave her a glance so admiring that she blushed. "What she said was true enough."

"And when I told him I hadn't seen a slave, that was true," Christy maintained. "Because you'd run away to freedom, Justus. You decided you *weren't* his slave." Christy hugged herself with excitement. "Please, Mother, may I go across the creek before school tomorrow and hunt for where the fox ran?"

"I think you'd burst otherwise." Ellen laughed. "Yes, Thos, you may go, too . . . after your chores."

"Let us thank God for mercifully protecting us tonight," said Jonathan. "Let us pray He will guide Justus safely to freedom and one day reunite him with his loved ones."

They all bowed their heads.

"Let justice flow down like a mighty river," Jonathan ended.

They all said "Amen."

Chapter Eight

Next morning, Christy's mind fled her lessons, leaping from the man in the loft above them to the opening beneath the ledge that she and Thos had found before school. It was too small for her to crawl through, but surrounding cracks in the limestone made them hope the entry could be enlarged. What luck it would be if it led to the passage! Seeing Thos fidget, she knew that he, too, was itching to get to work with a pick and crowbar.

She thought school would never end, although, at noon, Hester Ballard tearfully appeared to say Bishop Jardine and Lafe had come to her house that morning after spending the night at Charles Hamelton's, Jardine's proslavery friend.

"They couldn't find hide nor hair of the runaway," Hester told Ellen Ware. "I'm so mortified Lafe came bothering you that I'm ashamed to show you my face. Can you forgive me?"

"Goodness, Hester, you didn't do anything!" said Ellen, hugging her. "You've always been wonderful to us." She fumbled for words of consolation. "Boys . . . well, they get wild sometimes. . . ."

"I couldn't stop him hanging around Watt Caxton," Hester lamented. She drew a tremulous breath. "That's why I decided to let him go with Bishop Jardine. I'm hoping being away from home . . . driving a team and being with a lot of men . . . will straighten him out."

How good it would be not to look up to find him staring at her scar. Christy swallowed a glad exclamation, relief tempered with sympathy for Hester.

Ellen pressed the other woman's hand. "Work, earning some wages, may be just what he needs, dear. You'll miss him, but, at that age, it's hard to keep them at home. Look at our Charlie."

Somewhat comforted, Hester went out with the rest of them to admire the progress Ethan Ware and Lige Morrow had made on the well. "Ground's getting damp," Ethan said. "With luck, we'll hit water tomorrow. That was a mighty fine water witch, to locate this place that goes down between the rocks. Where'd you say he was from?"

"North of Trading Post," said Jonathan vaguely. The Hayeses had never given their views on slavery but only the most fanatical Free Staters approved of Brown's slaughter of unarmed men.

Watching Ethan swing the pick made Christy wish he could be enlisted to help clear a way into the hidden river, but that would be too risky. Most people who didn't hold with slavery still wouldn't break the Fugitive Slave Law that made it a crime to aid runaways or not return them to a master. Christy was sure her parents wouldn't burden a friend with any part in Justus's escape unless they knew that friend shared their horror of bondage.

The afternoon dragged. After school was out and Morrow sauntered off with Ethan and his boys, Jonathan got the pick, Christy lugged a crowbar, and Thos brought a shovel.

"Why, it's like that rock was already cracked inside!" Thos cried as Jonathan swung the pick into a fissure and it lengthened and split into shards of crumbling stone. "Here, Christy, give me the crowbar. You clear away the rubble."

Since Thos could put more strength into plying the iron bar, Christy accepted the lowly chore of clearing away the results of her father's and brother's exertions. They chipped and pried and delved till at last a whole slab fell under Jonathan's assault.

The fox's narrow entry broadened enough to accommodate a man and dimly reveal a larger grotto. Moving into it, Jonathan only had to duck his head a little. As their eyes adjusted to the faint light, Thos and Christy exclaimed and pointed at the same instant: "Look!"

Guarded by fantastically shaped stalagmites and stalactites was a narrow opening. Thos squeezed through it.

"Careful, Son," Jonathan warned. "Don't take a step you don't test first and don't go far! Someone will have to go back for a lit candle if it seems we really have something to explore."

Thos's voice floated back, resounding eerily. "It got wider after just a little way, but I'm crawling now. . . ."

"Mind you don't crawl into a pit!" Jonathan called. "Thos, Son, you'd better come back. Christy, run for a candle."

She was on her way when Thos's shout stopped her. "I'm in a *big* place and I hear water!"

Christy's heart leaped high, pounded with relief. That had to be the secret passage! A hiding place, and a safe way for Justus to cross into Kansas.

"Come out," Jonathan commanded Thos. "You and Christy will bring Justus here when it's dark. He can sleep tonight in this chamber. I'll ride over to the mill and ask Simeon Parks if he knows where John Brown is or who else might help a fugitive go north."

Thos rejoined them, and, although he squirmed, Christy couldn't keep from giving him a hug of congratulation.

"Let me bring a candle in the morning and take Justus to the sinkhole by Whistling Point," she begged.

"I found the tunnel," Thos reminded. "Please, Father, don't you want me to take Justus across the line?"

"But *I* found the underground river!" Christy wailed.

"Maybe your mother will think you should both go," Jonathan said, dropping an arm on a shoulder of each. "Now get the spade and crowbar and we'll tell her and Justus the good news."

Justus was for going to the cave immediately to lessen the Wares' danger, but they insisted he stay till night would hide him from any inquisitive eyes. When it was dark, Justus, equipped with quilts, a coat, and socks and shoes of Jonathan's, set out with Christy and Thos who carried food and a candle in a tin lantern.

"Will you be all right?" Christy asked when a pallet was made. The lantern winked in the shifting, wavering shadows, turning the growths from ceiling and floor into grotesque creatures that might at any moment engulf a trespassing mortal.

Fortunately Justus wasn't cursed with her imagination. "Bless you, missy. Soon's you're gone, I'll kneel and thank Jesus and then I'll go to sleep." He smiled his trust. "Nothin' bad's goin' to happen now. I feels it in my bones."

"I'll stay if you want," Thos offered. From the glint in his eyes, he hoped for more adventure.

Justus gave him the gentlest push. "Get on with you, missy, young master! I declare, I slept fine today, but I'm tired again. Don't that beat all when I ain't done a lick of work?"

"Have a good night," said Christy, picking up the lantern.

"We'll come in the morning," added Thos.

Back in the cabin, Christy and her mother knitted while Thos mended a bridle. The baby slept in the little box bed Jonathan had made for her to nap in since her crib was in the other cabin and Ellen wouldn't leave her alone there. It seemed a long time before Jed's whicker and Queenie's answering neigh proclaimed Jonathan's return.

Thos ran out to take charge of Jed. Jonathan came in and bent to kiss Ellen exultantly. "Simeon Parks will hide Justus till John Brown can spirit him north. Christy, young Dan O'Brien will meet you and Thos and Justus near Whistling Point in the morning and take him to the mill. That is, if you still want to take him through the cavern. Thos could do it."

"Father! It's *my* cave. And Justus . . . in a way, he's sort of mine, too."

"You feel responsible for him, dear." Ellen touched her cheek and smiled. "You and Thos will both go, then, but you'll hurry back so we won't have our hearts in our mouths. And now, Jonathan, it's time we had our prayers and got to bed."

Eating buttered corn pones and carrying some for Justus, Christy and Thos made their way to the fox cave in the first gray light. They had an extra candle as well as the one in the lantern, lit from the fireplace.

Christy smothered a cry as a shadow moved from beneath the ledge. Once again, it was Justus. "You look like angels, you do for sure." He smiled lop-sidedly. "I slept sound after you left last night but an ole hootie-owl woke me up. Been in a cold sweat ever since."

Christy gave him the warm corn pones. "It's all taken care of, Justus. A Quaker family that has a mill over in Kansas will keep you till someone can take you north." She lit the spare candle off the one in the lantern. That way, if one flickered out, they'd have the other. She handed the lantern to Justus and flourished her candle. "Let's go."

The river was a flow of dark melted sky, narrowing between stalagmites spearing into stalactites, sometimes eddying almost to the feet of the intruders in this secret world. The atmosphere was warmer than outside, but Christy shivered to remember how Dan had tested and picked their way in utter blackness, that desperate underground journey when it had been far from certain they'd find a way out.

He'd be waiting for them. That made the blood dance happily through her veins. She hoped he'd think she was a little bit brave even though she'd been nervous of his foot log across the Marais des Cygnes, and she couldn't ride after Border Ruffians the way he had. If that sort of trouble kept on. . . .

Don't let there be a war, she prayed silently. *Not a war with Dan and Thos and Charlie and Matthew fighting, maybe even Ethan and Father and Andy McHugh and Owen Parks. . . . Please, not a war! Let the slaves go free without that.*

"I was this way before!" she called back to Justus. "It's not much farther."

"Christy?"

The voice reverberated through the passage, but even sepulchrally magnified she knew it. Her heart seemed to burst right out of her and fly to him. "Dan!"

Rounding a rose-streaked pinnacle, she saw him, hair aflame with light spilled from the sky above, the blessed, shining, blue sky that lit his smile as he came forward.

He looked taller, not so thin, although it was only two months since she'd seen him. "You . . . you've piled rocks right up close to the top," she said.

He chuckled. "As I remember, you didn't favor being pulled up by the wrists."

Christy's face heated. If he remembered that, did he recall how she'd thrown her arms around him? Turning from his grin, she said: "Justus, this is Dan O'Brien. He'll take you to the mill."

"That I will not." Dan put out his hand. After a moment's hesitation, a dark one accepted it and brown eyes looked into gray ones. "It's to John Brown himself I'm taking you, Mister Justus. He's waiting at Andy McHugh's with a wagon. They'll take you to Reverend Corder, who's part of the Underground Railroad in Lawrence."

Justus took a sighing breath. "It's too good . . . too good to believe! You . . . both of you young masters, and you, missy, you're all too good. . . ."

"You've got to get out of the habit of calling white men 'master'," Dan growled. He glanced up through the glory of rust sycamore leaves and the golden ones of oak. "Sooner we go, the sooner you'll be out of Kansas, Justus, and into the free states."

"Amen to that, young mas. . . ." Justus checked himself. A smile widened his face. "Dan, point me the way to go. Now I'm out of Missouri, I reckon there's not a hound or slave hunter can catch me." He gripped Thos's and Christy's hands between his big ones, squeezed them hard and long. "Bless you, young 'uns, and your mama and daddy and little baby sister. Bless you all. I'll pray every day for you the rest of my natural born life."

He climbed up the pile of stones that shifted here and there beneath his weight. Dan followed lightly. "You can walk back outside," he suggested to Christy and Thos. "Save your candles."

So, after all, he did give Christy a hand up and squeezed hers hard before he let her go and started briskly toward Whistling Point and the blacksmith's.

★ ★ ★ ★ ★

Seth Cooley, Mordecai Jardine's partner, squinted over his ledger as he figured out Charlie's pay. "Can't keep you busy all the time," he drawled, scanning Charlie with keen gray eyes, "but, if you'd like to winter at my farm outside of town and do some short hauls with mules, you'd get room and board and a dollar a day when you're freighting. Jim Mabry's a tough wagon master, but he speaks well of you. Hopes you'll freight with him next year."

"That's real good of Mister Mabry." Charlie hesitated. During the winter, he couldn't be much use at home. That dollar a day even part of the time sounded pretty good. But although Bishop Jardine hadn't spelled it out, Charlie knew he was expected to see Travis Jardine safely home and, while on night guard he'd watched the Big Dipper, he'd dreamed of Melissa Jardine's shining eyes, the fleeting, just one-time brush of her fingers on his arm.

He wanted to see his own family, too. He'd thought of them often, especially his mother and Christy, as he walked beside his oxen or rolled up in his blankets to keep the mosquitoes off or wished he had cool buttermilk to drink instead of brackish water.

"I'd sure like the job, sir. But could I go home first?"

Cooley studied him. "Will you undertake to be back by the middle of December?"

"Sure as I'm alive, I'll be back, Mister Cooley."

"I'll count on you then." The wiry gray-haired man, leather-skinned from years on the trails, opened his safe and counted out more money—gold pieces—than Charlie had ever seen at one time. "Don't flash that around, son. There's plenty of rascals, some of 'em female, who'd cut your throat for just one ten-dollar gold piece." He sighed. "Sorry to say one of the worst is a neighbor of yours. Lafe Ballard."

Charlie frowned. "Lafe? What's he doing here?"

"Seems he helped the bishop chase a slave . . . who got away . . . but Mordecai felt obliged to the kid and hired him, sent him to me." Cooley's mouth tightened. "It's the crack of the whip moves oxen along. No need generally to give one more'n a flick. First day out, Lafe opened a slash down his lead ox's flank. Wagon master fired him then and there."

"Who's he working for now?"

"The devil, mostly, and at that no more than he has to."

"I'm sure not going to tell his mother that. She's a real nice lady."

"Then I pity her. The way that cub hells around, he won't live to grow up."

Charlie dropped the coins in the buckskin pouch that held a few copper cents and some small silver. The gold, he thought, banishing Lafe from his mind, had a special ring, mellow and—well, *golden*.

"The bishop asked me to watch out for a couple of good horses that you and Travis could ride to his place," Cooley said. "They're in the stable at the wagon yard and your saddles are in the shed." He cleared his throat. "Might be a good notion to hunt Travis up and start right now. About the only thing young sprouts your age can do around Independence when they're not working is get into trouble."

Travis could do that without any help. During the freighting trip, Charlie had kept him from shooting at some Indians, who'd come to camp to visit, and smoothed over several arguments that were heating towards fights. Freighters were an independent lot and wouldn't put up with a high-handed pup even if his father paid their wages.

"I want to buy my mother and sister something nice," said Charlie. "If Travis comes in here, sir, will you tell him I'll meet him at the wagon yard in an hour?"

Cooley snorted. "I won't see him again. He drew his wages as soon as the oxen were unyoked yesterday evening. Didn't even help drive them out to my farm for the winter."

Not only that, Travis hadn't helped tote the six, heavy wooden yokes to the warehouse. Leaving them where he'd taken them off the oxen, he'd simply vanished. Charlie lugged them to the warehouse, but that was a bone he meant to pick with Travis no matter how he tried to laugh his way out of it.

None of this was for Mr. Cooley's ears, of course, or Bishop Jardine's. *I'm the steady horse they've harnessed the wild colt to,* Charlie thought with a wry grin. *I've dragged him along the best I could, but, if he won't start pulling his share of the load, I'm breaking out of harness.*

"Thank you kindly, sir. I'll be back as soon as I can."

"Good." Cooley offered his hand, just like Charlie was grown up. Charlie shook it, proud and happy, and stepped outside with the soft clink of his first earned money like music in his ears.

Independence, the seat of Jackson County, was four miles from the Missouri River and boasted about 3,000 inhabitants, a number of two-storied brick buildings, a log courthouse, a ferry, and a teeming dock where steamships unloaded, but its real fame lay in vying with St. Joseph and Council Bluffs as the jumping-off point for the West where travelers and wagon trains outfitted for the Oregon and Santa Fé Trails. A weekly mail stagecoach ran from here to Santa Fé, and there was a monthly mail stage to Salt Lake City. Blacksmiths shod mules and molded iron braces for ox yokes; Weston's factory built wagons to endure the rutted tracks and hazardous river crossings; wheelwrights made and repaired wheels, and merchants stocked everything westbound settlers needed to get there and make a start.

The town was much less crowded now than when Charlie left it in late August. The last emigrant trains had rolled out months ago, of course, and long-distance freighting was winding up for the winter as wagon masters brought in their outfits. Still, the streets were filled with a prosperous bustle. A new brick bank building was going up and Charlie heard one onlooker brag that it would have three stories.

What would his mother and Christy like best? Keeping an eye out for Travis as he went in and out of shops, Charlie regretfully decided against an ornate gilded soup tureen and a porcelain angel with unfurled wings. Neither would be safe behind his saddle. The biggest mercantile solved his problem with a grand array of fabrics but impaled him on the thorn of deciding which cloth to buy.

"You fancy that velvet, sonny?" A plump, gray-haired woman bore down on him as he reached out to touch a beautiful material that reminded him of moss, except that it was dark red.

He jerked back, but stood his ground, emboldened by his earnings. "I . . . I'm looking for some nice cloth for my mother and sister, ma'am. Can you wash this velvet stuff with lye soap and creek water?"

She flinched. "Gracious no, dearie!" She looked him over and drew conclusions which Charlie was sure flattered neither him nor his home. "What most ladies like," she said kindly, "is something pretty for church and parties but that won't be ruined if you spill something on it and won't show every little spot and smudge."

The woman pulled half a dozen bolts out where he could see them. "Calico and gingham cost the least and wear well. Can't go wrong with either." Sarah Morrow had looked like a brilliant flower in her red calico, but Charlie sensed it wouldn't be that becoming for his mother. "This poplin wears well, but I can tell by your face you don't want brown."

"They wear brown homespun mostly."

The woman nodded. "This Scotch plaid flannel is warm. The chambray's nice for summer, but you probably want something for all year round."

"Yes'm. I . . . I guess so." Charlie's head was spinning.

"What color are your ladies' eyes and hair?"

"Mother's are dark. Christy . . . um . . . her hair's black, but I think her eyes are blue or maybe gray or. . . ."

"Complexion?" Charlie stared. The woman elaborated. "Are they fair or rosy or a bit sallow or olive?"

"I don't think they're exactly rosy." How was he so sure that Melissa Jardine was, that her brown hair sparkled with reddish lights, and her eyes were the color of wild gentians? "Christy forgets her sunbonnet so she's sort of brown in the summer. They have nice skin, though," he added defensively. "Smooth and no lumps or spots."

"I may have just the thing . . . if there's enough of it." The woman bent to produce the remains of a bolt from beneath the counter. "This azure foulard should look well on both of them."

The glowing twilight blue was patterned with small scrolls and flowers. Charlie thought it marvelous. But it was so shiny and soft. "Will it wash all right, ma'am?"

"Yes, taking care, of course, for it's silk. No hot water and just a little soft soap. How big are the ladies?"

"Christy's no lady, ma'am, she's . . . well, I guess she just turned thirteen. She's skinny and comes about to here." He measured below his collarbone. "Mother has to look up at me a little."

"She's taller than me?"

128

"Maybe a tad. But she's . . . ," he broke off.

"Not as fat," finished the woman merrily. "There should be enough material. When you're cutting out two dresses, you can use cloth that would be scraps, otherwise, and can piece where it won't show. I can give you a bargain since it's the end of the bolt. And you'll want thread and buttons, and perhaps braid or ruching for trim."

"Whatever you think, ma'am. I'm mightily obliged."

"A pleasure, dear. Your mother and sister are lucky. Tell them that for me. Anything else?"

Boots, a leather coat, and a blue flannel shirt took a second gold piece. He couldn't flaunt his new things without getting Thos and his father flannel for shirts. Beth would love that cuddly lamb, and he should get some candy. A final yearning pushed then to the front of his mind.

Would Melissa Jardine think him presumptuous if he brought her a present? Would her parents object? She didn't need anything, he knew that, yet somehow he burned to get her something with his first earned money.

As he studied ribbons, artificial flowers, and trinkets, the store lady asked: "Do you need a nice gift for a special young lady?"

He blushed and jerked his head first yes, then no. "I . . . I mean, if there's the kind of thing that wouldn't give offence, ma'am."

"Well, there's these lovely embroidered hankies."

Maybe he should get them for Mrs. Jardine so it wouldn't seem peculiar he had a gift for Melissa. Then he saw just the thing, a translucent gold-brown stone with a reddish hue to its depths, the color of her hair. The polished oval was rimmed with plain gold and had a simple gold chain. He pointed at it. "Would that be all right, ma'am?"

"Jewelry gifts shouldn't be expensive unless you're engaged, but the amber isn't costly." She laughed. "I wouldn't look down my nose at you if you gave it to *my* daughter."

He took it and the hankies. When he left the store, arms full of parcels, cheek swelled with peppermints thrown in for a good customer, he'd spent $22 and couldn't have said whether he was more horrified or delighted. He did know one thing. It was a thrill to be able to buy things without worrying over every cent, and it was mightily gratifying to hear even the diminished jingle of his two remaining gold pieces among the copper and silver.

"Well, look at the big spender!"

Something tripped Charlie. He went sprawling, frantically trying not to let his purchases fall in the mud. The one with the azure material squeezed out of his arms and bounced in front of a carriage.

Still on his knees, Charlie lunged forward and grabbed for the bundle. The carriage splattered mud on it and him in his new coat, but the front wheel rolled over just the edge of the parcel.

The driver called back—"Sorry!"—but didn't stop. In a torment to see if the material was much hurt, Charlie peered inside the torn, muddied wrapping and rejoiced.

Bless the store lady. She'd wrapped several layers of newspapers around the cloth before tying it up in brown paper. The wheel had destroyed some of the paper but hadn't reached the fabric.

Then he saw Lafe Ballard. The eager light in those cold eyes, the twist of the girlish lips, told Charlie the tripping had not been accidental. He took off his coat, spread it on a pile of crates, placed his packages carefully on top of it, and smashed Lafe's grinning mouth.

"Hey!" Backing away, Lafe spat blood. More poured from his nose. "Can't you take a joke?"

"Here's one for you!" Charlie hit him again.

Lafe staggered, reached inside his coat. A knife flashed, a Bowie with both edges honed. People were gathering, including the store lady who held open the door and cried: "Run in here, son! Your mother. . . ."

Charlie would have obeyed. The knife froze him to the marrow. But he remembered a trick he'd seen in a fight between two teamsters. Swerving out of Lafe's way, he kicked up. There was a cracking sound as his new boot struck Lafe's wrist. At the same instant that shoulder was seized from behind and Lafe, howling, was swung around to meet Travis Jardine's fist to the jaw as the knife dropped to the street.

Charlie picked it up and wiped it off. "Guess this makes us even for the mess you made of my things."

"You . . . you broke my wrist!" screeched Lafe. "I'll get even! I'll. . . ."

A man in a dark coat with a gold watch fob across an ample front stepped up and took Lafe by the arm. "I'm a doctor and my office is next door. Come in and I'll see what I can do."

"Can you pay the doctor, Lafe?" asked Charlie.

"What's it to you?" snarled the other.

"I'll pay if you can't."

"Damned goody-good!"

The doctor gave Charlie a gentle push. "Go along, lad. I'll work things out with this young polecat. Maybe break his other wrist."

Refusing offers to buy him a drink from several rough-looking men who looked like they'd had too many, Charlie caught his breath and looked at Travis. "I'm glad you came along."

Travis laughed joyously, brown eyes sparkling. "So am I. Paid you back some for being such a good mama hen."

He exuded a smell that was a little like flowers and more like sweat. Charlie frowned. "Did you stay at your aunt's last night?"

Travis's surprised stare gave him away, although he recovered with a chuckle and affectionate smack on Charlie's shoulder. "She's someone's aunt, I'm bound, Charles."

Charlie frowned harder, remembering his night in the barn at the wagon yard and the way Travis had left his yokes on the ground. Travis gave him a playful cuff on the ear. "Well, old fellow, what was I to tell you without getting a sermon?"

Keeping low company was supposed to make a person get sick and look awful, but Travis was bursting with vim, and somehow, although he was a few months younger than Charlie, he suddenly seemed older, closer to being a man. What had he done last night?

"You didn't put your yokes away," Charlie began. "You told me a flat out lie. You. . . ."

"Oh, come along!" Gaily Travis took some of the packages and set off at an easy lope. "You can preach on the way. Since it'll take us four days to get home, that ought to give you all the time you need."

Chapter Nine

Except for timber-fringed swollen creeks across which they often had to swim their horses, Charlie and Travis rode mostly across lonesome prairie except for a chain of small settlements between Harrisonville and West Point where they crossed into Kansas to pick up the Military Road and were soon in wooded country.

They crossed the Marais des Cygnes at Trading Post. A few new cabins had been built on old foundations but others lay in charred ruins. At the Little Osage, they left the road for the ruts that led through the wintry forest to the Jardines.

Fallen leaves, some still scarlet, orange, and yellow, muffled the horses' hoofs. Trees were bare except for cedars, clumps of glossy mistletoe high in the tops of elm trees, and the black-barked black jack oak that would keep most of its fading red-brown leaves till spring, providing shelter for birds and the squirrel tribe. The colors of the timber came from trunks and limbs, a different beauty from summer's lushness or autumn's glory, but strong like bones stripped of flesh. Oaks were many hues from the pale gray of white oak to the black or dark brown of post oak. The red brown bark of young river birches stood out against the silvery white young sycamores, the white branches and yellow-brown trunks of old ones, the deep gray of hickories and dark brown of walnut.

"Did you get your mother and sister anything?" Charlie asked

Travis's eyes widened. "Why? Father takes them to Saint Louis every year to shop and visit my sister. Anything they need in between trips, he'll get in Osceola or Nevada, the Vernon county seat." He opened his coat to show a revolver in a new holster. "At least I've got this to show for my wages. Good thing I bought it before I got into that poker game . . . and other things."

Charlie well knew the Jardine ladies didn't need anything. Travis's attitude made him feel like a fool for daring to hope they'd appreciate his modest gifts. "You've been away," he floundered. "Some little thing would show you'd thought about them."

Travis sighed. "Preaching Charlie! I guess you bought something for your mother and sister."

"Yes," said Charlie, riling. "And my brother and father, too."

After a bemused stare, Travis laughed. "If I brought Pa something, he'd think I'd done something awful and was trying to put him in good temper before he heard about it."

They rode a few minutes in silence when a buzzing sound swelled gradually into a roar.

"Wild pigeons!" yipped Travis. "I'll try out my Colt. Take a bunch home for supper." He gave Charlie a triumphant grin. "That'll be my present!"

Drawing his revolver, he urged his horse forward. Amidst squeaking and tittering, a vast cloud of shimmering wings rose from the ground, then swooped low. Thousands of slate-blue heads ducked to catch up acorns in slender black bills while light played on crimson eyes and feet and glimmers of gold, violet, and rosy purple on the sides and back of necks. As far through the trees as Charlie could see surged a feathered ocean, gray and blue on their backs as the birds swept down, russet or wine throat to belly as they winged up, flashing white from belly to tail.

Migrating flights had passed over their farm in Illinois but Charlie had never seen pigeons feeding, or up close. How Christy would love this. Father would have called it one of the wonders of God. So enthralled was Charlie that the crash of the gun startled him almost as much as it did the birds.

They rose in a swirling whir through the roof of great oaks, but not before the revolver downed four more. Travis swung down and tossed his reins to Charlie.

"Good shooting if I do say so." He stroked the revolver before he holstered it. "Look! Blew the heads off two of them."

What Charlie saw were two birds flopping helplessly with shattered wings. He hitched both horses' reins over a dead tree, took the smallish heads, one at a time, and wrung the glistening necks. He could barely see through blinked-back mist in his eyes. Going back to his horse, he mounted and rode on.

Why was he so upset? He'd killed chickens, helped slaughter hogs. But to see the dazzle and radiant power of wings changed to bloody gobs of feathers—it was like fragmenting a joyous anthem into obscene curses.

"These won't be as tasty as spring squabs, but they'll go down well, fried in butter." Travis came abreast with Charlie in the silenced woods. He'd tied the pigeons' crimson legs with the rawhide strings behind his saddle.

Two on one side. Three on the other. Spread out, those drooping wings had spanned two feet of boundless air. Charlie counted twelve tapering feathers in each graceful tail. These had white edging, as if an artist had spared no pains to perfect the pattern.

Too full of the merits of his new gun to notice Charlie's

mood, Travis chattered till they rode out of the forest into the cleared fields of what he proudly declared the Jardine plantation.

"When the hands don't have something else to do, Pa puts them to clearing land." Travis waved an arm around the vista that included fields on both sides of the river, a large, rambling, white, two-story house with a verandah and lots of glass windows, numerous outbuildings, and about a dozen log cabins, each with a good-size garden patch. "We grow hemp, tobacco, and a little cotton," Travis went on. "Of course, we raise nearly all our food and sell corn, hogs, and the best mules in Missouri."

Charlie gulped. "It's sure a big place."

"Oh, not as plantations go." Travis shrugged with the worldly wise smile that so irritated Charlie. "The big ones in this state are along the Mississippi and Missouri. But when Melissa and I marry and take up land, Rose Haven will be right considerable."

"Rose Haven?"

"That's what Mama named it. Before she'd move out here, Pa had to promise she'd have a prettier rose garden than she did near Saint Louis . . . and she does."

Charlie thought of his own mother who'd nursed the climbing rose at their Illinois home till it ran all along the front porch. She'd be thrilled now with just one rose bush. And how crazy he'd been even to think of offering gifts to the women of Rose Haven. At least, he could give the presents to his mother. He wished he'd asked Travis to lead his mount here—that he himself had struck off afoot from Trading Post. Then he could have gone on hoping that Melissa Jardine might like him a little.

"Is your house built with milled lumber?" he asked, deciding he might as well swallow the worst.

136

"Lordy, no! When we first got here six years ago, we lived in a couple of log cabins with a breezeway between. More were added on and the slaves rived out clapboards to nail inside and out." He chuckled. "In spite of the verandah, Mama says that underneath it's still a plain old log cabin."

"Not very plain." Charlie decided he couldn't much like Mrs. Jardine. Sounded like she was spoiled rotten.

"Our trees bore fruit for the first time summer before last," Travis said as they rode past scores of young trees. "We've got apples, peaches, pears, plums, and cherries. Grapes, too, and the biggest, juiciest strawberries you ever ate. Too bad they're out of season or we'd have them with shortcake and cream."

As they neared the stables, a spraddle of hounds rose up and eyed them although they didn't bark. "Now whose could they be?" Travis frowned. "Mama can't abide dogs, so we don't have any."

"Those black and tans look like Watt Caxton's pack." Charlie remembered the way they'd piled into Lige Morrow's hounds at the cabin raising. "But what would Mister Caxton be doing over here?"

At that instant, a scream came from beyond the stables. The hounds erupted. They raced after a streak of gray that could only be a cat, closing in from several directions.

"Emmie! Emmie-e-e!" In a flurry of skirts, Melissa Jardine pelted toward the dogs and the cat that, caught in the open, arched its back and hissed balefully.

It had no chance at all, but it would rip some noses before it was torn apart. Melissa snatched up a fallen branch and flailed at the dogs, shrieking. They shifted out of her way but poised to rush at the cat.

Charlie sprang from the saddle and dived through the hounds, sweeping the cat high in his arms. The snarling, barking dogs leaped for it, tearing his sleeves and gashing his arms. He kicked through them and ran toward the stable with the cat clawing him.

A gun barked louder than the pack. Charlie stumbled over an animal that fell with the top of its head blasted. There was another shot, a dog weltering in spilled intestines. Then Watt Caxton was panting from the direction of the house, the bishop in his wake.

Cursing and kicking the hounds, Caxton subdued them. Melissa came up to take the spitting, scratching cat from Charlie. It had bit him repeatedly on the hands, and the dogs had gashed his arms.

"You damn' fool!" Travis was pale. "The dogs could have killed you!"

Caxton glowered at his dead hound and the one twitching its last. "No cat's worth two good hounds!"

"My cat's worth your whole pack!" Melissa blazed. Her deep blue eyes widened as she saw Charlie's hurts. "You're bleeding! Your coat's all torn! Oh, you were brave!"

The look in her eyes paid him a hundred times for his pain and the ruination of his sleeves. She caught his upper arm and tugged. "Come to the house, boy. Aunt Phronie will fix you up. She's got some wonderful salve!"

"Travis," said the bishop, "go with Charles. Now then, Caxton, you had no business bringing your pack to Rose Haven."

"You've been glad of 'em in the past, Bishop," Caxton whined.

The bishop's voice dropped but Charlie could still hear, although Melissa's closeness and the scent of her curling mass of auburn hair drove even the aching sting of the bites and scratches from his mind. "It's true I may need your hounds again since I keep none, Caxton. For that reason, I'll pay to replace these two. But never bring them on my property again unless you're told to and they're on chains."

Why would the bishop hire Caxton and his dogs? Not for 'coon hunting, that was sure. Unwillingly Charlie remembered the runaway Lafe Ballard had helped chase. Lafe hung around Watt Caxton. Had Caxton's pack trailed the fugitive?

With his flesh torn by the hounds' teeth, Charlie felt sick at the notion of a man chased by a pack as if he were a 'coon or fox, and he'd never liked that, either. His revulsion faded, though, with the warmth of Melissa's hand on his shoulder, the scent of her clothing and hair.

"In here." Travis steered him into a clapboarded cabin behind the big house. "We have the kitchen out here so that if there's a fire the main house won't burn."

Melissa ran in first, putting the gray cat on the sunny windowsill with a final caress. "What do you have for dog bites and cat scratches, Aunt Phronie? That nasty Watt Caxton's dogs would have killed Emmie if Charlie hadn't saved her."

"Well, child," snapped a tiny, yellow-skinned woman in a starched white apron, "don't let him bleed all over my floor. Here, honey boy, drip over this bucket while I fix some soft soap with warm water."

Charlie! Melissa had called him by name, not "Charles" or "boy" or "young man". He felt he could float right through the roof, but Aunt Phronie had him sit on a footstool and lower his arms into a tub of soapy water that was hot enough to make him yelp.

"Never mind, honey," adjured Aunt Phronie. "The heat helps draw out poison. Miss M'liss, fetch me some clean rags. You get yourself in to see your mama, Master Trav. She's been missin' you, Lord knows why, and you're just in my way."

Having disposed of her young master and mistress, the spry little woman held a sweetened mug of coffee with cream to Charlie's lips. "Gettin' chewed on's a shock to the system," she told him. Her hazel eyes were red-rimmed, probably from the constant smoke of the kitchen's great fireplace. "This'll perk you up." She glanced severely at Emmie, lying still and soaking up sun as if she hadn't ten minutes ago been in peril of at least her first life. "Miss M'liss is plumb foolish about that silly cat, but why you should be . . . ?"

"Miss Melissa ran to help the cat. I was afraid she'd be hurt." He didn't want to admit that he couldn't watch the cat be torn apart.

"Mmph." Aunt Phronie lifted his arm, lowered it gently, and nodded. "Still bleeding. That's good. What's bad with animal bites, or human either, is li'l bittie punctures that breed pus and corruption and maybe blood poisoning. You'll take these scars to your grave, but at least they won't *be* your grave."

"Sorry to make you so much trouble, ma'am."

She looked startled, almost scared. "Lord, honey, don't call me that! I'm Aunt Phronie. Anyhow, this ain't a patch on the mess we'd have with my missie if the hounds got her blamed kitty."

Melissa hurried in with an armful of snowy cloth that looked like it'd been cut or torn from good sheets or such. Charlie had watched his mother and sister card and spin and weave too much not to be aghast at such waste.

"Oh, don't use that good cloth!" he protested. "There's an old shirt in my things. . . ."

Aunt Phronie ignored him. "Make a pad for each arm," she instructed Melissa as she herself selected a cloth bag from a number hanging in the darkest corner. "I'll grind this inside bark of slippery elm and mix it with water till it's all soft and spongy. That'll sop up blood and help the wounds heal. Hold up your right arm, honey boy. We'll fix it first."

"Your poor arm!" cried Melissa as blood trickled down to drip into the water.

"Aw, it's not bad," Charlie scoffed, although in spite of the coffee he felt sort of weak and dizzy.

"Missie, put the pad on soon as I have the bark in place," said Aunt Phronie. She wiped Charlie's arm and molded the pulpy mass of wet bark over the gashes. Melissa held the pad while the old woman wound a cotton strip around the arm.

"Your arms'll feel better with slings holdin' 'em," Aunt Phronie said, and grinned a little. "You'll be a sight, though, both arms tied up."

Charlie grinned back. "Well, I just hope I don't meet a bear while I'm walking home."

"You're not walking home!" Melissa decreed. "Trav will take you, but you're not going till we're sure you're all right. Is he, Mama?" She turned to the slender woman who came in supported by a cane and Travis's arm.

"Charles is surely welcome as long as he'll stay." Mrs. Jardine's voice was surprisingly resonant for such a frail woman. Her eyes were not the brilliant blue of Melissa's but a softer shade, and her hair was silver with the faintest hint of brown. Dimples showed in both cheeks. "I fear neither of us can shake hands easily, Charles, but I am delighted to meet you."

He was already on his feet, arms awkward in front of him even though Aunt Phronie had tied one sling a bit higher than the other. His uninjured hands rested at the sling edges.

He inclined his head and groped for something fitting to say to her. He could see why she had her roses and anything else. When he'd been here overnight before, he and Travis had left for Independence, and he'd only known she was ailing. No one had said she was crippled.

141

"The pleasure is mine, Missus Jardine." He hoped that sounded proper. "I'm fine, though. No need for a fuss. Please. . . ." He didn't want her on her feet because of him, but he didn't know how to say it.

"Come into the house, then," she invited, turning with a slight limp. "Phronie, will you have Lilah bring cheese biscuits, or something tasty, to the conservatory?"

She was leaning heavily on her son and the cane by the time she entered the door Melissa held open, and sank down in a wicker chair on wheels. She smiled, though, as she gestured at a rustic bench and other chairs.

"Sit down, Charles. Travis, ask your father to bring our guest a medicinal brandy. No, none for you, dear. *You* weren't bitten."

Settling on the bench—funny how a person's balance was affected by having both arms secured in front—Charlie gazed about in wonder. Clapboarded log walls rose waist high on the south side, but panels like long, glass windows stretched from there to the roof that covered the other half of the sunny room. Two large windows were cut in the north wall. Roses climbed trellises to the roof, flourished in half barrels, and rioted in a wide log planter built along the southern wall to catch the sun.

"It's . . . it's like fairyland, Missus Jardine," blurted Charlie.

Indeed, except for the aching sting of his arms, he felt as if he had been magicked into another world, one whose queen was this woman with moon-bright hair, one where Melissa was a princess who smiled on him.

The roses were every hue from ivory and yellow to bronze and crimson. Their odor fuddled the senses. One end of the roofed section was latticed into a cage for two green-glistening birds that turned yellow heads with orange cheeks toward the humans and chattered grumpily. Charlie had chased flocks like them out of the corn that summer and knew they were Carolina parakeets.

They raised a din when a green-eyed, honey-skinned girl of perhaps Melissa's age brought in a tray of tiny golden biscuits, salted nuts, cubes of cheese, and slices of pickle. Charlie filled the small plate she offered and tried not to make a pig of himself.

Lilah had to have more white blood than black. How white did you have to be before it would seem strange for you to be a slave? There'd been plenty of white-skinned slaves in Greece and Rome. Why had American slaveholders decided only black people should be slaves?

His hostess' pleasant voice snapped this train of thought. "Soon now a roof that shelters the glass from snow will be fitted to the permanent one and reach out to those posts. The posts *are* there, four of them, though they're covered with honeysuckle and jasmine. Except on cloudy, bitter days, the glass still gets enough sun to warm this room nicely." She smiled at the birds that were attacking apples with their pale yellow beaks. "If it gets cold, Hither and Yon squawk till someone fetches braziers of coals."

"I found that pair in the bottom of a hollow tree after . . . well, after I cleared out a swarm that was tearing up our apples and pears," said Travis.

The bishop appeared in the doorway, holding two glasses. He strode to his wife and put one of the glasses in her hand. The atmosphere of the rose room changed. It was as if the flowers dimmed and their scent faded. The parakeets hushed and the sunlight altered.

"That Caxton rascal! Naturally those hounds you shot, Travis, became blue-bloods, the pride of his pack. If I didn't need him for certain things. . . ."

Mrs. Jardine drew her shawl more closely around her. "I don't trust that man, my dear."

"Lige Morrow has hounds," Charlie said, and then wished he hadn't. He couldn't imagine Lige tracking slaves, but there was no use tempting him.

The bishop shook his head. "Morrow and I can't agree." Jardine's gaze swept over Charlie's bandages. The glimmer of a smile touched his lips. "I see Phronie's been at you. Hurt much?" Before Charlie could answer, the bishop offered him a glass. "Brandy and water, lad. It'll help. Another stiff one at bedtime and you should feel pretty fair by morning."

"Oh, I can't stay over, sir, thank you," Charlie stammered. "I need to get home."

"Stay at least the night," Mrs. Jardine urged. "We want to be sure the bites won't cause serious trouble. Besides"—here she smiled at her husband and children—"tomorrow's our twenty-fifth anniversary. Please stay and help us celebrate."

"Please!" importuned Melissa.

"I have to help get in the winter wood and shuck corn before I go back to work for Mister Cooley."

"So Seth wants you to go on short hauls?" inquired Jardine. "That's as a good recommendation as there is."

"You can't cut or chop wood till your arms heal a little," argued Travis. "Listen, Charlie, if you miss Aunt Phronie's special cake and syllabub . . . well, I pity you."

A day or two wouldn't hurt. Charlie looked at Mrs. Jardine.

"If you're sure, ma'am. . . . But I don't have any good clothes."

"You can wear some of mine," said Travis. "No fear of your busting out the seams."

"Take Charles to Miles's room," Mrs. Jardine told her son. "That'll be the quietest after Yvonne and Henry arrive with their little ones. That's my daughter from Saint Louis," she explained. "I expected them before now, but it's quite a journey, especially with the children."

"Especially with *those* children," Travis muttered once they were out of earshot. "Vonne lets them rampage through the house like a tribe of monkeys, and Henry pays them no mind unless they tread on his toes."

"Maybe they'll have tamed down since you saw them," Charlie suggested.

"I wouldn't bet on it," Travis growled before he flashed a grin. "And I sure do like to bet."

There was no missing the arrival of the St. Louis family. Racketing footfalls and shrill voices filled the wide hall. After considerable banging of doors, the uproar moved outside and faded with distance except for an occasional extra loud shriek or bellow.

Charlie was amazed, when Travis called him for supper, to be seated near four seraphic blond children who smiled on him benignly while translucent eyelids drooped over sky blue eyes.

Mrs. Jardine presented Charlie to Yvonne and Henry Benton. Slender Yvonne's high-piled auburn curls were striking with her creamy skin and sapphire eyes. Her fair-haired husband was large, slow-moving, and frequently emitted a rumbling laugh.

"Starting with the big girl at the end, the grandchildren are Rebecca, Annette, James, and Tod," said their grandmother, beaming.

Charlie tried not to stare as he murmured his—"Pleased to meet yous." How could these well-behaved if sleepy children, ranging from Rebecca's perhaps six to toddler James, be the same ones clambering through the hall?

"It's belladonna," Travis whispered in Charlie's ear. "Without it, they won't settle down to eat. Aunt Phronie thought of it when Vonne's doctor couldn't figure something out."

So peace reigned through soup, vegetables, ham, chicken, and a special dish of Travis's pigeons. Charlie passed them on. He still felt a pang to remember the sheen of thousands of wings dipping and lifting.

"So you never got back that hand you bought out of Indian Territory?" Henry Benton said to his father-in-law.

"He may wish he was back when he finds out Yankee hearts are cold as their weather," shrugged the bishop. He frowned. "I still can't see how he gave us the slip, unless someone hid him." He examined Charlie with piercing russet eyes. "Your folks likely don't hold with slavery."

"No, sir, they don't."

"Mordecai," began Mrs. Jardine, "please. . . ."

"Don't fret, Vinnie," her husband soothed. To Charlie he said: "You'd oblige me, lad, by taking a good look at how our people live and telling your parents about it."

Relieved at such a reasonable request, Charlie nodded. "I can surely do that, sir."

Melissa smiled at him. His heart swelled till he thought it would carry him right through the roof and into the sky.

The cabins had hard-packed dirt floors like many settlers' houses, but these were cozy with braided rag rugs or sheepskins and the beds were spread with good quilts. There was a chest at the foot of each bed and pegs held clothing. Several chairs and a bench faced the fireplace.

"Single hands sleep four to a cabin," the bishop explained. "They can cook for themselves or eat at the cook house. Couples have cabins to themselves, of course. Phronie lives in the double cabin near the kitchen with her granddaughter, Lilah, four unmarried older women who work in the house, and my wife's bedridden old nurse, Aunt Zillah.'"

"I don't see any children around, sir."

"No. I don't keep brood mares and I don't keep breeding women. Only consider, lad. Children are a total loss, eating their heads off and wearing out clothes, till they're at least nine or ten. They don't pay their keep till they're thirteen or fourteen. A hand's in his prime from full growth at seventeen or eighteen till about thirty. With luck, he'll do a full day's work for another twenty years, and can perhaps be useful another ten years, but, after that, he has to be fed and housed till he dies."

"I suppose it is a problem," Charlie admitted.

"One Northern factory owners don't have," Jardine snorted. "If their workers don't have enough to eat, and sicken or die, they're replaced by other poor people, and God help them when they're too old to work. Of the three men now living on my bounty, one was ever stiff-necked and rebellious. The others were good hands. Sam gave me a full thirty years labor and ten of half time. He's earned his pork and corndodgers. But poor Titus was gored by a bull when he was forty-five and hasn't been fit for anything since but mending harness and making shoes." The bishop blew out his cheeks. "Instead of buying new hands, I think I'll hire them. There are always planters with more men than they need who'll let them work somewhere else for about a hundred dollars a year and board." He grimaced. "Where there's plenty of cheap Irish and German help to be had, they do the dangerous work. No one wants to lose an expensive slave."

"You might try what my father says a North Carolina planter found good," suggested Charlie. "He discharged his overseer and told his people, if they worked well, he'd split the overseer's salary amongst them at the end of the year. They worked better than they ever had, cheerfully, too. Some saved up to buy their freedom."

Jardine frowned. "They must have been older ones who were going to start costing the owner in a few years. I hope those darkies went North. It's not right to have free Negroes living where they'll give slaves rebellious notions. Nat Turner. . . ." He shuddered.

Charlie went cold at the very mention of that slave uprising twenty-five years ago in Virginia. Nat Turner's God led him to gather about seventy other slaves and murder fifty-five white men, women, and children as they swept through the county. Turner was hanged, of course, with eighteen other rebels.

"I think it waste and aggravation to raise pickaninnies," went on the bishop. "The boys in whom carnal nature burns have found wives at nearby farms." He laughed at Charles's unspoken question. "Bless you, the wenches' owners think it a fine thing to increase their work force so the arrangement suits everybody."

Except the married couples who couldn't live together. The voices floating from the gin house were joking and light-hearted, though, and three men in the carpenter shop whistled as they sawed and hammered. An old man in a cabin smelling of leather hummed over a sole he was shaping to a last. The blacksmith hammered out some kind of tool while his helper pumped the bellows. Delicious odors permeated the air around the cook house, and women's bantering voices drifted out.

Bishop Jardine surveyed his kingdom and smiled. "I hope you'll tell your father what you see here, Charles. All my servants are well fed, well clothed, and housed as snugly as most whites. They're nursed through sickness and cared for when they age. All are baptized and attend the services I hold every Sunday." He gave a wry laugh. "Perhaps you know that in the 'Forties, the Baptists, Presbyterians, and my own Methodist church split North and South over slavery, but I'll defend the institution against any blue-nosed Northern preacher." He gestured at the peaceful scene. "Tell me true, son. Aren't these darkies happier and better off under my care than they would be if they were freed and left to shift for themselves?"

Charlie didn't want to anger Jardine but he knew what his father would say. It was on his lips before he knew it. "But if they could choose, sir, how many would rather be free?"

The bishop's jaw clamped tight. " 'Free' echoes finely in the ears. I've no doubt pernicious whispers of Abolitionist rubbish have reached Rose Haven. But you might as well ask ten-year-old children if they want to be free. It would be cruel folly to take them at their word."

"What about Lilah?"

Jardine reddened. "You can see that Phronie is a mulatto," he said after a moment. "Her father was the overseer on my father's plantation and her daughter, Lilah's mother, was the result of a guest's inebriation, the only slave ever born on my property." The bishop sighed. "Her beauty would have tempted even Saint Paul. To avoid . . . problems, I sold her to a neighbor."

"He didn't avoid the problems?"

"No. Lilah's mother died in childbirth. I had let Phronie go help her, of course. Phronie brought home the infant and appealed to my wife, so we had to keep her. To give my neighbor his due, he made my wife a gift of the baby."

"His own daughter!" Charlie gasped.

The bishop turned even redder and made some inarticulate mumble. Charlie thought the neighbor might rather have given his daughter to her grandmother or possibly freed her and sent her to be raised and educated in a convent. It was stirring up a hornet's nest, but Charlie had to speak.

"It doesn't seem fair, sir. Lilah's only one-eighth Negro. Looks like the other seven-eighths would count most." His imagination flashed ahead. "If she has a child by a white man, it'll only be a sixteenth black. If a white fathers a baby on that child, it'll be a thirty-second. Are you claiming a drop of Negro blood has more power than quarts of white?"

"The child of a slave mother is a slave, Charles. Any other system would be pandemonium."

"Sounds like this one is."

The bishop glared a moment, then laid a paternal hand on Charlie's shoulder. "You argue from ignorance and your Universalist upbringing. As a Methodist, I have to give Baptists this much . . . they know slavery is sanctioned by God and is the best means of saving heathen souls. Servitude in this life is a small payment for eternal bliss."

"If slaves go to the same heaven as whites, will they be servants there?"

Jardine blinked, then chuckled. "You've a subtle mind, lad. To be sure, God's mysteries are beyond us, but His word tells us that in heaven there will be no marriage and neither bond nor free. So leave it to Him, and let's get ready for the celebration."

Charlie couldn't wear a coat with his slings, but Travis helped him into a handsome maroon velvet waistcoat and fine wool trousers made by a St. Louis tailor.

"They sag a bit," Travis admitted. "These suspenders will hold them up, though, and won't show under the waistcoat. You should keep these shoes. They pinch my toes and raise blisters on my heels."

"They're just like new. . . ."

"They don't fit. And they sure won't fit Pa or Henry." Travis appraised him. "Your hair looks better now it's washed, but you're shaggy as a shedding buffalo. Aunt Phronie can trim your hair good as any barber."

She did, although in a swivet with preparations for the feast. "Don't you look fine as new paint?" she enthused when she'd finished snipping a bit here and a tad there. "If your arms get to smartin', honey, drink more of the syllabub. For sure and certain, it's more whiskey than cream and eggs. Now take yourselves out of my kitchen, Master Trav. I got rolls to make and the cake to frost and. . . ."

"What kind of cake, Auntie?" Travis peered hungrily at round layers cooling on the table. Charlie thought that, stacked on top of each other, they'd make a cake big enough to feed the whole plantation. Would the slaves get a piece?

"It's Queen Cake, honey, just like my mama made for your mama's wedding. Plenty of wine, brandy, cream, currants, and spices, with six eggs and well nigh a pound of fresh butter to each pound of sugar and flour. I'll use just a tinch of cochineal to make the frosting a real pale pink." She handed each boy several ginger cookies. "Now go along and get in somebody else's way!"

The way they found to get into was Melissa's. While her sister visited with their mother in the conservatory and the Benton children whooped and ambushed each other amongst the arbors and walks of the rose garden, Melissa and Lilah arranged flowers on every available surface in the dining room. Leaves had been added to the table and silver, crystal, and china reflected light from lace-curtained windows.

Fussing with a few bronze roses till they perfectly graced the table's centerpiece, Melissa paused to scrutinize her brother and his friend. "Charlie, you *do* look nice."

He felt his chest expand at her praise. When would he have

a chance to give her the amber necklace? If he had a chance would he dare?

"Trav," she went on in a sisterly chide, "do something with that ridiculous cowlick! Aunt Phronie made Pa some excellent hair grease out of lard and oil of jessamine. Ask him for some. And I hope you remembered to get an anniversary present in Independence . . . at least something for Mama."

Travis squirmed. "I . . . uh. . . . Fellows don't keep things like that in their heads the way you females do."

"Trav!" she wailed. "You forgot!"

He hung his head. Charlie's inner struggle was brief. It would never do for him, an outsider, to have a gift for Lavinia Jardine when her son didn't. "Travis, I've got some nice embroidered handkerchiefs. They aren't much, but if you'd like to give them to your mother. . . ."

Travis looked as if a weight had been lifted off him, but Melissa fiercely demanded: "Were the handkerchiefs for your mother or sister, Charlie?"

He was glad to say truthfully: "No, Miss Melissa. I got them other things. . . ." He halted, realizing that must sink Travis even lower in his younger sister's regard.

"See?" She withered her brother with a dark blue glance. "I declare, Travis Forsyth Jardine. . . ."

"Let's get the hankies," Travis said hastily.

Gentleman farmers from miles around shared the festive dinner—suckling pig, saddle of mutton, wild turkey stuffed with rice and nuts, sirloin of beef, rolls of wheat flour, fluffy whipped potatoes and other vegetables, pickled eggs and onions, and a bewildering array of sauces and relishes, the whole followed by puddings, pies, and the rich, moist Queen Cake.

Aunt Phronie's poultices had drawn much of the soreness from Charlie's wounds. He slipped his right arm out of the

152

sling to use his fork, but Travis cut his meat and Melissa, on his other side, buttered his rolls.

The house servants joined in toasts made with syllabub Jardine ladled from a crystal bowl. Charles recognized the genial heat of brandy and smoothness of cream. His head buzzed as he sipped. It was delicious but he declined a second helping. He'd rather die than slip under Melissa's table in a drunken stupor.

She nodded approvingly at his decision and wrinkled her nose at Travis who gave Lilah his glass to be refilled. "A helping of this is plenty for anyone, Trav."

Travis gave her a superior glance. "My dear little sister, you've never even caught a whiff of the skull varnish freighters drink. I could have half a dozen of these glasses and never show it."

"That's because you act wild all the time!"

"Me? I'll have you know I'm the one who rescued our sober-sided Charlie when he was about to get carved up by a no-account Pa hired and Seth Cooley fired."

To Charlie's embarrassment, she had to hear the story, and by then guests were leaving the table and chatting as they made leisurely farewells. The sun set early this time of year. It was prudent to get home before night, especially if creeks or the river had to be forded.

When the last carriage rolled away, Mrs. Jardine's old nurse, Aunt Zillah, was brought in to recline on a sofa, while Aunt Phronie and the household gathered around. Mrs. Jardine opened gifts that Melissa and Yvonne handed her and passed them on to the bishop to admire.

The distant sons sent presents from Oregon and California: a crate of smoked salmon from Miles, dried figs and pickled olives from Sherrod. Henry puffed out his chest as Yvonne presented their gift, a splendid silver-framed mirror.

The three older Benton children, escorted from their playing by Lilah, offered their gifts with angelic demeanors. Rebecca, holding Annette's hand, put a gilt box of bon-bons into her grandmother's lap. James strode manfully to his grandfather and handed him a box of cigars.

"May I have one, Grandpa?" he besought.

"If your mama allows, you may have a puff," said Jardine gravely. "That could be all you want."

James stuck his tongue out at Rebecca. "I get a puff but you don't 'cause you're just a girl!"

Lilah, catching Rebecca as she screeched and started to kick her brother, quickly hustled the youngest members of the family away. Yvonne brushed a kiss across the bishop's knitted brow. "Aren't they wonderfully high-spirited, Papa? Oh, look, Mama! Auntie Zillah made you this lovely soft shawl! It just matches your eyes."

The frail white-haired woman, face wrinkled as an old potato, raised on an elbow to peer through filmed eyes at her nurseling. "Took Phronie a mort of time to get the dye right." Her proud voice was a wisp of hard-breathed air. "It becomes you, Miss Vinnie, darlin'. It'll warm you in the chill winds."

"She's blind as a bat," Travis whispered.

Charlie knew she saw with the eyes of love, and his own misted. Mrs. Jardine, supported by her husband and son, limped over to embrace and thank her nurse. Melissa's gifts were an embroidered nightgown and nightshirt. Aunt Phronie gave an afghan knitted in soft shadings of rose. The other house servants spread a quilt over their mistress' lap, each square an appliquéd bird or flower.

"How beautiful!" Mrs. Jardine's gaze went from one woman to another. "Much time and care is in this. I promise you that I cherish every stitch."

The women smiled joyfully. It was clear they adored

Lavinia. Probably Phronie saw to scolding, if any was needed. Lavinia apparently supervised the work of the household, but her actual work was limited to tending her roses as much as she could and working with her women to make the cotton, wool, and linsey-woolsey clothes of the slaves and sew sheets and other such needs for the whole plantation.

Melissa had shown Charlie the room given over to this work. "The married women have spinning wheels in their cabins," she said, "but they do their weaving here. This is Mama's special loom. Her cloth is so fine that our everyday dresses and Papa's and Charlie's shirts are made from it."

There were three other looms, four spinning wheels, and a long, plank table. "That's where Mama and Aunt Phronie cut out clothes. The cloth's too dearly made to let just anyone whack away at it."

"Can you weave and spin?" Charlie asked, hopeful of finding some way where this rich girl's life was like his mother's and sister's.

"I can, but I hate it when the weather's fine and I'd rather be riding or outside." She glanced at the fireplace where the makings of a fire were laid. "It's all right on cold or stormy days. We keep the kettle on for hot chocolate or tea and sing and talk and tell stories."

Rising now, the bishop fastened a diamond pendant around his wife's neck and kissed her cheek. "I pray the Lord, dearest, to give us twenty-five more years."

"I pray that, too, my love." She handed him a slender book. "Yvonne bought this in Saint Louis at my request. It's by a Harvard professor who uses the meter of an ancient Finnish epic in the story of a young Indian who grew up knowing the speech of birds and animals and became a wise and good chief."

" 'The Song of Hiawatha'," mused the bishop. "We'll

read it together, Vinnie. You know how much I like to read about Indians before they became debased, thieving lovers of firewater."

Charlie knew his father would say that a legendary Northern Indian was easier to deal with than the Osages and Shawnees treated out of this region eighteen years ago. Travis stepped forward and bent to kiss his mother, slipping a tissue-wrapped parcel into her hand.

"Not much, Mama, but they come with lots of love."

She shook out each of the half-dozen handkerchiefs and exclaimed over the embroidery. "Lovely!" She looked up at him with shining eyes. "These will be useful, but pretty, too. Thank you, darling."

Charlie wished he'd had a gift, but it was far better that Travis hadn't disappointed his mother. That made Charlie think of his own. He vowed to leave next morning. Walking fast, he'd be there by noon.

It had been a tiring day for Mrs. Jardine. She graciously thanked everyone and wished them a good night before the bishop and Travis helped her to her room. The Bentons withdrew, and the servants were clearing up.

Melissa spoke softly: "It was truly good of you to give Travis those handkerchiefs." Her hand closed on Charlie's wrist below the bandages. More warming than brandy, her touch sang through him, sweet dizzying fire. "Thank you, Charlie, ever so much."

Scarcely able to breathe, he said: "I have something for you, Miss Melissa." He'd put the necklace in the waistcoat pocket in case he had enough chance and courage at the same time to give it to her. Now, clumsily, he fished it out. Firelight turned the amber into golden flame. "I . . . I sure hope you'll accept it."

She caught in her breath. Dark lashes swept up from those

deep blue eyes. "Amber! How gorgeous! Oh, Charlie, I'll keep it always!"

Either she was pleased or a mighty good actress, and, if she was acting, it was to gratify him. That, Charlie figured, was fine either way. Then her face fell. "I wish I had something for you."

"You do."

Her eyebrows arched. "What?"

The perfume of her hair reached deeply into his senses, rousing feelings he'd had only in those troublesome dreams that had started plaguing him a few years ago, feelings it made him ashamed to have near Melissa.

"You've got plenty of it." He tried to joke a little to ease the tightness around his heart. "Could I . . . could I have a lock of your hair?"

"My hair? This old red stuff?"

"It's the prettiest auburn in the world." He searched for words. "Like a . . . a blood bay horse."

"Hmph!" She tossed her head like a mettlesome filly.

"I . . . I'm sorry! I mean. . . ."

She smiled at his confusion. "It's all right, Charlie. Horses are better-looking than most people." She crossed to a graceful writing desk and opened a drawer. "Here." She produced a pair of scissors and handed them to him. "Take any curl you like . . . so long as it doesn't show."

He chose a piece that curved against her ear and back of her neck. One careful snip and it was his. "Thank you, Melissa." He choked on the words. "I'll keep it always."

"Will you?" she teased.

He was solemn. "Yes." *I'll always love you, Melissa Jardine.*

She rose on tiptoe. Before he knew what she intended, her lips brushed his cheek and she fled.

Chapter Ten

Christy didn't know whether she liked Travis Jardine or not. He had kept Lafe from knifing Charlie, no getting around that. The way he laughed, so carefree and rollicking, made you want to laugh with him, but sometimes she felt he was laughing at them. He was charming to her mother, complimenting her almost too much on their simple fare. To her father, he was always respectful. He played peek-a-boo and "this little pig" with Beth till she squealed gleefully, and he treated Thos like a younger brother. Christy he mostly ignored.

Maybe that was the trouble. Christy frowned as she stepped backward three or four steps, turning the spinning wheel with her right hand, drawing out the thread with her left. Her mother, working the foot treadles of the loom, threw the shuttle carrying the weft thread through the warp with expert speed. She could weave two and a half yards in a long day if her husband or one of the boys filled the bobbins, but usually carding wool or cotton into fluffy rolls, spinning these into thread, and weaving were done at night or when an hour or two was found between daily tasks.

It was Saturday. There was no school so Ellen Ware hoped to spin at least a yard today. Jonathan Ware and the boys, including Travis, were using wedges, mauls, and axes to split cleared trees. The muffled sound of their labor reached inside the house. Travis was helping because Charlie had to content himself with trimming branches off the logs. His arms were still sore from the dog bites.

Christy shivered to think what those fangs could have done to Justus. Because Travis was there, the Wares hadn't told Charlie about helping the runaway. All too soon now Charlie would have to leave for his winter job with Seth Cooley. It was grand that he'd be earning cash money— Christy thrilled all over again to remember the excitement of his producing parcel after parcel from his canvas bag—but how they'd miss him at Christmas! She hoped Travis would take himself off in time to let them have Charlie to themselves for at least a day or two.

Soon the men would come in for dinner. Stew simmered, smelling of onions and herbs. The butter Christy had churned last night would soak deliciously into corndodgers, and as a treat, because Travis was company, there was Indian pudding—cornmeal and milk cooked with butter, eggs, and honey from Sarah's bees.

It was some comfort to hear that Travis's mother and sister spun and wove and sewed. Fifty slaves! Just keeping them clothed would be a major task. It would be interesting arithmetic to figure out how many slaves it took just to clothe the others. Seven yards for a dress, two for a shirt, three or four for trousers. Then there were sheets, towels, counter-panes. . . . Christy's head whirled at the thought.

More resigned to her chore, she held the end of a new roll of wool, clipped from the Suffolk ewes and already dyed blue with wild indigo, to a thread attached to the spindle, turned the wheel till the fiber joined with the thread, and walked forward to run up the thread.

Dyeing the cloth was an adventure, sometimes a disappointing one when wild plum roots produced, instead of purple, a muddy shade that couldn't be dyed over, or when hickory bark yielded a dirty sulphur hue instead of pretty yellow. This at least could be rescued by dyeing the cloth brown with walnut roots. It just took *more* work, and meant you wore somber brown instead of happy yellow.

Christy dreamed a moment of the beautiful dresses she and her mother would have from the azure foulard Charlie had brought them. Imagine. Real silk! She hoped she'd stop growing so she could wear it a long time. It seemed like magic to have cloth you hadn't worked for hours and hours to make. Sewing Christmas shirts for her father and Thos from Charlie's gift of plaid flannel was going to be a pleasure.

Beth toddled about the room clutching the fleecy lamb Charlie had brought her, murmuring in her private language as she investigated everything but the fire. At sixteen months, she often dropped to her knees and crawled till frustration with getting her skirt caught under her provoked her into pulling herself upright. Stooping to collect a bit of mud fallen from someone's shoe, she started to taste it.

"No, Bethie!" Christy warned. "Nasty!"

"Nas-ee," the dark-haired child echoed. *"Phu-ee!"* Wrinkling her snub nose, she dropped the mud that crumbled into grainy bits. The mud didn't smell, but suddenly Beth did.

"Will you change her, Christy?" Ellen stood up, flexing her fingers. "I have to make the corndodgers."

Christy changed her sister quickly. She didn't want Travis to catch her at the task. Unfortunately the little homespun gown was wet. Christy changed it, too, put Beth down with a pat, and carried the pail of accumulated baby things out to what they all thought of as John Brown's well. Drawing up a bucket of water, she poured it over the garments and went a safe distance to rinse them before filling the pail.

Back in the cabin, she added soft soap, and put the pail on

the dogtrot to soak, although ordinarily it would have set in a corner. She had to grin ruefully at herself, going to such trouble not to offend His Majesty Jardine's delicate nose.

Before warm weather, her father would build a well house with big water troughs to cool foods that might spoil, but for now it was cold enough that milk kept sweet on a shelf at the far end of the cabin from the fireplace. Christy brought pitchers of sweet and buttermilk to the table and fetched a crock of butter and smaller pitcher of cream for the Indian pudding.

Her brothers trooped in with her father and Travis, washed in the basin by the door, smeared a clean towel dirty, and eagerly pulled up chairs and benches. Her mother ladled out stew and passed corndodgers while Christy filled mugs according to the drinker's request.

"Milk . . . sweet, please." Sun through the window struck gold from Travis's laughing brown eyes. Had he meant that "sweet" the way it sounded to her?

Deliberately she filled his mug with buttermilk. His eyebrows shot up, but he didn't protest. She gave him a small, grim smile. He was only teasing, of course, but she wanted him to know he couldn't score off her without getting jabbed back.

Her father had just said grace when Robbie set up the jubilant barking with which he greeted Lige and Sarah Morrow, any of the Hayeses, and Hester Ballard. Poor Hester! She'd brought a special balm for Charlie's wounds. No one had the heart to tell her that Lafe had lost his job and attacked Charlie with a knife.

"The kindest thing for Hester may be for Lafe to just disappear," Jonathan said as she rode away.

"Jonathan!" cried Ellen. "That would be terrible, not to hear now and then where he is and what he's doing."

Jonathan shook his head. "Knowing, my dear, might be more terrible."

He went now to the door and called in pleased surprise: "Why, hello, Dan! Get off that horse and have a bite with us."

Dan O'Brien! Christy's face heated. She hadn't seen him since he'd helped her out of the sinkhole near Whistling Point and taken charge of Justus, but he was often in her thoughts.

Strange, but it wouldn't have occurred to her to set the baby clothes outside because he was coming. Hadn't he taken care of his own little sister? There wouldn't be much he didn't know about babies—or being hungry. After the dread and hope he and she had shared the night they turned the bears loose and groped their way along the underground river, Christy felt their lives were bound together—for better or for worse.

He followed Jonathan in, smoky blue eyes settling at once on Christy. Then he saw Travis and his smile faded. They spoke since apparently they'd met at Parkses' mill the day Charlie and Jonathan had taken corn to be ground.

With his flame of hair and thin face, Dan put Christy in mind of a fox, wary and shy. Beside him, Travis seemed an overgrown, ebullient puppy. As he ate, Dan answered Ellen Ware's questions. The Parkses all were well and sent greetings. Andy McHugh and Susie Parks were engaged but hadn't set a wedding date. To replace the cabin burned by proslavers, James Montgomery's friends had helped him build a veritable fort house of upright logs eight inches thick squared out of the heart of big oaks, grooved and pegged together so tightly no bullet could enter.

"There's only one small window set above the level of a man's head to light the whole downstairs," Dan said. "The loft has portholes. A few people shooting through them can defend 'Fort Montgomery' against dozens of raiders. There's a tunnel dug from beneath a trap door in the floor that comes out near the hill rising above the colonel's house."

"You seem to put a lot of stock in Montgomery." Travis spoke in a disdainful tone. "Pa says he's a mad-dog Abolitionist who ought to be strung up beside John Brown and all his sons."

Dan gave a hard, angry laugh. "I was with Colonel Montgomery when he chased Major George Clarke's gang of cutthroats back into Missouri. They didn't make much of their chance to hang him . . . or John Brown, either, though another gang shot one of his sons while he was just walking along the road."

Travis half rose, eyes stormy, but Jonathan raised a hand. "Political discussion is one thing, but there'll be no wrangling at this table."

"But, sir . . . !" Travis cried.

Jonathan quelled him with a look. Jaws clenching, Travis stared at his food. Dan buttered a dodger, praised it and the stew, and asked Charlie how he'd liked freighting. That carried them through dinner, although Travis didn't join in the conversation.

"So it's back on the trails you'll be next summer, Charlie?" There was a wistful note in Dan's voice.

Charlie nodded. "Why don't you come, Dan?" At Travis's scowl, he added: "There's lots of freight contractors. If you can't hire on at Independence or Westport, for sure you can at Leavenworth."

"I'd admire to see those far prairies and mountains," sighed Dan. "Maybe there'll come a time when I won't be needed where I am."

"And you, Travis," Jonathan asked, "will you go freighting, too?"

"My parents are determined that I must go to school, sir."

Travis made a grimace. "Pa wants me to attend a theological seminary. Mama prefers the University of Missouri, but we've finally agreed on Kemper Military School at Boonville." He looked at Dan with a gleam in his eye. "That way, it won't be a complete waste of time if war breaks out."

War might settle Travis, perhaps six feet underground, but Christy doubted that the strictest military academy could.

Dan said: "We're doing a little drilling ourselves."

"That bunch of Quakers and Northern farmers?" Travis derided. At Jonathan's glance, he muttered: "Sorry, sir." He didn't look it.

"I delivered your parcel, Missus Ware," Dan said to Ellen.

He must mean Justus was safe. Christy's heart swelled with thankfulness as Dan turned to her. "Remember that cave I told you about? I went back in it a long way, last week. No telling where it comes out." A way of telling her he'd explored onward from the Whistling Point sinkhole. He got to his feet. "Thank you kindly for dinner, Missus Ware. It's to Mister Hayes's tannery I'm bound, so I must be riding."

"Oh, first you'll have Indian pudding!" Christy urged. She didn't want him to leave, didn't want to him to go till they'd had a few private words.

"Indian pudding, is it?" He sat down quickly like the boy he still was.

Around the table, pudding and cream vanished with avid plying of spoons.

Making his farewells again, Dan went out. Christy followed, trying to manufacture some message to Susie and Lydia. She babbled as Dan tightened the saddle girth on Breeze or Zephyr—she couldn't tell the Parkses' bay geldings apart.

Dan gazed at her in a way that made her breath catch and silenced her. Looking stern, eager, and questioning all at once, he seemed about to speak when Travis came out and made a great bustle of getting wood from the dogtrot. When he'd carried in two loads, he came out swinging the water bucket.

With a sound of disgust, Dan mounted. Desperately, for Travis wouldn't be long out of earshot, Christy blurted: "Dan, I'd like to see where the cavern goes. . . ."

"Seems like Travis Jardine keeps too tight a watch on you for that."

"Dan!"

He was already riding away.

Wrathier than he knew he had any right to be, Dan reminded himself that Travis was Charlie's friend and had to be credited for helping with the chores Charlie wanted to be done so he could go to his winter work with a clear conscience. It wasn't Christy's fault that Travis was there.

Yes, but what had given the hulking spalpeen the notion that he had a right to clutter up their parting? Dan gritted his teeth, as furious with himself as he was with the planter's lordly son.

Why had he snapped Christy's plea off like that when he had offered to run the errand to the tannery for no other reason than to stop at the Wares' and ask Christy if she could investigate the farther reaches of the underground river with him? Her parents might have insisted that Thos come, too, but Dan thought they'd allow the excursion in order better to prepare for more runaways.

John Brown might not always be around to take fugitives North. It would be useful to know how far the passage reached and where it ended. With luck, it might open into a secluded valley or wilderness where it was possible to live in hiding for a time.

Dan decided he'd make up his harshness to Christy later—if, indeed, she wasn't taken in by young Jardine—but he wouldn't stop by the Wares' again today. He'd take a short cut across the ridge above their farm. The Hayeses' cabin and tan yard were in a gradually sloping hollow that ended at the creek. The clearing was in a forest of blackjack oaks that yielded the bark used for tanning, and a lively spring burst out of serried limestone in between the double cabin and the tanbark house next to four large wooden vats buried in the ground, tops level to the surface.

Ethan Hayes was making the most of having his yellow-headed boys home from school. Luke, the youngest, urged on Ethan's white mule, the halter of which was attached to a bar fastened to a tall post that revolved on a pivot as the mule drew a roller over large pieces of tanbark spread around the post.

Twelve-year-old Mark dumped a bucket of small bits of tanbark into one vat. Matthew and Ethan had stretched out hides lifted from the vat of strong limewater that loosened hair and flesh so they could scrape them off with knives. Only after this could the hides go into one of the tanning vats.

The acrid smell of the vats stung Dan's nostrils, eyes, and lungs. Tanners earned the hide they kept from every two that people brought them. At a safe distance from the tanbark house were ashy remains of the log pyre built to heat limestone rocks till they were white hot and could be put in a vat with water to leach out the lime.

Ethan greeted Dan and bade him get down from his horse. As Dan complied, Ethan removed a last bit of flesh from a hide that looked like it came from a deer and lowered it into the middle vat of brown ooze.

"Mister Parks ready to make shoes for all of you?" Ethan said, and smiled. With his lithe body and bright hair, he looked young enough to be the elder brother of his stair-step sons. Simeon Parks ground his grain and got leather in return.

"We have to make some new harness," Dan said. "And repair the old stuff."

"Come up to the shed," invited Ethan, "and we'll get you just what you need . . . heavy leather for harness and soles, softer and thinner for shoe uppers."

Ethan bundled the tanned hides together and tied them with rawhide strips to fasten behind Dan's saddle. "You happen to know the Wattles folks who've taken up land north of Sugar Mound?"

"Heard of them." Mill gossip had it that the Wattles families were Presbyterian, vegetarian, and the women and girls wearers of bloomers that reached to the ankle beneath skirts that dipped a few inches below the knee.

"The brother called Augustus brought cash money for leather a couple of weeks ago, but I didn't have any on hand. He asked me to keep the money and send the leather when I could. It bothers me to have a man's money when he doesn't have what it paid for."

"I can take the leather to the mill," Dan offered. "Unless someone heading that way comes by in the next few days, I'm sure Mister Parks will let me or Davie deliver it."

So Ethan added two more hides to the bundle, and Dan went his way. Fretting at Travis's presence at the Wares' and, even more, at the way he'd snapped at Christy, he didn't enjoy the outing anything as much as he'd expected to and was heartily glad when the mill came in sight.

As it turned out, Lydia and Susie Parks took over his errand. "From what I hear of the Wattles, we have much in common," Lydia said. "Augustus Wattles and his older brother John, with their wives, ran schools for freed slaves in Ohio. Amongst them they have several daughters close to our age, Susie."

"The most remarkable thing about those Ohio schools is how they came to be," put in Simeon Parks. "Back in Eighteen Thirty-Two or so, a young Kentuckian named Thom attended Lane Seminary at Cincinnati which was headed by Doctor Lyman Beecher, father of Henry Ward Beecher who's preached so powerfully against slavery and Harriet Beecher Stowe who wrote *Uncle Tom's Cabin*. Remember the uproar when it was published in Eighteen Fifty-Two?"

Lydia nodded. "For Christmas, Papa, I hope you'll give Susie and me her new book. I think it's called *Dred, A Story of the Great Dismal Swamp*."

"I've already ordered it, my dear." Simeon looked perhaps even more fondly at Lydia, the plain daughter, than at Susie, the pretty one. "At any rate, young Thom was so turned against slavery that he converted his father who freed all his four hundred slaves."

"Four hundred!" echoed Dan, dazed to think of one man having power of life and death over that many souls. Even slaveholders agreed Negroes had souls. The English had never been sure about the Irish.

"Some planters own a thousand or more workers." Simeon shook his head. "Most Southerners, though, have no slaves at all or only five or so who pretty much live and work like the master's family."

"What happened to Thom's slaves?" Davie asked.

"Freed Negroes aren't allowed to live in Kentucky. Ohio wouldn't admit them unless they had a promised livelihood, so the elder Thom gave money to buy tracts of good Ohio farmland for his former slaves. They've lived there peacefully for twenty years. After the children attend local schools, they can attend Oberlin College if they wish."

Dan's head spun. College-educated Negroes! "So some masters free their slaves?" he pondered.

"Yes, out of conscience or affection," Simeon added grudgingly. "A number free their own children born to slave women . . . often educate and give them a start in life. Not only Thom's emancipated slaves, but many others live in the Ohio settlements. The Wattles brothers and their wives taught until the men's health forced them to take up less demanding work."

"They chose to come here and help make Kansas a free state," Lydia finished. "Papa, may we take some wheat flour to them? You know how tiresome cornmeal gets, especially if you're not used to it."

"David, tomorrow morning you and Dan hitch up the team and load a bushel of wheat flour into the wagon," Simeon instructed. "A bag of oats as well."

Lydia and Susie Parks added pickles, relish, wild plum preserves, a jug of Sarah Morrow's honey, a loaf of wheat bread, and a pound cake. They set off in high spirits and returned, tired but happy, about sundown.

"We had dinner with both Wattles families." The sparkle of Lydia's dark eyes brightened her thin face till no one would have called her plain.

"And don't forget those two handsome young Morse brothers, Orlin and John," teased Susie. "They set up a store at Wattles' crossroads, but they let people take away so much of their stock on credit that they gave up the store and started making furniture. Which one did you like best, Lydia?"

"They're too young for me." Lydia's blush belied the austerity of her tone. "Though they'd be eligible for you, Susie, were you not pledged to Andy McHugh." Dismissing flirtations, Lydia went on enthusiastically. "John Wattles graduated from Yale and is a close friend of William Lloyd Garrison. The daughters are young, but accomplished."

"Celestia played the piano so beautifully I almost wept," added Susie. "The Augustus Wattles have four children. The son, Theodore, is about your age, Dan. Emma's fourteen and a bit rackety. Mary Ann's so smart she terrifies me, though she's only ten. The oldest, Sarah Grimke, is eighteen. We had a grand visit while we cleared up from dinner and washed dishes."

"She's named for the daughter of a South Carolina judge who owned a thousand slaves," explained Lydia to Dan who was the only one who didn't understand the Grimke name. "She and her sister, Angelina, came to loathe slavery so much that they've devoted their lives to fighting to free the slave . . . and women."

"Sarah Wattles told us something her namesake wrote," added Susie, and quoted, " 'All I ask of our brothers is that they will take their feet off our necks, and permit us to stand upright on the ground which God has designed us to occupy.' "

Owen rolled his eyes. "Good grief, Suse! I don't have my foot on your neck!"

"Not physically." Lydia skewered her brother with a stare. "But you can vote. So can any drunken, filthy, tobacco-spitting lout, but Susie and I cannot, nor can your own Harriet."

Perhaps to head off an argument, Owen's young wife asked: "Do the Wattles ladies truly wear bloomers?"

Lydia and Susie exchanged bemused glances. "Why, yes, they do." Susie giggled. "At first, it was all we could notice, but, you know, as the day passed, we forgot all about it. I must say it's perfectly modest. The bloomers fit loosely till they fasten at the ankle. It's a great saving to skirt hems."

"I suppose," sniffed Lydia, "bloomers shock prudes with the evidence that women have legs. So do men, but no one seems to find that scandalous."

Simeon looked so uneasy that Susie laughed and hugged him. "Don't worry, Papa! We've already decided not to outfit ourselves in bloomers."

"We've no wish to embarrass some of the crude men who come to the mill," said Lydia, looking down her nose. She hesitated as if torn between opposing feelings. "Owen," she said to her younger brother, "the Morse brothers are drilling regularly near Sugar Mound with Colonel Montgomery and his men. The colonel told the Morses how much he hopes you and Dan and Andy will join the drill when you can."

Susie lost her smile. "The colonel says it's not a question of if the proslavers will raid across the border again, only of when. He wants to be ready."

Dan glanced at Owen. Almost in the same breath, they said: "So do we."

Chapter Eleven

May 19, 1858, dawned to a bright sky. The excited bustle that had filled the Parks home for days rose to fevered intensity. "You've picked a grand day for your wedding," Dan told Susie at the breakfast she scarcely perched to eat. "Now if Andy doesn't forget. . . ."

Susie kicked Dan under the table. "Don't even tease about it. We've already had to put off the wedding twice because of rumors that Clarke's bushwhackers were coming."

"Thank goodness they were just rumors," murmured Lydia. "We've been expecting a bushwhacker raid ever since Colonel Montgomery smashed the whiskey barrels at the Trading Post store and told the proslave men who hung around there that they weren't welcome in Kansas."

Dan laughed to remember how the sod-corn whiskey sloshed for a hundred yards down the Military Road. "Yes, and back in January the colonel smashed the ballot box at Sugar Mound and stomped the ballots to pieces to protest the Lecompton Constitution drawn up by the proslave legislature."

"Even without Sugar Mound's ballots, the proslave constitution was voted down ten to one," said Owen. "At this rate, Kansas may never enter the Union."

"Minnesota just did." Simeon brightened. "That makes seventeen free states to fifteen slave." Then he grew somber.

"As the slave states lose power in Congress, I fear they'll shatter the Union. These border troubles are just a hint of what's ahead."

"We've drilled with as many guns as we could get nearly every day this spring," said Dan. "But day before yesterday we decided the scare was all talk and we had to get back to work."

"We'll dance at your wedding today, Suse," teased Owen, "but tomorrow we must dance behind the plows."

"Well, right now, you can dance outside and lay planks on sawhorses for tables," decreed Lydia. "The Wattleses and Morse brothers are coming, and Colonel Montgomery and his family and. . . ."

"And the Wares." Susie shot a roguish glance at Dan. "Christy's what . . . almost fifteen now?"

Dan was only too aware of how Christy seemed more a young woman each time he saw her, which wasn't often since that early December day a year and a half ago when he'd found Travis Jardine behaving like a member of her family.

He probably would be, one way or another. Charlie, when he wasn't freighting, spent about as much time at the Jardines as at his own home, and the bishop spoke of him approvingly. He needed an honest, hard-working son-in-law more than a rich one, a young man who could gradually take over the running of the plantation. Travis, who had been expelled from two military academies and the University of Missouri in less than a year, was now attending a military school in Arkansas and had accepted the discipline to the extent that he'd declared his intention of seeking a commission in the cavalry.

No, not for a long time would Travis care to manage the plantation. By then, if war clouds burst into full storm, there might not be a plantation to run.

Here on the border a sort of off-and-on war had gone on

for years although it was more threats and fear than actual killing. Dan and Owen had several times ridden with Montgomery's Sharps-armed volunteers to recover stolen livestock or scare off bushwhackers. This made life safer for Free Staters, but there was no true peace—and couldn't be till the quarrel between North and South was over.

In the last year or so, many new settlers had taken up land in this eastern part of Kansas. Most of them wanted to ensure Kansas' entering the Union as a free state, but some were just as interested in profiting from a railroad proposed to run from Leavenworth to Fort Scott and Fort Smith.

Dan had still not shown Christy the passage he'd explored by entering the Whistling Point sinkhole and going the other direction, instead of making for the concealed opening they now called the Fox Hole. Twice, though, she had sent word by Thos to meet her and an escaped slave at Whistling Point at night and arrange a way to spirit the fugitive northward.

The first time it had been a young woman with a baby, fleeing to her husband who had previously escaped. The second runaway was a young hand like Justus, his bare back lashed into scabbing ridges because he'd tried to keep the overseer from forcing his sister who was barely of an age to menstruate.

"My little sister, she in his cabin now, that fat old white man's." Tears ran from the man's eyes. He swallowed hard. "I kill him if I stay, or he kill me, more likely. Better I run. Maybe save up enough to buy my sister."

Christy had struggled not to cry as she wished the man a safe journey and thanked Dan for taking charge in a polite but cool way that told him she hadn't forgotten the jealous way he'd thrown Travis Jardine in her face.

Those meetings at Whistling Point were truces. Dan

wanted peace. More than he could have dreamed, he wanted Christy to be his friend again—yes, even if she had fallen for Travis's easy charm. If only today she'd smile at him, Dan vowed to keep a curb bit on his tongue.

Hughie Huston, the Irish veteran of the Mexican War Dan had met after the defeat of Clarke's bushwhackers, had taken Christy's fugitives to Lawrence since John Brown had been away. Hughie, a minister of the Church of United Brethren, would perform a service today to satisfy guests who might not think the simple self-pledging of Quakers a binding enough marriage. The Parkses esteemed Colonel Montgomery, who was a Campbellite preacher, but Susie didn't want her wedding to be the occasion for one of Montgomery's impassioned sermons against slavery.

Even on a wedding day, it was important not to waste the four or so hours before time to clean up and greet guests arriving for the noon ceremony. Oats and potatoes had been planted in late March and corn was being planted as the fields were plowed. That put in several weeks ago showed bright green blades struggling with lustily growing weeds. Dan and David attacked the weeds with hoes, while, in the next field, Owen and Simeon Parks used Zephyr and Breeze to haul at stumps and roots.

It was late morning when Simeon peered under his hand toward the rumbling of a wagon. "Hurry, boys!" he called loudly enough to reach Dan and David. "Here comes the bridegroom!"

Working had heated all of them. Rather than get in the harried women's way to wash up, they pulled off their shirts and splashed on chill water from the river, then dried in the sun as they pelted for the cabin. In their loft, Dan and David scrambled into clean clothes, including socks knitted by Lydia and Susie and shoes made by Simeon.

Remembering Travis's unpatched garments, Dan sighed a little at his hand-me-downs from Owen, patched neatly on elbows and knees. He appreciated his foster sisters keeping his clothes from falling apart. Besides, there'd be more grown-up men and women with patches than not at the wedding, but someday Dan was bound he'd have a whole brand new outfit, store-bought top to bottom.

He instantly chastised himself. He was lucky not to be under the Irish turf alongside his parents and baby sister. What would they say to his hankerings when he hadn't gone hungry a day since Uncle Simeon had taken him in, or lacked clothes to cover his ungrateful bones? He scowled in the little tin mirror at his broken nose and slicked his wet, fiery hair as flat as it would go.

Uncannily David turned green eyes on him. "How much longer do you aim to stay here, Dan, getting just your keep? You could hire on as a freighter like Charlie Ware and make good money."

"Your pa fed me a good many years when I couldn't earn my keep." Dan shrugged. "Reckon it's only fair to make it up a little." He grinned and cuffed the younger boy. "You trying to get shut of me?"

David cuffed back. "You know better than that! But Pa wouldn't fault you. . . ."

"I know. One more reason I need to pay back what I can. No way to pay it all." For a split second, Dan was six years old again, begging his tiny sister to rouse. *Wake up, colleen! Dannie has a nice bite for you. . . .*

She couldn't wake, never again, and the bite had been a moldy bit of turnip he'd snatched from a pig trough. Mother of God! Here he was, full-bellied, craving new clothes!

Blinking at the sting in his eyes, Dan swallowed. "Anyhow, even if the militia's quit drilling for now, there's no telling when the bushwhackers may ride back. I want to be here when they do."

"It's not fair, you and Owen drilling while I have to plow and plant," David groused.

"Your time'll come, lad." Dan, by way of consoling David, tousled his just combed curly black hair and got in response an indignant punch in the ribs. "Your time'll come."

A chill fingered Dan's spine, the sensation old Catriona McHugh said was someone walking on your grave. His grave or Davie's? *Holy Mother!* In spite of his Quaker upbringing, Dan still reverted, in distress, to words learned in his mother's arms, the Virgin hazily assuming his mother's sweet face and tender voice. *Holy Mother, if one of us must die in what's coming, let it be me, not Davie. Please let it be me.*

"Don't stand there like a moon calf!" David called from the ladder. "Here come a whole tribe of ladies in . . . in . . . I guess they're bloomers. The Wares are unhitching. Preacher Hughie's just come. Oh, Dan, hurry!"

Dan did, forcing away his fit of dread. Between helping guests take care of their teams and saddle horses and improvising more benches as the crowd multiplied, Dan had no chance to do more than greet Christy along with the rest of her family, but when he didn't have to look somewhere else, his eyes found her as a magnet needle finds north.

That dress! The scoop-necked bodice accentuated Christy's blossoming shape and the full, full skirt flowed like melted sky. The sleeves fitted close to the elbows where they were caught with velvet ribbon to fall in gathered flounces. Only Susie's cream satin and lace gown, inherited from a grandmother, was anything as beautiful. No, wait! Mrs. Ware wore a dress of the same heaven blue cut in a different style.

Relief overwhelmed Dan. For a crazy flash, he'd thought that Travis—but, of course, the Wares wouldn't have permitted such a gift. The costly material must be a gift from Charlie.

Rejoicing, Dan had to snatch a few more words with Christy. Skirting the crowd, he caught up with her as she added plates and utensils to the Parkses'.

"That's a dress to suit the Lord's angels, Christy."

She turned cool gray eyes on him. Dan groaned inwardly. Could she be mad at him after all this time, after they'd twice met at Whistling Point to help runaways? But that was in the dark, hidden as the underground river. Here in full daylight, her face was unreadable, although intentionally or not her lips were invitingly parted.

She'd kissed him when they were children. Would she ever do it again? The hope that she might compelled Dan to brave her aloof stare. "Charlie must have got you that dress in Saint Louis," he said desperately. "Looks like it came from . . . from London or Paris."

"Independence." She laughed, warming suddenly. "Charlie brought the material home that first autumn he freighted. I pestered Mother to help me sew it up as soon as we could. She told me I was growing so fast that I'd be out of it in six months, but I could decide." Had that dimple always been in her cheek? "I'm glad I waited."

"So am I!"

Soft color glowed from her throat to black curls swept up with velvet bows, and she glanced away. "Isn't Susie lovely?"

"So are you."

"It's the dress."

"No, it isn't." She had the clean fresh scent of lilacs. His heart pounded in his ears. He said huskily: "We still need to see where the cavern leads, Christy. When . . . ?"

"We'll talk later. See, Lydia's calling everyone inside." Christy rushed away.

At least, praise be, she was ready to talk to him. And how she shone, prettier by far than the other girls, even the bride. Dan stood with the other men at the door of the cabin. The end opposite the fireplace was banked in lilacs and plum and apple blossoms. Taking their places in the bower, faces flower-like in spite of their gray and brown homespun and those distracting bloomers, the three oldest Wattles girls sang, accompanied by brown-haired little Celestia on the violin. From the sweetness of their voices, no one would guess they had founded The Moneka Women's Rights Society in February to work for rights equal to men's and prohibit alcohol. Lydia and Susie were members, of course, and came home from meetings full of excitement over petitions they'd sent the legislature and the constitutional convention.

The sisters concluded with "My Love is Like a Red, Red Rose". Andy fidgeted at being the center of attention, but the way he looked at Susie showed that he agreed with every word of the song.

Hughie Huston lengthily blessed and admonished the young couple. They then placed rings on each other's fingers and promised in the Quaker way to help and cherish each other all their lives.

Few eyes were dry, but Lydia made everyone laugh when she announced in a stern tone: "There'll be no kissing of the bride. You may shake Susanna's hand as you do Andrew's. Then kindly make room for others by stepping outside." She raised her voice above the commencing hubbub of jokes and congratulations. "As soon as we're assembled at the tables, will you ask a blessing, Colonel Montgomery? After that, all of you please take plates and help yourselves."

Those first in line obeyed Lydia although they pumped Susie's small hand with such energetic good will that Dan reckoned she'd have preferred kisses even from the whiskered

179

gents. When Lige Morrow, however, uncoiled his lanky form from the doorway, he strode forward, beaded fringes swishing, took Susie in his arms, and kissed her soundly.

"No offense, Miss Parks," he drawled to Lydia. He swept a courtly bow to Susie who was blushing but not displeased. "And sure none to you, Missus McHugh, but I didn't come all the way over here to shake the bride's hand."

"Lige!" Sarah scolded, but she was laughing, and so was everyone except Lydia. The fact that she remained a spinster at twenty-four was hurtfully emphasized by her sister's marriage. Not that Lydia lacked proposals. A number of widowers with children and an urgent need for a woman to do the work of the household had frequented the mill till they got it through their heads that Lydia preferred keeping her father's house to any of theirs.

As soon as the remaining guests wished the couple happiness, everyone trooped out to the sheet-draped tables laden with good things that gave out tantalizing smells. Most of the guests had contributed a special dish, from the Morrows' golden honeycomb to Mrs. Ware's richly creamed marble-size new potatoes. Most relished of all, perhaps, were crusty rolls and loaves made of the Parkses' fine-ground wheat, lavished with butter.

Mrs. Ware and the Wattleses had brought plates, cups, spoons, and forks to fill out the Parkses' supply which included one of Susie's gifts from her family, a set of blue and white ironstone dishes. With filled plates, people sat down wherever they could. Dan, one of the last in line, perched on a stump next to the Morrows and their lazing hounds.

Sarah Morrow, in her yellow calico, looked like a tiger lily among the prevalent grays, browns, and blues. She handled her eating utensils gracefully, but Lige Morrow, wielding his skinning knife, was having troubles.

"Give me a good hickory trencher any day," he grumbled. "No chasin' your food all over it like you do on these dog-gone' slippery plates. A body can't stick his knife in 'em, either."

"Well, honey, we'll bring your trencher next time." Sarah's tone was soothing but she had a wicked grin.

"Now, Sarah. . . ."

The sound of horse hoofs rose above the talk and laughter. Lige was on his feet in an instant, knife in hand.

"It's just someone late for the wedding," Sarah guessed.

"No!" gasped Dan. "That man in the middle's being held in the saddle by his friends." Dan hurried forward with Lige. They were joined by most of the men.

"Why, it's Reverend Reed!" cried Hughie Huston when the face of the man sagging on the middle horse could be made out. "He came last year to work among the Indians. Brought fifty Sharps rifles to help Free-State men defend their families. God have mercy! His bowels are sticking out of him."

Lydia Parks was the first to reach the wounded man. "Owen! Dan! Bring a wide plank from a table and carry him to my bed."

"Bless you, ma'am." Husky Eli Snider, who had a blacksmith shop near the Nickels' farm, supported Reed on one side while his brother, Simon, held him on the other. "We knew it was bad for the reverend to bring him like this, but we couldn't leave him. Them murderin' devils might come back!"

James Montgomery laid a steadying hand on the blacksmith's trembling arm. "Who, Eli? Who did this?"

"Charles Hamelton and a gang of bushwhackers . . . maybe thirty of 'em. Lined up eleven men in a ravine, shot 'em, and skedaddled."

"Where?"

181

"Back to Missouri, most likely. Hamelton's been living over there since he cleared out of Kansas last year."

"Maybe we can catch them." Montgomery was the smallest man in the crowd, but all eyes fixed on him. "Any man who has a horse and gun and is willing to chase the killers, get ready to ride with me. If you have to go home for a gun or horse, do that, and try to catch up." He swung back to Eli. "Did the bushwhackers kill the other ten prisoners?"

"Five certain dead." Eli shuddered. "Austin Hall played dead even when they kicked him, but wasn't hit at all. One bushwhacker put a pistol to Amos Hall's cheek and the bullet nearly tore off his tongue. He's alive, though. The others may pull through."

"Is someone helping them?" called Jonathan Ware.

"We met Missus Colpetzer with her boy, Frank, and Missus Hairgrove driving a wagon with bedding and water, following the bushwhacker's tracks. They were scared something awful would happen when their husbands were prisoner." The brawny smith choked up. "We . . . we had to tell them. Colpetzer's dead. Hairgrove's so bad hurt, he seems sure to die."

"The ladies drove on to pick up the wounded," said Simon. "Brave they are, and so is young Frank. Only twelve years old and his father murdered."

"I'll go help them," Jonathan Ware said.

"I'll come with you." Ellen Ware was heedless of her fine silk gown. "Christy, do as Lydia bids you and take care of Beth."

Dan held one side end of the plank, Owen, Andy, and Jonathan Ware the others, as careful hands eased the ash-faced minister onto the board. Each struggling breath pushed blood and intestines through the bloody hole in his clothes and abdomen.

"Can someone lend me a horse and gun?" cried Thos.

"Come home with me," said Andy, yielding his side of the litter to Simeon Parks. "We'll switch the wagon and harness for saddles. You can borrow my shotgun." Andy swept his weeping bride into his arms. "Sweetheart, stay here till I come for you. You know I have to go."

She nodded mutely, then promised between sobs: "I . . . I'll look after your mother."

"Belike I'll look after you!" Old Catriona hobbled swiftly toward the house, clearing a path for the plank litter. "Gabbling whilst this poor man's entrails dry entirely! Fetch your scissors, Susie, so we can cut away the dirty cloth and get at the wound. And then be changing that bonnie gown so the granddaughter you're going to give me can be a-wearing it for her wedding!"

Lydia ran to fetch a clean wet cloth and placed it over the protruding loops of intestine. "Tincture of yarrow," she told Catriona. "After we've cleaned the wound with more yarrow water and sewn it up, we'll put on a slippery elm poultice."

"*Och*, and it's a wise woman you be." Catriona looked with respect at this sister of her new daughter-in-law. "I know the cures from Skye, but you'll ken best what to use here." She called to the litter-bearers: "Leave the reverend on the board, laddies. He can bear its hardness better than being jarred about."

The minister was gently lowered to Lydia's counterpaned bed. As Dan hurried out, he caught a glimpse of Christy, trying to comfort Beth who wailed at the uproar and screamed for her parents. They'd be back, but some fathers wouldn't ever again hold their children.

The Wattles brothers, not joining the pursuit because of poor health, took charge of sorting out what horses could be spared and how families could be gotten home. As Dan and

Owen saddled Zephyr and Breeze, Simeon and David hauled out of the barn three old but sturdy saddles that had been left as payment for cornmeal.

"Please, Papa, let me go!" David begged.

"You're too young. Besides, Son, Quakers don't hold with violence."

"Owen's going!"

"Owen's a man who must choose his path. So can you . . . in seven more years."

"Dan's not that old!" yelped David.

"Dan's dear to me as a son," replied Simeon. "God has lent him to us for a time, but I don't have the same rights over him as I do with you."

"Davie, you keep an eye peeled for bushwhackers!" Dan called over his shoulder. "They could swing back this way."

"Our Theo will ride with Colonel Montgomery," Samuel Wattles said. "He can take one of the three Sharps we have in our wagons. John and I will keep the other two and stand guard here till we know the killers are gone."

Snider brothers in the lead with Colonel Montgomery, the party jogged along, soon joined by Andy McHugh and Thos Ware. "Hamelton's gang came through Trading Post and took John Campbell who was keeping the store," Eli explained more fully. "They stopped for Sam Nickel, but he's off acting as a county judge. The raiders held a gun to Missus Nickel's head, but, since she wasn't hiding Sam, there wasn't anything she could tell them. Reverend Reed was marched along with two men he'd met along the road. Hamelton dragged young Amos Hall out of his sick bed and caught his brother, Austin, as he was coming home from getting a scythe sharpened at my forge. . . ."

Eli Snider was unable to go on. His brother Simon took up the story. "The gang took William Colpetzer away from his wife. She saw the raiders coming and begged him to hide, but he wouldn't because he said he hadn't done anything wrong."

"Hamelton found William Hairgrove and his son Asa," said Eli. "Also Michael Robertson and a friend visiting him from Illinois. Herded them along like cattle. When one poor man asked to drink from a stream, they told him he could drink in hell."

Dan was thankful that he didn't know the Hall brothers or Michael Robertson, and that his acquaintance with the other victims was slight since they had all moved recently into the area. It was horrible to think of the terrified men on that cruel march and the helpless dread of their wives. It was just luck that Simeon hadn't been taken, or Andy, or Owen. Or himself, for that matter.

"When Hamelton had the prisoners lined up in the ravine about a quarter mile from our forge, he and four of his Bloody Reds tried to get us, but three of us had guns so. . . ." Simon's voice frayed. "So they rode back and shot down those poor fellows."

"The marvel is they didn't kill them all," grated Eli. "They went around kicking bodies and putting bullets into anyone who didn't seem completely gone. Cold-blooded murder of unarmed men!"

Dan's own blood chilled but he couldn't help thinking the same was said of John Brown's slaughter of proslave men— and the Doyle brothers, still in their teens. He also thought of Mrs. Nickel with a bushwhacker's pistol to her head, after being burned out of her cabin less than two years ago. Could anything heal this border before everyone on both sides was killed off?

As the riders neared Timbered Mound, Montgomery called: "Here come the ladies with the wounded!"

One sunbonneted woman cradled a bandage-swathed

man on the plank seat, supporting his head and shoulders. The woman in back, beside a body that didn't move, spoke reassuringly to the four men lying on featherbeds, some groaning, all crudely bandaged to stanch blood that still soaked through.

The tow-headed boy, walking beside the yoked oxen, halted the team at the horsemen's approach. He moved stiffly, as if he might break. His freckled face was blanched. Young Frank Colpetzer would never forget this day.

"We're taking the wounded to that cabin over there, just north of Timbered Mound," explained the woman on the seat. Her garments were stained with her husband's blood. She must be Mrs. Hairgrove. "Austin Hall wasn't hurt. He's gone for Doctor Ayres."

"Can we help you in any way?" asked Montgomery, doffing his hat.

The woman's dazed look changed to one of fierceness. "Catch Hamelton and his murdering bunch."

"We'll do our best, madam. Do you have any notion of where they went?"

From the back, Mrs. Colpetzer called: "Austin Hall crawled up the slope and saw the gang looking back from Spy Mound yonder! Then they tore off north and east in twos and threes. I expect by now they've crossed the border."

"We can cross the border, too." Montgomery bowed to the women, raised his hand, and the pursuers rode on.

Chapter Twelve

Where various fresh tracks sheared off from Spy Mound, Montgomery halted. "We'll split up here, boys, and follow each bunch of tracks. If you run into any suspicious-looking fellows who draw guns on you, shoot to kill, but take prisoners if you can. We'll give them a fair trial."

"I bet we sight neither hide nor hair of 'em," said Eli Snider gloomily.

"That's as Jehovah wills." Montgomery's piercing gray eyes traveled over his men. "Let's meet before nightfall at Jerry Jackson's store. Jerry's good-hearted and as upright as a slave-holding man can be and has always let Free-State settlers buy on credit. I think he'll have a shrewd idea of who was with Hamelton. If we can't catch them now, we'll come back later."

Dan rode with Owen Parks and brown-haired Theo Wattles, who looked to be about Dan's age. Tracks slicing up bits of turf in damp spots led east from Spy Mound, north of the dense woods along the Marais des Cygnes. After a few miles, the hoof prints veered toward the river.

"They figure on losing us by riding in the water," Owen growled.

"They'll have to get up one bank or the other sometime," Dan reasoned. "When we find a place to cross, I'll ride along the other side while you and Theo stay over here."

"Don't forget we're in Missouri, or soon will be," warned Owen. "We may run into plenty of men who'd have been with Hamelton if they'd had the nerve."

"Doesn't take much nerve to shoot unarmed men," argued Theo.

"Hamelton gave up on the Sniders pretty fast when he saw they had guns."

Dan glanced at the sun, now halfway down the sky. Was it only a few hours ago when they'd been at a wedding feast? Poor Susie! What a memory to link with her marriage, even if Andy rode home unscathed.

"We're supposed to meet at Jerry Jackson's by nightfall," he reminded the others. "These fellows we're after could hole up at almost any cabin or barn." *Or cave,* he thought, remembering Christy's Fox Hole. "If we don't find them in a couple more hours, we'd better head back. The river doesn't look real deep here. I'll go across."

The current never topped Zephyr's knees. On the other side, Dan led the horse to keep from dodging boughs in the dense timber. How long could those bushwhackers stay in the river? It was bound to get deep sometime and force them out.

Tracks at last. Scarring the bank, kicking up rotting leaves and twigs. They threaded out of the timber, across a stretch of partly cleared bottomland with a cabin and outbuildings, and vanished at an expanse of plowed fields that must have covered fifty acres.

At the far end, a half-grown boy urged along a yoke of oxen hitched to a breaking plow. On the side near Dan, a man drove a team dragging a triangular harrow. The killers wouldn't have to cross the river again. They had disappeared into the woods somewhere beyond the broken ground.

"Mister!" called Dan, cupping his hands. "Mister!"

The man with the harrow stopped his team and wiped his brow. "Yeah? What do you want?"

"Three horsemen must have passed by a couple of hours ago. Did you see which way they went?"

"Youngster, I make it a practice to see nothin' that don't concern me."

No telling where his sympathies lay, if he had any, but Dan had to try. "They were with a gang that just shot down eleven unarmed men a few miles east of Trading Post. Five died. Several of the others may not live."

The man spat out a blob of tobacco. "Dang' Free-State Abolitionists should've stayed up north."

"Charles Hamelton, who led the bushwhackers, came from Georgia."

The farmer shrugged. "I got a field to harrow, boy. Iffen I was you, I'd scoot back to Kansas. And stay there." He grinned at something behind Dan. "Don't get wrought up, Hallie. The young sprout's ridin' on."

Dan looked over his shoulder. A woman with gray hair straggled into a knot had a double-barreled shotgun pointed at his mid-section. From twenty paces, there was no way she could miss. From the look of her narrowed eyes, she wouldn't be offering him a glass of cool buttermilk.

"Good afternoon to you, ma'am," he said.

When he glanced back from the timber, she still held the shotgun.

It was twilight when the empty-handed searchers rode wearily up to Jerry Jackson's store on Mulberry Creek. A few slaves were still unhitching teams near the barn behind the slave cabins and clapboarded house. As Dan, Owen, and Thos arrived, Colonel Montgomery had evidently just told

Jackson of the massacre because the big, ruddy-faced store-keeper was shaking his graying blond head.

"William Colpetzer killed?" There was no mistaking the horror and pity in Jackson's voice. "He had the best mind of any man I ever knew, and was civil and honest like you'd expect from Pennsylvania Dutch. Never worried me a bit that his bill climbed to over a hundred dollars. If his poor wife doesn't know that, I sure won't tell her! Why, Hairgrove was from the same part of Georgia as Hamelton and tried to be neighborly, but Hamelton turned him away. And Reverend Reed, a real saint for sure. The Indians he teaches brought him furs and venison last Christmas and all of them kissed him on both cheeks." The storekeeper went to his shelves. "Let me send some brandy for him and Hairgrove and the other wounded. I'm glad the Hall brothers weren't killed . . . mighty fine young men."

"You haven't seen Hamelton?" demanded the colonel.

"He and his brother and a few other men reined up while I was sweeping out the store. . . ."

"When?"

"Early afternoon. We'd finished dinner a little while before. I had a snooze on the verandah, like always in nice weather, and had just walked over here to the store."

"Did Hamelton say anything?"

"Just that he was going to Westport. They took off north in a big hurry. I suspicioned then they'd been up to something, 'specially after a neighbor stopped by and said there'd been a big meeting of proslavery men up near West Point yesterday, maybe four hundred of them. He said they worked themselves up to cross into Kansas and kill a bunch of snakes."

"Indeed?" murmured James Montgomery.

Jackson nodded. "Judge Barlow tried to talk them out of it. He followed to where they camped on the border that night and told them the truth . . . that their squirrel rifles and shot-guns would be up again' Sharps rifles and Colt revolvers. According to my neighbor, most of the mob plumb melted away."

"Except for Hamelton and his worst cut-throats." Eli Snider's tone was bitter.

Jackson looked sorrowful. "Let me fetch that brandy. And some vittles for the widows and orphans."

"Maybe we could still catch at least the Hameltons!" cried Eli Snider.

Plainly warring with himself, Montgomery shook his head. "We're not prepared for a three- or four-day chase, and the Hameltons can hide out at any number of places."

"Then what are we going to do?" blurted Andy, although he, of all of them, must have wanted to go home.

"Right now I propose that we ride back, care for the wounded, bury the dead, comfort their families, and plow and plant their fields."

Someone swore. Unruffled, Montgomery continued. "We'll make a list of the bushwhackers if the survivors recognized them. It's likely lots of them live around West Point . . . remember that's where Clarke's rabble crossed over when they raided us summer before last. When the planting's done . . . we all have to eat, and so do the murdered and wounded men's families . . . we'll ride over to West Point, collect as many bushwhackers as we can and. . . ."

"Hang them to the nearest tree!" yelled Doc Jennison who had just galloped up with a few other men.

"We'll turn them over to Sheriff Colby at the county seat in Paris." Montgomery's voice didn't rise but it cut like the flash of a blade. "Friends, in God's name, let it never be said that we're no better than bushwhackers."

"I say they deserve their own medicine!" howled Jennison.

Even his tall, comical hat and slight build couldn't detract from his blood-stirring urgency. "I say let's not waste this jaunt across the border! Jerry Jackson may not be a bush-whacker, but he lets them hang out around his store. He owns slaves! Let's burn him out and teach these Missouri pukes a lesson!"

"No burning, Doctor." With thanks, Montgomery accepted a bag from Jackson and helped him tie it on behind the saddle before he turned to face the younger man and said firmly: "We'll be glad of your company on the way home, sir."

Jennison glared around, found no support, and spurred angrily ahead. The storekeeper brought out two more bags that were lashed on behind Andy and Owen. "Tell the ladies I'm purely sorry," the big man sighed. "Tell them they can have credit at my store for anything they need. I'll deliver their supplies if they don't have any way of sending for them."

"Thanks, Jerry," said Andy. "But we neighbors aim to look after the families." He paused. "Did you hear Doc Jennison?"

"I heard." Jackson's head drooped before he lifted it. "But what can I do, Andy? I live here. Everything I have is tied up in my farm and store."

Two weeks later, after the corn was planted, Dan O'Brien, Owen Parks, and Andy McHugh rode with Montgomery's band as they followed the Military Road to West Point. North of Timbered Mound, earth had been broken, but not for seed. It was a common grave for William Colpetzer, John Campbell, Patrick Ross, and Michael Robertson. Andy had made a wrought-iron marker with their names and date of their murder. It would be a long time before more than that was needed to explain what had happened. William Stillwell had been buried at Mound City.

Montgomery called a halt. The men took off their hats and bowed their heads as he prayed for the victims' families and for God's help in bringing the killers to justice. Montgomery had a list of the bushwhackers. Some, like the Hameltons, had fled beyond reach. The name of Fort Scott Brockett was crossed out because survivors testified he'd wheeled his horse away from the ravine when he realized Hamelton intended to kill the men. "I'll shoot in a fair fight," he had cried, "but I'll have nothing to do with such a thing as this!" Some of the other bushwhackers started to ride off with him, but Hamelton cursed and exhorted them back into line and gave the order to fire.

The slaughter outraged Free-State sympathizers throughout the nation. James Lane, the fanatical Abolitionist known as the Grim Chieftain, gathered militia and scoured the border. Old John Brown started building a fort not far from where the blood of the massacre stained the grass and earth. Strangers were brought to him to explain what they were doing in the area.

In spite of all this, none of the assassins had been caught, and Montgomery's band found none in three days of peering into lofts and smokehouses, poking pitchforks into hay, and even looking in privies.

"They're gone, boys," admitted Montgomery that night as they ate roasted prairie hens and rabbits. "We have to get back to our work. But I'll keep the list. If any of them come back, be it ten years from now or twenty, they'll answer for their crime."

They were breaking camp next morning when a singular person rode up on a claybank horse. Even in this mild weather, he wore a shabby bearskin coat over a calfskin vest and overalls that could not disguise his thin, bony frame. Lank dark hair stuck out in every direction. He scanned the party with quick black eyes before his lips parted in a grin that revealed tobacco-stained teeth.

"Colonel Montgomery? General Jim Lane, Commander of the Army of the North and Kansas Militia, at your service, sir."

Montgomery inclined his head. "We may not agree on methods, General, but I believe we both serve freedom. As you see, we've found none of the killers."

"No more have I, sir, though we searched Westport top to bottom, and hunted along the border." Lane had a peculiar voice, husky and rasping, of the timbre Dan would expect to hear at a camp meeting. "My men have gone back to their farms and businesses, but I jogged south in hope of encountering you."

To Montgomery's lifted eyebrows, Lane placed his hand on his heart. "You are a preacher, Colonel Montgomery. You see before you a repentant sinner who craves baptism. The water in this stream looks deep enough. Will you do it?"

Montgomery's features softened. "I am bound to, General, if you're in earnest."

"Never more in my entire life, sir."

Divested of coat and vest, Lane was quickly dunked under. Once back in his malodorous outer garments, he thanked Montgomery and shook his hand before he climbed on the claybank and rode north.

As Dan led Zephyr to water, Andy warned: "Don't water that horse downstream from where Jim Lane got baptized."

"Why not?"

"Because whatever the man's got, we don't want to give it to an unsuspecting beastie!"

They had thought Montgomery too far away to hear, but

he reined his horse in beside them. "Do you hold it against Lane that he was a proslave Democrat back in Indiana where he was lieutenant governor?"

Andy scowled. "I hold that against him less than the way he sold his wife's property, spent the whole ten thousand dollars to run away from her to start new in Kansas, and is now suing her for divorce."

"Andrew," admonished their leader, "if Lane has repented, he'll atone for his errors. If he lies, God will judge him. Let's go home now and fight weeds out of the corn so our families can eat."

This busy season kept men and boys in the fields from dawn to dusk, but, as they rode, the men shared out the work of the dead men so their families could survive. Dan wondered if God was responsible for the five dead men, the widows, and orphans? The bloom of Dan's baby sister, crushed so soon? Had God just made the world and turned it loose? Was there any use to pray?

Yet Dan couldn't stop the worship welling through him at the scores of shadings of fresh green from grass to stately oaks, at drifts of fragrant hawthorn, pink blossoms of wild crab-apple, carpets of prairie roses, dogwood's creamy blooms and pink-veined snowy flowers against the dark green leaves of wild plum. His heart sang with the meadowlarks that flashed yellow breasts to the sun, beating their wings, then gliding as if for joy.

This beauty was as real as the blood-soaked earth in the ravine draining down to the Marais des Cygnes. He would hold fast to that. As they neared the common grave by Timbered Mound, Montgomery turned to his little army. "We've had no luck this time, men, unless baptizing General Lane counts, but remember what I say . . . deeds like this massacre will arouse the nation and free the slaves. We who hate slavery are called 'disunionists' by proslavers, but it will be they, not we, who shatter the Union."

A chill shot through Dan as Montgomery raised a hand in the air and his voice rang like a bell. "You may count on the fingers of this hand the years that slavery has to live! By then, there'll be no slaves in Kansas, or Missouri, or anywhere throughout this country. When we dug a grave for these brave men, we also began to dig the grave of slavery." He paused and gave that smile that touched Dan's heart. "Thank you for going with me. Next time we ride, may it be with better results."

James Denver, the territorial governor, traveled to Fort Scott in June to make peace between the proslavery men who controlled the Bourbon County government, and the Free Staters. On his way back, he promised Montgomery to station sixty militia along the border for the rest of the summer.

The truce was further helped along by rumors of gold in the Rockies of western Kansas where a town named for Governor Denver was already being platted. The lure of gold drained off some of the wilder, unrooted adventurers on both sides. Dan was never tempted. What he intended was to work his own farm someday, something no ordinary person in Ireland could dream of. After starvation, he prized corn and wheat more than gold.

To support Governor Denver's peace, when William Hairgrove recovered enough from his wounds, he went with Sam Nickel to visit Jerry Jackson. Representing people from both sides of the Missouri line, they promised to warn and aid those threatened by either Kansas jayhawkers or Missouri bushwhackers.

Meanwhile, farmers, whatever their politics, waged another kind of war, attacking weeds to keep them from choking

out the crops. As rain washed the blood of the massacre into
the soil of the ravine and grass healed the broken earth of the
grave by Timbered Mound, Dan took turns with Andy,
Owen, and David in helping cultivate the Colpetzers' fields
and helping young Frank keep fences and buildings in repair.
As Dan followed the plow through rows of corn that cut off
any cooling breeze as it grew higher, hoed weeds around potato plants, or scythed the golden wheat, he often called
Christy to mind, lived over the few moments they'd had together at the wedding.

He dreamed of her in the gown of twilight blue, but more
often he saw her in moonlight as she'd looked when they
freed the bears, or blurred in the darkness by Whistling Point
where he was keenly aware of her voice and scent and presence because he couldn't study her face and try to figure out
whether her eyes were deep gray or hazel.

In the middle of August, the men were still at work in the
fields when twilight revealed a heavenly body halfway down
the northwestern sky. Simeon Parks declared it was a comet
with a tail. "Whatever directs them in their celestial journeys,
I believe they have no message for us except to declare the
wonder of God's handiwork," the miller said reassuringly. "I
well remember the autumn of 'Thirty-Three, when meteors
fell like snowflakes and many people thought it was the end of
the world."

Autumn was a blaze of gold and scarlet with wild geese
flying on the first gusts of winter. Corn was cribbed, oats and
wheat plowed under, and, when the stubble rotted, next
year's wheat was harrowed in. The Parkses' barn was full of
wild grass hay and so was Mrs. Colpetzer's. Dan and David
filled her lean-to with firewood, including a good supply of
oak backlogs small enough for her and Frank to handle.

The time had come for neighborly visiting when the

weather was mild enough. Although John Brown chided Simeon for his Quakerish beliefs when the sword of the Lord and of Gideon was needed, the gaunt old man sometimes came to the Parkses, usually with a few of what could only be termed disciples.

The two Dan liked best were only a few years older than he. John Kagi was the son of Austrian emigrants. His dark eyes burned when he blasted slavery, but they softened when three-year-old Letty sidled up to cast flirtatious glances through her long brown lashes. When sweet hickory sap bubbled out of the end of a burning, green hickory log, Kagi would scrape it off with his knife and give it to her.

Sometimes Brown did that, a smile bending his craggy features. After her first stranger-shyness, Letty didn't fear him and clambered freely into his lap as he discoursed on the methods and ethics of war while his young followers hung on every word. Kagi's close friend, Richard Realf, looked like a blond angel. Newly arrived from England, he was a poet like his relative, Lord Byron, and would recite at length from "Mazeppa" or "Childe Harold".

"Byron died for Greek freedom," Richard said one night as they sat around the orange-tongued fire, savoring spiced cider. Owen was mending harness, but the other men folk cracked hickory nuts and ate all they wanted while filling a crock to be used in cooking. Lydia carded wool and Harriet and her mother knitted.

The two Parks households, Owen's and his father's, had supper together and usually spent the long winter evenings in Simeon's house. It saved firewood, but also made company. They all missed Susie's smile and happy nature, and it must be especially hard for Lydia who had mothered Susie. Andy brought her and Catriona over every Sunday when weather allowed, but they had to be home in time for chores.

"Had Byron lived," went on Realf, "he'd be too old to fight in this battle except with his pen, but you may be sure he'd have done that." He drew a folded page from his pocket. "Have you seen Whittier's poem about the Marais des Cygnes? A friend clipped it from the September *Atlantic Monthly*."

"Oh, read it, please!" exclaimed Lydia. "Mister Whittier is my favorite living poet. He's not tedious like most Abolitionist writers."

"He's a Quaker, too," approved Simeon.

"Oh, Papa! That wouldn't signify were he a bad poet!" She turned back to Realf, sparkling with eagerness. If she always looked that way, thought Dan, she wouldn't be an old maid.

"I have it almost by heart." The young Englishman smoothed out the page and turned it over to catch the lines:

> **From the hearths of their cabins**
> **The fields of their corn,**
> **Unarmed and unweaponed,**
> **The victims were torn.**

When the passionate voice fell silent, Simeon repeated: " 'The crown of this harvest is life out of death.' God grant it."

"Amen." After a moment, John Brown raised his gray head and looked at Dan. "Could we have your fiddle tonight, lad, some of the dear old hymns?" Nearly always, he asked Dan to play.

Dan played all the hymns he knew. The bitter grooves at Brown's mouth seemed to smooth. He helped Letty onto his lap where she soon fell asleep, soft curls stroked by a hand that had sabered men down.

When Dan stopped, Brown thanked him. "Your music flows through my soul like cleansing waters. Would there was a way I could hear it always." Rising, the haggard old man put Letty in her mother's arms, bade them good night, and went out with his companions.

Chapter Thirteen

Early in December, volunteers from Lawrence, Osawatomie, and Emporia joined Montgomery's men camped at the head of the Little Osage River in the north part of Bourbon County. In spite of Governor Denver's truce, Fiddlin' Judge Williams kept sending out warrants for the arrest of Free-State men. He had two of them chained to the floor of an old building in Fort Scott with winter coming on and their only bedding a few quilts. The federal judge wouldn't give Ben Rice and John Hudlow a trial or set bail, so Dan, Owen, and Andy were riding with Montgomery to break the prisoners out of jail.

Eli Snider grumbled: "We ought to burn that vipers' nest of proslavers to the ground and roast Judge Williams and his officers in the coals! I'll bet my forge and anvil that the Marais des Cygnes massacre was hatched up down here, just like George Washington Clarke's raid in 'Fifty-Six."

Colonel Montgomery moved into the flickering light, a slight, dark shadow against the blaze. "Now that we're all together, gentlemen, we need to elect a leader. I don't seek that responsibility, but I must make one thing clear. As either leader or follower, I'll have nothing to do with needless bloodshed or destruction. Our aim is to free the prisoners and show Judge Williams and his marshals that we won't tolerate such treatment of Free-State men."

Sam Wood, the young, brisk leader of the Lawrence squad, came to stand by Montgomery. "I'm a Quaker, sir. None of us want killing, only justice. My men and I respectfully urge you to take charge of this expedition. I've spoken to our friends from Osawatomie and Emporia. We are all agreed."

In the chancy glow of the firelight, Montgomery's face showed pleased surprise. "Then I humbly accept, gentlemen, and will do my utmost to see that this enterprise is one you'll be proud, not shamed, to tell your grandchildren about. Now we'd all better rest."

"What's your plan, Colonel?" asked Wood.

"We'll leave our horses with some guards where the military bridge crosses the Marmaton. When it's light enough to see but still so early that most folks will still be in their warm beds, we'll go straight to the old government building at the north corner of the square and bring out Rice and Hudlow."

"How about Fiddlin' Williams?" demanded Eli Snider.

A smile flitted over Montgomery's grim features. "We may burn his law books since he pays no attention to what they say about speedy trials and setting bail. Sleep well, men. We'll need clear eyes and steady nerves tomorrow."

The prairie grass, dried stems still smelling of summer, made a passable mattress and Dan slept close to Owen, but he had the great outdoors on his other side except for where his saddle gave some protection. Whether he turned his back to the wind or his front, he was soon chilled through his blanket and quilt. From trees along the little creek below, an owl hooted and the shrill *yip-yip* of coyotes seemed to answer. Dan snatched catnaps in the intervals before his warmed parts got cold again.

He was cold inside, too. Montgomery didn't want killing, but what if Fort Scott people started it? Riding into a sleeping town where women and children might be caught in crossfire was a far cry from chasing Clarke's bushwhackers or hunting Hamelton's bloody gang after the massacre. Still, two men lay chained to the floor of their prison, had been there for months, simply for being against slavery in Kansas. Dan was glad when Montgomery called: "Up, boys! Eat whatever you have for breakfast, and let's be on our way. We'll drink our coffee in Fort Scott."

Dan munched on cornbread and a hunk of Lydia's excellent cheese, saving a bite of bread for Zephyr who dearly loved it. He whistled and the hobbled horse came to him out of the darkness, daintily lipped the bread. Dan was saddling up by feel more than sight when he heard the muffled sound of hoofs on grass.

"Who is it?" called Montgomery.

"John Brown with two of my sons and Bondi, Kagi, and Realf."

August Bondi, a Viennese, was another of Brown's most ardent disciples. Foreigners often became fiery Abolitionists when they saw the promise of liberty that had drawn them here was tainted with slavery.

"We've come to join you."

"You're welcome," Montgomery said. "So long as you agree that our aim is to free Rice and Hudlow and teach Judge Williams that he must leave off fiddling his proslave tune."

"I say we burn the den of bushwhackers to the ground and kill any who resist!" thundered Brown.

"We want none of that, Captain Brown." Sam Wood, the Lawrence Quaker, spoke with soft force. "We've chosen Colonel Montgomery as our leader. You are, indeed, welcome, but only if you obey his orders."

"I had expected to assume command," said Brown.

There was embarrassed silence. At last a man from the

Osage said: "Captain Brown, I and thirty or so of this band trade in Fort Scott and have friends there. Not all proslavery men are bushwhackers."

"Then they shouldn't keep such company." Brown's voice rose.

"Remember our slaughtered at Marais des Cygnes!"

"Remember Osawatomie," someone muttered.

"We must ride, Captain Brown." Montgomery spoke from his saddle, he and his horse only a little darker than the night. "Come with us if you will, but keep to what we've agreed on."

Leather creaked and metal jingled as the small army mounted. "I'll go my own way!" Brown cried. Dan was glad the group had rejected Brown's proposal, but he couldn't help feeling pity for the fierce old man's humiliation. This changed to dread as Brown cried: "I'm going to cross into Missouri and bring out slaves! Will none of you ride with me?"

There was no answer but the sound of seventy-five horsemen trotting southeast.

Three hours later, Dan's nose wrinkled at the smell of burning leather-bound law books and the furnishings of Judge Williams's court. Dan's rifle formed part of the pen of Sharps surrounding Judge Williams, Judge Ransom, and several marshals and deputies.

Ben Rice stood next to Dan, a wide grin on his face as he pointed a Sharps toward the officials who'd put him in jail. John Hudlow, on Dan's other side, called to Williams: "Keepin' warm, Judge?"

The portly man chuckled. He'd retained his dignity and good humor even though he'd had to dress in haste with rifle muzzles leveled at him. "It's good of you to care, Mister

Hudlow. So long as you don't burn my fiddle or that old wardrobe that's been in my family for generations, I'm well content."

A big, mean-mouthed man from the Little Osage sauntered up with a beautiful violin that sent a thrill of admiration and yearning through Dan. His own fiddle had been left him by a crippled-up old man back in Pennsylvania for whom Dan had done chores, the old man who'd taught him to play.

"Reckon your fiddle will jig a merry tune in the fire, Judge," taunted the big man.

Dan, moving instinctively, caught the fiddle and bow as the other man started to hurl them into the blaze. Giving the fiddle and bow into the judge's hands, Dan's mouth went dry as he met the angry glare of the man with the cruel mouth.

"Who pulled your chain, boy?" the man rasped.

"No need to ruin a fiddle that can be making music long after we're all dead." Dan was surprised he sounded calm when his innards felt like a bunch of wasps swarmed inside them.

"We won't wrangle amongst ourselves," decreed Montgomery. He gave Dan a half smile. "The world needs all the music it can get."

"Music, my foot!" Judge Ransom was red with fury as he glanced around at his captors. "You'll all go to prison for treating officers of the United States in this scurvy fashion! And someone will hang for shooting Deputy Marshal John Little!"

"He used his shotgun on us first, and wounded two of our men," said Montgomery. "Most courts, perhaps even yours, sir, would scarcely find it strange to shoot back. Still, I regret it."

Judge Williams squinted over his shoulder. "Can it be?" he asked in tones of disbelief. "Colonel Montgomery, can some of your high-minded followers be looting that store yonder?"

It was the store from which Deputy Little had fired into Montgomery's men, but the colonel whirled and shouted in a voice that carried: "Men! Get out of that store and board it up!"

They obeyed, but some had suspicious bulges in their clothing. Several came out chewing tobacco they hadn't had when they reached Fort Scott.

"We'll bid you good day, gentlemen," said Montgomery. "I hope you understand, Judge Ransom and Judge Williams, that we won't allow you to harass Free-State men. In fact, you might find the climate of Missouri more salubrious." Montgomery's gray eyes went over the marshals and deputies. "I earnestly advise you not to pursue us."

"Colonel Montgomery"—bowed Judge Williams—"I'll gladly fiddle you out of town." He tucked the mellow wood under his chin and broke into "Old Dan Tucker".

Montgomery's men withdrew, supporting their wounded, rifles in hand, watching behind. At the bridge, they mounted, Rice and Hudlow on horses brought by the Osage men. They rode off to the lilt of the fiddle.

Heart pounding with relief and triumph, Dan grinned at Owen. "You've got to like a man like that."

"Not if he kept you chained to the floor," Ben Rice said.

Early in January, John Brown, Richard Realf, and John Kagi stopped at the Parkses and had dinner with the family. "My work here is finished," the gruff old zealot said. "We brought eleven slaves out of Missouri and now we must see them on their way to freedom. My good friend, Augustus Wattles, has upbraided me for breaking the so-called border truce, but I cannot think I did wrong though one master was killed when he tried to stop us from freeing his slaves. His blood is on his own head."

"That's not the way the governor of Missouri sees it," remarked Simeon Parks dryly. "He's asked the governor of Kansas to arrest not only you, but Colonel Montgomery."

Brown smiled. "What did the good governors do after the massacre at Marais des Cygnes?"

"Denver did his best to make a peace," said Owen.

"They say peace, peace, but there is no peace!" Brown's eyes blazed in the light. "There can be no peace while there is slavery." With visible effort, he controlled himself. "I came to bid you farewell, not to wrangle. Dan, my boy, would you play some of the old hymns?"

Dan could not deny him, this man so terrible yet so bent on what he saw as right. As Dan played, Brown closed his eyes and his breathing grew deep and steady. When Dan played "To Be a Pilgrim", Lydia sang.

**Who would true valor see, let him come hither,
One who will faithful be, come wind, come weather. . . .**

Brown opened his eyes and rose with a sigh. "Bless you for the songs." Reaching into his pocket, he brought out a tattered little leather-bound book. "Have this to remember me by."

"It's your New Testament," Dan protested.

"I have much of it by heart. Keep it, lad. In the times to come, you'll need it more than I will." Brown offered his hand. Its bony roughness penetrated Dan's nerves and fiber. He wondered if the others with whom the old man shook hands felt branded by his touch.

Chapter Fourteen

Christy listened to five-year-old Mary Hayes chant the alphabet and felt sisterly pride that Beth, a year younger, knew it perfectly. The little girls were a delightful contrast, Mary with the Hayes' gold hair and blue eyes, Beth with glossy dark curls and hazel eyes. On the wall map of the United States, Christy's father was showing Luke Hayes and Tressie and Phyllis Barclay the location of the first silver strike in the country, out in Nevada Territory.

That was where Hester Ballard thought Lafe was. Christy hoped he'd stay there, although she felt sorry for Hester who still hoped Lafe would grow out of his wildness. It wasn't wildness. He was plain mean.

The little school had shrunk. At fifteen, Mark Hayes, never a keen scholar, chose to stay home and help at the tannery. He was needed more now that his older brother, Matt, had started freighting that summer.

So had Thos, as soon as the corn grew tall enough to hold its own against the weeds. Christy took over his milking. She did the older, gentler cows while her father milked the young, more fractious, ones. She was also now the principal carrier of wood and water. What the family needed, Christy thought, was a boy in between her and Beth who could grow into the chores of his older brothers. Beth, bless her usually willing little heart, perched on a high stool to dry dishes, set the table, made beds, and brought in kindling, but Christy still felt stretched between inside and outside tasks.

At least, unlike Charlie who made short hauls out of Independence, Thos would be home through the winter and help with plowing, planting, and cultivating till the corn was well up. Christy often hugged her small sister tighter to warm the chill of loneliness that came from feeling that Charlie was more the Jardines' now than his family's.

He still came home in late autumn from his last trip to Denver or Salt Lake City. He brought lovely dress material for his mother and Christy, flannel shirts for Thos and his father, and dolls for Beth, although she loved her battered Lambie best. Before he left, he helped cut and split the winter's wood. But he went to see the Jardines before he came home.

Christy sighed, absently prompting Mary as she sounded out: "Kuh-a-t. Cat." Charlie would turn twenty in December. Even if he couldn't have Melissa, he'd marry someone. Then he really wouldn't be theirs any more. It was a comfort to look across the room at her mother who hummed softly as she worked the treadles and sent the shuttle through the warp threads.

Ellen Ware never seemed to change although her husband teased her a little about the few gray hairs showing at her forehead. Christy knew that she herself was changing, and not just because the blue foulard needed gussets under the arms that spring in order not to fit painfully tight across her breasts. She had changed in the way she felt when Dan O'Brien's smoky blue-gray eyes touched her, then veered away as if he'd been burned. All his growing had gone into height. He was still so thin that he was only muscle and bone beneath his skin. The flame of his hair had darkened a little, but it was as unruly as ever although he apparently tried to slick it down with some concoction before he came to Sunday morning service at the Wares'. He'd been doing that since the border troubles quieted down after the uproar over John Brown's carrying those slaves out of Missouri. In reprisal, proslavers raided Kansas, and, to get even for that, last Christmas Eve Doc Jennison and his jayhawkers looted and burned Jerry Jackson's house and store. Enough reckless Free-State men had come into southeast Kansas to give Jennison his own following. He no longer deferred to Montgomery who was stern but just.

Now that fraudulently elected proslavers no longer ruled the territorial legislature, a fourth convention had framed a Free-State constitution in July. Overwhelmingly ratified by the voters, it would soon be presented to Congress. Thank goodness, the bitter struggle over whether Kansas would be slave or free was all but over.

Dan came to worship, carrying his Sharps rifle, but he also had John Brown's New Testament in his pocket. Ellen always invited him to stay for dinner, but he and Christy were never alone. Christy somehow knew he'd never again ask her to explore the underground river beyond Whistling Point, that they could no longer share that kind of childish adventure.

Did she want him to come courting? Christy blushed at the thought. How could she be mysterious and interesting when they'd met while she was still a child? They knew each other too well, yet Christy often felt she didn't know him at all. When he rode off toward the border, she felt cheated, as if something hadn't happened that should have.

One of the horses neighed, to be answered by a whinny and the sound of hoofs. "Why, it's Dan," said Ellen.

Christy's heart leaped into her throat. Why was he here on a weekday? Let it be nothing wrong. "Mary, help Beth with the primer," Christy directed, and reached the door as Dan was looping Zephyr's reins around the sapling trunk that served as a hitching post.

This wasn't an ordinary visit, although hides lashed behind the saddle indicated that he was on his way to the tannery. His face told her a bad thing had happened. "Come in, Dan," said Jonathan from behind her. "Is something amiss?"

"It's John Brown, sir." Dan's voice was through changing, but it broke now.

"What's he done?" Jonathan demanded.

Dan gulped. "He and twenty-one men seized the federal arsenal at Harper's Ferry in Virginia."

"What?" cried Ellen, rising from the loom.

"That was on October Sixteenth. They held it for two days. Brown was counting on slaves to rebel and join him."

"A slave insurrection," Jonathan groaned. "The thing Southerners dread above all things."

"There wasn't any uprising," Dan said. "Marines under a Captain Robert E. Lee overwhelmed Brown's party. Killed a number of them, including two of his sons."

"Brown lives?"

"For now. He was beaten to the ground with bayonets and sabers. By now his trial should be under way. He'll be tried for treason against the State of Virginia and criminal conspiracy to incite a slave rebellion."

Jonathan bowed his head. "God have mercy on him. He has done terrible deeds but against a terrible evil."

"Do you think he's crazy, sir?"

"Sometimes we call men crazy to convince ourselves that we are sane. How did you get the news?"

"Some stage passengers from Leavenworth heard it after it came in by telegraph, and told the people at Trading Post. Uncle Simeon heard about it when he went to the post office yesterday."

Christy's breath caught. These awful things! Was war coming? How could it? Yet how could it not? Dan would fight. Her brothers would—Charlie at least. Being a Quaker hadn't kept Owen Parks from fighting bushwhackers. She couldn't imagine Andy McHugh staying at his forge. Matt Hayes and Mark. . . .

Surely it wouldn't happen. The President and Congress knew how frightful it would be to have the country torn with the kind of struggle, many times magnified, that had gone on for years along this border.

"You'd better have a bite with us, Dan," said Ellen.

Dan shook his head. "I'm taking some hides to the tannery. Have to hustle to get home in time for chores."

Christy was already filling a mug from the buttermilk jar. "You'll have this."

He raised an eyebrow, almost grinned. "Yes, ma'am."

Their hands brushed. Warmth curled up her arm, jolting her heart. If only she could take both his hands—no, throw her arms around him and hold him close till the storms passed.

"Thank you kindly." He gave back the mug.

Was he careful not to touch her this time?

After Dan was gone, Jonathan went to the map. "Here's Harper's Ferry," he told his students after a moment. "It's a name that'll be in any history books written after this."

Luke and Phyllis were eleven, Tressie a shyly budding thirteen. By the time they were Christy's age, what would have happened to them? Or the little girls bent earnestly over their primer? Kneeling beside them, Christy hugged Mary and Beth so hard they wriggled and looked at her in surprise.

"I see a c-c-cat," labored Mary.

A lump swelled in Christy's throat. The children would be

caught in whatever was coming. This was like seeing one of the autumn fires sweep toward them, but having no place to hide, no place to run, as everything caught fire.

On a Sunday in mid-December, a haunted-looking Dan brought word that John Brown was hanged on December 2nd. Six of his men would die later. "I went with Colonel Montgomery, Augustus Wattles, and men from Lawrence, to try to rescue old John."

"You did?" gasped Christy. "Oh, Dan, how?"

"We went separately by train from Saint Joseph to Pennsylvania and met in Maryland, across the river from Virginia. Only one of our people was allowed to see Brown, and then only under strict guard, but there was someone friendly to him who managed to get messages back and forth." Dan turned up his hands and let out a long breath. "Brown wouldn't try to escape."

"Why not?" breathed Ellen Ware.

"He said his jailer and his wife had been kind to him and he had been given special privileges in return for his promise not to try to escape. He didn't want to be the cause of more bloodshed." Dan paused. "Most of all, he hoped his death would rouse the nation against slavery. He said . . . 'I am worth more to die than to live.' On the way to the gallows he passed his jailer a note. It said he had once hoped the nation could be purged of its crimes with little loss of life, but now he was convinced it would only be with blood."

Jonathan Ware put a hand on Dan's shoulder. "Still, it must have strengthened him to know friends came all the way from Kansas to try to save him."

"I wasn't his friend." Dan shook his head as he looked at Jonathan. "I don't know what I was. I played my fiddle for him and he gave me his New Testament."

"God rest him," said Jonathan. "And his men who must die, and those they killed."

Dan pulled out the well-worn little Testament. "Here's what the chaplain read when Brown's body was lowered into the grave . . . 'I have fought the good fight; I have finished my course; I have kept the faith; henceforth there is laid up for me a crown of righteousness. . . . ' " Dan's voice wavered.

Blinded by tears, as much for Dan as the God-or-devil-ridden old man, Christy put her arms around Dan's thin body. His face pressed against her hair. She felt the damp warmth of tears. Then he straightened.

"We heard plenty of talk on our journey and back East. Did you know Abraham Lincoln back in Illinois, Mister Ware?"

"No," said Jonathan, "but I voted to send him to the House of Representatives, and, of course, I followed his debates with Stephen Douglas."

"He's made talks this month in Leavenworth, Atchison, and other Kansas towns. He says slavery is wrong, but he's willing to leave it alone where it already exists. That won't be good enough for the South if he's nominated next summer and wins the November election."

"Only a strong proslavery President can satisfy slave owners." Jonathan's tone was rueful. "Oregon came into the Union free early this year. If Kansas is admitted under its Free-State constitution, that will make nineteen free states to fifteen proslavery. The pity is that most Southerners don't own slaves, never will, and may wind up dying for the interests of the planters."

Dan looked from Christy and the little girls to Ellen Ware. "It's been bad enough along the border, but if war really comes. . . ."

"Maybe the President and Congress will just let the

Southern states go their own way." Christy almost wished for this, although she knew it was cowardly. Then she thought of Justus and the other slaves she'd helped get away and knew that couldn't go on.

"No person should own another," Ellen said, eyes meeting her husband's. "No one has the right to separate families, to whip, and even kill."

"Charlie and Thos may have to fight!" Christy protested.

Ellen winced. "If I could, I would go in their place."

"Maybe there'll be a way out of it short of war." Dan put John Brown's Testament back in his pocket. "I have to get on to the tannery, folks. Thanks for the drink, Christy."

She watched him and Zephyr fade into the leafless trees before she sat down again with Mary, Beth, and the primer. After school was out, she went to draw a bucket of water from the well John Brown had witched, and whispered a prayer for him in all his blood and terror—whispered a prayer for them all.

Thos got home that night, seeming a foot taller, hair streaked from sun. Charlie, having stopped at the Jardines', came home a few days later, in time for his twentieth birthday. Bronzed and strong from months on the trail, he looked a man grown.

"Good thing they hung that maniac, old Brown." Charlie snorted. "He claimed he never planned a slave rebellion, but, if he didn't, how come he ordered lots of heavy pikes? How come he armed the slaves who were with him when he took the arsenal?"

His views surely echoed Bishop Jardine's. Jonathan said peaceably: "Let's leave him to God, my son. Is it as dry on the prairies as it is here?"

"It's dry. Creeks and rivers are down. But we ought to get

rain or some good snows that'll put moisture in the ground for spring planting."

"I hope you're right." Jonathan gazed at the bright, cloudless sky. "We had a good harvest, thank the Lord, but we needed those fall rains."

"We can't do much about that," said Thos, "but we can sure help get in the wood."

Charlie worked hard, but his mind seemed far away.

Hurt that he didn't pay more attention to her, Christy teased: "What's the matter, Charlie? Mooning over Melissa Jardine?"

"Miss Jardine will marry some highfalutin' gent from Saint Louis," he snapped. "When she visits her sister there, Trav says the young bloods cluster so thick you can't stir them with a paddle."

Amazingly Travis was still at the military academy. When Charlie was home over Christmas last year, Travis visited the Wares for a few days. He did look handsome in his uniform, but he positively strutted. He'd waylaid Christy on the dogtrot one night. She scrubbed at her lips even now at remembering the rough, hot taste of his mouth. She'd wrenched loose and slapped him so resoundingly that, although he waited half an hour to follow her in, his cheek still showed the mark of her palm. He pointedly ignored her and left right after breakfast next morning.

To Christy's relief, he didn't come this year. Charlie was grown up now, and Thos almost so. There was no telling if they'd be home next Christmas. *Please, please, let there not be a war they'd have to go to . . . that Dan would fight in!* The worst dread, the one so awful that Christy pushed it away the instant it shadowed her mind, was that Charlie might be so influenced by the Jardines that he'd fight for slavery.

This Christmas Eve, though, before the Wares had their

own dinner, they lit a lantern and trooped, escorted by Robbie, to give the animals their Christmas treats. For the geese and Silver-Laced Wyandottes, Cavalier and his many wives, Ellen had cracked corn soaked in buttermilk. Patches, Evalina, and their spotted progeny wrinkled their snouts appreciatively at a soup of potato peels, turnips, and cabbage.

Jonathan had never been able to bring himself to butcher either of the original Poland Chinas, but each fall one of their offspring was slaughtered, skinned, and cut into hams, bacon, and side meat. On that day, Christy wished her family was vegetarian like the Wattleses, although, at least, as Lige Morrow teased, nothing was wasted but the squeal. Ellen made sausage or deviled ham of scraps, pickled the trotters, and made headcheese of the head, ears, and tongue.

The dark-faced Suffolk ewe matriarchs, Mildred, Cleo, and Nosey, *baa*ed their approval of the oats Thos tipped into their trough before filling those of their score of descendants who furnished wool for blankets and winter clothing. The old ewes had supplied the Hayeses, Parkses, Hester Ballard, and other neighbors with the start of flocks. No sheep had been killed for meat, but they discovered ways of killing or maiming themselves so mutton or lamb occasionally appeared on the table. Over the years, in spite of Robbie and the fence, five sheep had crawled under or through the fence and fallen prey to wolves or panthers. Jonathan called it their tax paid to wilderness. Ellen was less philosophical.

Now, in the barn, Beth dipped fodder into molasses to feed Moses and Pharaoh, crooning to the gentle white oxen who snuffled their delight and rubbed against Thos, brass knobs on their horns gleaming, glad their favorite human was home. The same treat went to the soft-eyed but temperamental Jerseys, Lady Jane, Guinevere, Bess, Goldie, and the now grown calves they had produced on the way from Illinois—Clover, Hettie, Maud, and Shadow. Yearlings were sold off or traded. Jonathan didn't keep a bull so Ethan Hayes brought over what Ellen called his "male brute" when the cows needed his attentions.

Beth stroked and crooned her way along the cows. As she rubbed the whorl of hair between Shadow's gentle eyes, she looked up at her father. "Can they really talk at midnight, Daddy? Hester says they can! It's a gift from Baby Jesus because the animals let him sleep in their manger."

"Maybe we should let that be their secret, Bethie." Jonathan smiled at his youngest and picked her up to shield her from the chill wind as they walked to the stable.

Jed nickered as the family entered. Golden lantern light mellowed the rich bay of him and Queenie and burnished the haunches and head of Lass, the chestnut four-year-old. Charlie poured oats in their mangers while Beth offered molasses-dipped fodder.

"Merry Christmas," she murmured to each horse in turn, caressing soft muzzles. Her eyes shone as she gave her mother an exuberant hug around her legs. "We're their Saint Nicholas, aren't we?"

"Where's your pipe, then?" teased Charlie, swinging her to his shoulder as they stepped outside and barred the door. "Where's your round little belly that shakes like a bowl full of jelly? Where's your reindeer?"

"Char-lie!" She giggled and drubbed him about head and shoulders. "You're my reindeer. On, Prancer! On, Dancer! On Donner and Blitzen!"

He capered and bucked with her all the way to the house, set her down, breathless and laughing, by the fire. When dishes were done after supper, Jonathan read "A Visit from St. Nicholas" as he did every year, from Clement Clarke Moore's *Poems*. Only Charlie and Thos could remember before it was part of the Wares' Christmas ritual. Then they gathered around Ellen at the piano and sang all the carols they knew, Charlie's tenor reinforcing his father's.

" 'Joy to the world!' " exulted Christy, loving her family as she looked from one to the other, so grateful for them that she felt her heart would burst.

So good to have Charlie home. And Thos was there till summer. Those were the best gifts. The only other thing Christy wished was that Dan was part of their circle, cheek bent to his fiddle while the candle made a blaze of his hair.

IN MEDIAS RES

Author's Note

Rural settlers in western Missouri, Arkansas, eastern Kansas, and Indian Territory lived much as their colonial grandparents had. It was only after the Civil War that harvesting machines, threshers, binders, and the like came into wide use. Women often sheared their sheep and carded, spun, and wove not only wool but flax and cotton, into clothing, towels, and bedding. Each farm household was as self-sufficient as possible.

I spent my teen years in Missouri ten miles from the battleground of Pea Ridge. My grandfather told me stories his grandfather had told about Quantrill and the war. Like many Missouri families, we had members fighting on both sides. Thus the war was an early part of my consciousness but I hadn't thought of writing from both sides of that long, cruel struggle between neighbors till I read *Inside War: The Guerrilla Conflict in Missouri During the American Civil War* by Michael Fellman, who brilliantly shows in incident after incident how the world turned upside down, the outrages on both sides, and the twisted honor that boasted of not harming women although sons, brothers, and husbands were slaughtered in their arms. It was only when I read the true story of a slave woman who loved her white nurseling too much to abandon him when a band of liberators killed his parents and tried to persuade her to go with them that it struck me that such love was the underground river that flowed beneath the killing grounds and burned fields, that love, with hope, faith, and gratitude for the beauty and rhythms of the natural world, are the only answer to chaos, destruction, and hatred.

There are always varying eyewitness accounts of controversial events. Incidents along the border were especially numerous and confusing. I found five different dates for Clarke's 1856 raid, with estimates of his force ranging from 150 to 400 men. Probably this last figure included those who went on Reid's separate raid on Osawatomie.

My principal characters are fictitious but many of the others are real—John Brown, James Montgomery, the Wattleses—yes, the family really was vegetarian and the women really did wear bloomers and smash up the saloon at Mound City. I've altered timing in a few places for fictional purposes. Charles Jennison didn't move to the Mound City area till after the Marais des Cygnes massacre. For accounts of wildlife, farming, and daily life, I relied heavily on Wiley Britton's experiences in *Pioneer Life in Southwest Missouri*. First-hand stories of those who lived through that turbulent era are in *Linn County, Kansas* by William Ansell Mitchell. Finally, the WPA guides to 1930s Missouri, Arkansas, Kansas, and Oklahoma have a tremendous amount of information about towns and cities that existed in those days. As always, I referred often to *The Look of the Old West* by my mentor, friend, and teacher, Foster-Harris.

It is a kind of magic that lets us bring back vanished creatures of a vanished time, and show vast flocks of passenger pigeons darkening the sun for hours, settling in a great cloud to feed on autumn mast or capture the emerald glint of Carolina parakeets gorging on roasting ears after a family has battled weeds out of the corn for months. Who, in 1860, could believe these birds would utterly vanish?

Leland Sonnichsen wrote: "Truth is the sum of many facts. Truth is the forest, and facts are the trees which keep us from seeing it." Still, he would be the first to adjure us to have the right trees in our forest—and the right birds in the trees.

Jeanne Williams
Cave Creek Canyon, 2003

About the Author

Jeanne Williams was borne in Elkhart, Kansas, a small town along the Santa Fe Trail in 1930. In 1952 she enrolled at the University of Oklahoma where she majored in history and attended Foster-Harris's writing classes. Her writing career began as a contributor to pulp magazines in which she eventually published more than seventy Western, fantasy, and women's stories. Over the same period, she produced thirteen novels set in the West for the young adult audience, including *The Horsetalker* (1961) and *Freedom Trail* (1973), both of which won the Spur Award from the Western Writers of America. Her first Western historical romance, *A Lady Bought with Rifles* (1976), was published in 1976 and sold 600,000 copies in mass merchandise paperback editions. Her historical novels display a wide variety of settings and solidly researched historical backgrounds such as the proslavery forces in Kansas in *Daughter of the Sword* (1979), or the history of Arizona from the 1840s through contemporary times in her Arizona trilogy — *The Valiant Women* (1980), which won a Spur Award, *Harvest of Fury* (1981), and *The Mating of Hawks* (1982). Her heroines are various: a traveling seamstress in *Lady of No Man's Land* (1988), a schoolteacher in *No Roof but Heaven* (1990), a young girl heading up a family of four orphans in *Home Mountain* (1990) which won the Spur Award for Best Novel of the West for that year. The authentic historical level of her writing distinguishes her among her peers, and her works have set standards for those who follow in her path. *The Hidden Valley*, the second book in her *Beneath the Burning Ground* trilogy, will be her next **Five Star Western**.